Jill Paton Walsh was educated at St Michael's Convent, North Finchley, and at St Anne's College, Oxford. She is the author of three adult novels: *Lapsing* (1986), *A School For Lovers* (1989) and *Knowledge of Angels* (1994), which was shortlisted for the 1994 Booker Prize. She has also won many awards for her children's literature, including the Whitbread Prize, the Universe Prize and the Smarties Award.

She has three children and lives in Cambr

Praise for *Lapsing*:

'[JILL PATON WALSH] WRITES WITH LIMPID SIMPLICITY AND DIRECTNESS . . . A MOST AUSPICIOUS DEBUT'
The Times

'AN EXTRAORDINARY NOVEL: DELICATE, CLEVER, SERIOUS AND FUNNY . . . RADIANT WITH SERIOUSNESS AND PERCEPTION AND VERY CRAFTY WRITING . . . IT HAS A WONDERFULLY INNOCENT-SEEMING NATURALISTIC STRUCTURE WHICH ALLOWS DEPTH AND COMPLEXITY TO SHINE THROUGH IT'
New Statesman

'A BEAUTIFULLY WRITTEN BOOK. HISTORICALLY ACCURATE BUT NEVER SENTIMENTAL, SOLEMN BUT NEVER STIFF, IT BUILDS QUIETLY TO UNEXPECTED HEIGHTS'
Observer

'A NOSTALGIC AND DEEPLY MOVING NOVEL'
Financial Times

'A CHRONICLE OF LOSS OF FAITH IN THE FACE OF LOVE . . . TOLD WITH QUIET HUMOUR AND WRY HINDSIGHT . . . HAUNTING'
Irish Times

'A MOST UNUSUAL LOVE STORY . . . A NOSTALGIC AND SYMPATHETIC ACCOUNT OF LIFE IN THE PRE-PERMISSIVE SOCIETY'
Evening Standard

'A RARE COMBINATION OF COMEDY AND COMPASSION, PATON WALSH HAS CAPTURED BRILLIANTLY THE EARNESTNESS AND NAIVETY OF UNDERGRADUATE LIFE. HER LAST PARAGRAPH IS OF SUCH BRAVE BEAUTY THAT IT MADE ME WANT TO READ THE BOOK ALL OVER AGAIN'
Daily Telegraph

'A NOVEL OF FEELING, RECORDING SENSITIVELY TESSA'S RESPONSES TO HER RELIGION, HER STUDIES, HER FRIENDS AND THE WHOLE AMBIENCE OF OXFORD . . . JILL PATON WALSH WRITES ABOUT CATHOLICISM IN A DELICATE EXPRESSIVE STYLE THAT RECALLS ANTONIA WHITE'S *FROST IN MAY*'
Books and Bookmen

Also by Jill Paton Walsh

KNOWLEDGE OF ANGELS

and published by Black Swan

LAPSING

Jill Paton Walsh

BLACK SWAN

LAPSING
A BLACK SWAN BOOK : 0 552 99647 5

Originally published in Great Britain by George Weidenfeld & Nicolson Ltd

PRINTING HISTORY
Weidenfeld & Nicolson edition published 1986
Black Swan edition published 1995

Set in 11/12pt Linotype Melior by County Typesetters, Margate, Kent.

Black Swan Books are published by Transworld Publishers Ltd, 61–63 Uxbridge Road, Ealing, London W5 5SA, in Australia by Transworld Publishers (Australia) Pty Ltd, 15–25 Helles Avenue, Moorebank, NSW 2170 and in New Zealand by Transworld Publishers (NZ) Ltd, 3 William Pickering Drive, Albany, Auckland.

Reproduced, printed and bound in Great Britain by Cox & Wyman Ltd, Reading, Berks.

For Margaret

This is a work of fiction: a farrago of invented character and circumstance, and nobody who appears in it ever had any real existence unless, improbably, God did.

J.P.W.

Chapter One

LAPSING : INTROIT

'Bless me Father, for I have sinned. My last confession was three weeks ago. I have been ungenerous to a friend – spoken unkindly, I mean. I have been greedy, three or four times. I have spent money on a skirt I did not need. I knew I should have given the money to charity. I have been lazy. I missed choir practice, twice. I have forgotten my morning prayers, twice. I have had impure thoughts, four times. And there is something I would like to confess in case it is in any way sinful. I have kissed and caressed someone. I don't really think this was sinful, but I would like to confess it in case it is a venial sin. That is all, Father.'

'My child, are you a convert to Our Holy Mother The Church?'

'No, Father, I have always been a Catholic.'

'And are you a good Catholic, would you say?'

'I do try to be. I have always tried.'

And that, to an extent which would later astonish her, had been true. She had even, at Oxford, joined a cell. Not one of the extreme ones, just a group of the quietly devout, making temporary, renewable vows to undertake daily prayers, daily disciplines, and meeting every week for a little theological discussion and prayer. It was as a cell member that she had first encountered Theodore, who appeared as the new chaplain at the beginning of her second year, and spoke to them of the resurrection of the body.

All the time he was speaking, she could see in the corner of her eye, the little bird hopping, hopping on the golden leafmeal fallen early from the still nearly-green tree. She was leaning with unconscious grace against the trunk of the tree, sitting on her duffle coat, for though the day was warm and sunny it was, honestly, just a bit too damp for contact with the grass.

On such a golden afternoon one still had faith in summer. Warm sunlight bathed them, and warm pleasure at being together again after long separation; this was the cell's first meeting after the long vac. Only one new member had appeared to disturb the familiar society they had become to each other; a young research don, older therefore than the rest of them, and a potential rival to Hubert as the weightiest thinker of the group. Apart from introducing himself as Ben, however, he had spoken not one word in the entire course of the meeting. Strictly speaking the meeting was over: it had finished with prayers in the Chaplaincy Nissen-hut church half an hour ago, but the afternoon had tempted them into the meadow and the discussion continued under the trees.

They were discussing hair shirts. This was because Hubert wanted to wear one – it *would* be Hubert. Heroic virtue was what Hubert wanted, but he had been much reproved for pride, and the Abbot of a certain monastery at which he had taken repeated retreats, intended as samplers for the noviciate, had taken a dim view of Hubert, and told him he was best suited for holiness in lay life. Hubert hungered for more holiness than lay life seemed to offer him, but he had become cautious. What he really wanted was for someone to approve his decision to mortify the flesh by wearing a hair shirt on Fridays, and the approval seemed astonishingly hard to come by. Last year Father Anthony had been chaplain to the cell; he had told Hubert to practise self-denial by being content with ordinary pieties. Now Hubert, confronted by a new cell chaplain, was trying again.

The new cell chaplain was young – young for a priest, that is – slight, red-haired, and beautiful. He was in Oxford to do a doctorate, improving upon academic glories from abroad. He was, Tessa thought, pleased with the young people in the cell, with their keenness, and eager theological talk, and mutual affection. He was just as cautious about Hubert as his predecessor had been.

'Where would you get one from?' he asked of the hair shirt, with laughter in his tone.

Incredibly, Hubert said he had seen one offered in a mail-order catalogue.

'Could you work in one, Hubert?' Tessa asked. 'And if you couldn't . . .'

'Father Anthony was always saying,' said Alison, addressing the new chaplain, 'that we must first do our duty in our station in life, and only afterwards look for other virtues . . .'

'And you know, Hubert,' said Paul, 'God has put us in Oxford to study.'

'I expect I could work in the mildest one,' said Hubert dubiously, seeing his path to heaven once more disapproved of.

'The *mildest* one?' asked Paul. '*Hubert*, whatever . . . ?'

Hubert explained that you could get a hair shirt in three grades of discomfort, and he proposed to work up to the nastiest one gradually. His monastic mail-order catalogue recommended the first grade for novices at mortification; after a month or two one could move on to a harsher one.

'What do they cost?' said Tessa, seeing suddenly a possible way out.

Hubert looked guilty at once. 'They're not cheap,' he said. 'I expect they are a lot of work to make.'

'It's probably like picking hemp,' said Dominic, 'and the poor monks get bleeding fingers . . .'

Tessa wondered if there was any way in which she could explain to Father Theodore, without being rude to Hubert, who was having a hard time already, that he was rather rich, whereas the rest of them were fairly hard up. Looking up she saw the priest's sharp intelligent gaze bent on Hubert, and decided he could work that out for himself.

'It's an odd thing to say,' she said, 'but you know, Hubert, buying a hair shirt is buying something for yourself. Why not put the price of one into the poor box instead?'

'You want it so badly, you see,' said Dominic, 'that your self-denial is doing without one.'

'You don't understand!' said Hubert, now very dejected, 'I . . . oh, hell!'

They all looked at Father Theodore; they had done their best with Hubert, but it was his job to deal with it. They were not up to it themselves; that was why the cell had a chaplain.

'We are told,' he said, speaking softly, 'that we must love our neighbours as ourselves. It is implied that we love ourselves as we should our neighbours. Would you impose a hair shirt, Hubert, on these friends of yours?'

Hubert shook his head. He was near to tears.

'We don't hear much of a duty to love ourselves as we love others,' Father Theodore was saying. 'Very few people are tempted not to; it would be a somewhat unnecessary sermon. Nevertheless, each of us is a child of God. We must care for ourselves so that we go before God whole and unharmed.'

'I am only trying,' said Hubert, 'by doing penance, to save my immortal soul . . .'

'We are not souls,' said the priest. 'We have bodies too. It is not as disembodied souls that we shall stand before the judgement seat, but as resurrected bodies. If Hubert scars himself by wearing a mortificatory gadget he will carry the scar at the last day, before the throne of God.'

'But won't we be, well, glorified?' asked Paul. 'Made whole; all young and beautiful?'

'We don't know much about resurrected bodies,' said Father Theodore thoughtfully. 'But we do know a little. They are real, material bodies; they can be touched. And I'm afraid, Paul, you are wrong about being made whole: St Thomas could put his hand into the wound in Christ's side, you will remember; that wound had not disappeared. But we will be beautiful; think of the Transfiguration; of Christ in the garden, shining to the Magdalen; scarred or whole, we will be glorified.'

'I must say,' said Ben, 'I had never really thought of resurrected bodies as *real*. But if we are to have real bodies, why won't there be marriage and giving in marriage?' Discreetly interested in the newcomer, Tessa studied him. He was dark, with a rather wide-browed, untroubled face. He looked no older than the rest, though a little older he had to be. Tessa had not lost the child's expectation that every calendar year would bring a visible transformation. Ben was sprawled on the grass, his head propped on his hand, his eyes bent intently on the priest. 'How can it be heavenly, being a physical being without physical satisfactions?' he asked.

'Our physical appetites will be purer,' said Father Theodore. 'We shall love without the need to possess and the consequent fear of loss. We must continue to have physicality if we are to be in any meaningful sense still ourselves. So there will still be human affection. We shall see each other, face to face as we do now. We shall be able to sit in heaven, and discourse together . . .'

'Oh, but then, let's promise ourselves,' said Tessa, entranced, 'that we shall do just that! We will move across the plains of heaven, among the thousands of the blessed, and seek each other out, and sit down together and remember today!' Her affection expanded easily to encompass both the newcomers, russet Theodore, and raven Ben.

'Some of us might not be there to be found,' said Hubert glumly.

'However unworthy we feel,' said Father Theodore, 'God can save us. We must not despair of the mercy of God.'

'Father,' said Hubert, suddenly perking up, 'there's a text about "If thy right hand offend thee, cut it off, better to be saved without a hand than be cast whole into hell-fire" – something like that? And surely cutting off hands or plucking out eyes is worse than just getting scratched by a hair shirt?'

'"If thy right hand offend thee . . ."' said Father Theodore. 'Does your body offend you, Hubert? Is it to overcome some hard temptation that you want to discipline your senses? Do you find it hard to resist the lusts of the flesh?'

'Well, no, not really,' said Hubert. 'Not more than other people, I don't think. In fact that's why I want to do something special. Otherwise it all seems too easy!'

A suddenly dark and rueful expression crossed the priest's face. 'It isn't that,' he said, 'and no-one long finds it so.'

'I am so happy here!' said Hubert miserably.

'If you want hardness,' said Father Theodore, 'you must choose the harder path. You can simply be one of this cell, keeping the cell rules like all the rest, just being one of these good people, or you can buy and wear a hair shirt. Do whichever thing comes harder to you, and God will reward you.'

The chill of the autumn ground beneath the grass was making itself felt. The deep bell of Merton College marked the hour and they got up and stretched, and frightened into flight the little hopping bird.

At the Broad Walk they went different ways, Alison and Tessa and Paul made off towards Rose Walk. Before them, behind the ancient golden stones of the City Wall, Oxford spread a panorama of the towery City and branchy between towers. Late roses clambered the south-facing walls of Merton; beyond the Botanical Gardens Magdalen's Lily Tower stood tall and pale on a translucent water-colour sky. If cities too were corrupted and then resurrected, glorified, this might well be just such a transfigured town, Tessa thought.

'He's not much like Father Anthony, the new man,' said Paul. 'Do you suppose he's a heretic?'

'Oh, rot!' said Alison. 'Father Max would never give us a heretic!'

'But I thought hair shirts were OK,' said Paul. 'Didn't Thomas More wear one? I must look it up.'

Tessa thought there might be some relevant difference between Hubert and Thomas More but she didn't say so, for the thought was overtaken by another one.

'I say though,' she asked her companions, as they reached the bottom of the High, 'whatever *else* do you suppose you could get from Hubert's mail-order catalogue!'

However, Tessa would wonder later, had she managed to take everyone except Hubert seriously? Including herself; especially herself!

Though any photographer knows how the light changes all the live-long day, how various it is under every passing cloud, in every different climate, latitude, season, hour, for most people the medium of seeing is invisible – a constant white. We can hardly believe that the fabric samples, carefully matched under the lamplight, can so treacherously clash by daylight. 'The colours change,' we say. Just so, for the most part, we treat our own consciousness, by whose flickering light we view the world, as an invisible medium of seeing: its quirks and tints, and shadows, and changes of hue simply projected as changes in the world outside. Eagerly and hungrily viewing the whole word, the young particularly treat themselves as the invisible constant; so that – though retrospective understanding will later illuminate every one of their friends, enemies, companions – it will always be hardest to find for themselves. Whatever thoughts and actions seem most entirely natural will occasion the most astonished incomprehension later; later everyone's behaviour will seem explicable except one's own; and thinking back across years about Hubert's hair shirt, Tessa will, of course, be able to see clearly everyone in the circle except herself.

Why, for example, since Oxford was her great escape from the world of the convent school, had she spent so much of her time there in company with Catholics? She had not intended to, having a good opinion of her own power to resist the company of the heathen, whatever the nuns had thought. And it was, partly, an accident. For the college said they would fix lodgings, and when she had received a deckle-edged letter from the warden of a place called St Winifred's offering her a room if she cared to apply for it, she duly applied, supposing this was her official offer. Only when she arrived in Oxford did she discover that she was in a hostel some distance from the college, and run by nuns, whose peculiar form of good works was keeping Catholic girlhood in a secluded by-water of the dangerous deep pool of the university. By then the dean for lodgings had filled every secular hole in Oxford, down to the meanest known bedsit, and Tessa had to put up with St Winnie's.

In her first year, since she came from a school nobody had ever heard of – she was, indeed, its first-ever Oxford 'place' – and sported a surname resonant of absolutely nothing, she had been put in a kind of broom cupboard at the top of the back staircase, with a window looking out on to tiles and guttering. Tessa kept asking, in vain, for a change of hostel. But in the third week of her second year the nuns suddenly moved her, not, it is true, into a sunny room (those were all occupied, allegedly by the luck of the draw, by girls from Ascot and Mayfield), but into a not unpleasant north-facing room, high up, with a window-seat, and a prospect of lawn and trees in the University Park. There was a coarse cotton counterpane in orange stripes, a bamboo bookshelf and a solid desk. Tessa liked the room, and gave up trying to remove herself into the wicked world.

The isolation of her first-year room, and its vulnerable position – very near the swinging baize door to the sacred part of the building – had ensured Tessa a very quiet life. The predatory hordes of young men who walked the corridors of St Winnie's, hoping for tea and sympathy, or even more, seemed seldom to knock on her door, innocently feigning to be lost. She always got nought out of ten at the score parties held among freshers at St Winnie's, and indeed, only went to them to make the coffee, and listen to the talk. At a score party, a mob of first years all tumbled into somebody's room and conducted a head-count of how many men each participant had been dated by so far that term. The incredible scores claimed by such as Anna and her friends were then gradually chipped away in discussion. First you redefined 'dates'. Being taken for coffee didn't count; for dinner did. Much passion was expended on the question whether being escorted to some free college society or concert should count.

Then you disallowed the large majority of men. Oxford was full of wistful fellows sitting on walls and benches, gazing at passers-by and saying, 'Gee, I'm so lonesome!' GIs were accordingly disallowed, along with delivery boys, decorators, shop assistants (even in Blackwell's) and a self-employed sculptor. Only undergraduates – or, a fortiori, graduates were to count. Finally the Par Rule was applied. Since there were at least seven or eight men undergraduates for every woman, only seven plus counted. However the score was computed, Anna was always top, Tessa bottom of the list. For as long as she continued to go, that is. As the year wore on, and she made friends and got invitations, she quietly stopped going to score parties; she preferred, somehow, not to register her considerable degree of success.

Being moved into a better room, however, had consequences. The first of these was Stefan. On her third afternoon in a proper room, a knock on her door had announced Stefan, entirely unknown to her, standing in the corridor and saying, 'I am in such trouble. Can you help?'

'What's the matter?' Tessa asked. Stefan was nobody's idea of an Oxford Idol, being older than average for an undergraduate, with a receding hairline and a portly circumference.

'I am looking for a partner. I have to find partner. And I have tried all the girls I know, and knocked on every door on this floor. No luck. You are the last. Please?'

'A partner for what?' asked Tessa.

'The Polish Dance. I must go to the Polish Dance, and I have to have partner. What can I do?'

He sounded really distressed. He said 'Poelish' with a beautifully rounded 'o'.

'Well, it can't be that difficult,' said Tessa. 'When is it?' Somehow, without her quite having meant to let him in, she found Stefan had eased his way past her, and was sitting on her bed.

'It is at eight,' said Stefan, brightening at once. 'I fetch you at seven-thirty.'

'Tonight?' said Tessa, looking at her watch. It was half-past four. 'Well of course you can't find anybody for tonight. People need some notice.'

'But you are beautiful girl, and I have found you, OK?' said Stefan.

'Not for tonight, you haven't,' she said. 'I haven't got a dress. I was going to buy myself one, and I haven't got round to it. And no!' (he was looking at his watch now) 'There isn't time before the shops shut. There really isn't. You honestly should have thought of this before.'

'But it doesn't matter what you wear,' he said. 'You would not need special new dress. Anything will do. Anything. Something silk . . . you know. Or perhaps not silk. Only must it be long . . .' he added uncertainly.

'Well that's it. I haven't got a long dress. Sorry. I really am sorry, but I can't go with you.'

'What can I do?' cried Stefan, dropping his head dramatically in his hands.

'Keep looking, I should think,' said Tessa. 'And would you go, please, because I have an essay to write, and I want to get started by supper time.'

Stefan went, but not for long. In a few minutes he was back, with Barbara from seven doors along. 'Barbara! My dear friend Barbara, she lends you a dress!' he announced.

'If it's really only the dress,' said Barbara, trying to catch Tessa's eye. But Tessa was not made of stern enough stuff to throw up another defence against such determined attempts. She did not yet know anything against Stefan, he appeared to be well known to other people at St Winnie's, and he *was* rather het up about it all. So he departed with his date accepted, and Tessa and Barbara were left to manage the dress.

Barbara's dress was caramel-coloured taffeta, with a rustle like chips frying. It probably looked good on her; Barbara had blazing red hair, and always wore muted colours. It had an amazing effect on Tessa, however, exactly matching her tawny hair and hazel eyes. It quenched her completely, producing a monochrome effect like a sepia photograph. Also, although Tessa had not thought of Barbara as buxom, and thought of herself as excessively curved and heavy in crucial places, the impression was deceptive somewhere, for the dress hung limply from Tessa's shoulders to the hem, by-passing her contours completely. Tessa stared in the mirror, and Barbara stared at her with like dismay. Then Barbara grabbed a handful of the fabric from the back, and pulled the dress tight. The neck plunged down towards Tessa's cleavage, and the skirt swung with extra fullness.

'Better,' said Barbara.

‘But there isn’t time to take it in! How can that man be so silly?’

‘Stefan? Oh, he finds it easy! There isn’t time to take it in properly, but I’ll tack it on you just before you go.’

‘After supper then. I’m not appearing in the dining room like this!’

Then, of course, supper ran unusually late. Barbara cobbled up the fullness of the dress in great haste, and Tessa, feeling as awful as she looked, waited to be fetched by her partner.

At any time after seven the girls at St Winnie’s let themselves in by the side door with their keys. Young men – or young women, for that matter – wishing to call had to ring on the front door and be admitted by a nun, to wait in the hall while their young lady was fetched from her room. Waiting cavaliers could be seen from all the landings, and invariably were: students and nuns shared both curiosity and available viewpoints. Tessa realized, as she stumbled on her hem along the corridor, that someone interesting was waiting: she could hear the twittering excited whispers from the uppermost landing that betokened excitement among the nuns. It did not, till the moment she clapped eyes on him, occur to her that it could be Stefan causing the stir. But it was.

Stefan was wearing dark blue trousers with silk braid on the seams, and a jacket covered with braid and epaulettes of a vaguely military appearance. A blue ribbon round his neck carried a medal of some kind, discreetly tucked half visible into the ruffles of his extremely dressy dress shirt, and the whole thing was completed with an enormous dark blue cloak lined with brilliant scarlet, held by a silver chain and thrown nonchalantly back over one shoulder to display the scarlet to best advantage. He was carrying white gloves and wearing a dress sword. He looked like a bit-part in *The Student Prince*; whatever he might be wearing, nature had not equipped Stefan to look like the lead.

'Dear Lady, how beautiful you look,' said Stefan, absurdly, bowing and clicking heels at her. 'But you will be cold.' And sweeping his magnificent cloak from his shoulders, he put it round Tessa and led her out to the soft sounds of rapture from ecstatic nuns, and to a waiting car.

The dance was in the Town Hall. The lobby was seething with people, all dressed up. Grown-up people too – it was immediately obvious that this was not an undergraduate occasion, as Tessa had vaguely supposed it would be. Indeed, there was the Mayor of Oxford, complete with chain of office, standing on the pillared landing. As Stefan and Tessa walked in the voices changed pitch. Stefan gave his gloves and sword to the cloakroom attendant, and then offered Tessa an arm and swept her forward. People parted to make way for his determined advance. Stefan led her up the marble stairs, and for an awful moment Tessa thought the Mayor and Mayoress were at the top waiting just for them. Fool! she told herself, closing her eyes, and keeping in step with Stefan. When she opened them it was only too clear that the Mayor and Mayoress *were* waiting for Stefan and partner; they were beginning to move forwards, hands extended. As she took the last few steps, the cling of taffeta about her middle suddenly slackened. It loosened with each step . . . by the time she reached the landing the last of Barbara's tacking stitches was undone, and Tessa stood limply shining, shapeless from top to toe.

Heels clicked; Stefan bowed. Tessa, terrified, shook hands with the Mayor, and the Mayoress, who was regarding her with interest, and a dozen or more people in a line-up. Then they were in the ballroom. A small orchestra occupied a dais. Girls in Polish costume fluttered about like backstage ballet.

Stefan, gripping her firmly by the elbow, steered her out into the middle of the floor. 'We dance,' he said.

Tessa looked around in pure terror. 'Nobody else is dancing yet!' she said.

'They cannot till we do,' he said. The orchestra struck up a vigorous jolly chord. Down the hall beside them a double row of other couples assembled with a rustling of dresses. The orchestra stopped; the conductor looked around, tapped his baton briskly, and began again.

'But what is it?' hissed Tessa desperately at Stefan. 'Tango? Quickstep?'

'It is mazurka, of course!' he said. 'Dance!' For the orchestra had started, stopped, started again, like a record stuck in a groove on the first track.

'But I don't know how to mazurka!' Tessa wailed, forgetting to lower her voice.

'Why did you not say if you cannot dance?' said Stefan. 'You should not come to dances if you cannot dance. Now this is very embarrassing.'

The orchestra tried again a couple of times, but each try was shorter as they got more and more discouraged. A murmur of excited voices increasing in volume spread round them. Tessa's face burned, and tears of vexation sprang into her eyes.

And then, suddenly she was rescued. Bearing down upon them came someone she knew – Matchek, the tallest Pole in Oxford, Hubert had cracked, who belonged to the cell though he came only intermittently. A pretty dark-haired girl in white muslin and coloured ribbons was leaning on his arm.

'Change partners!' he said to Stefan.

Stefan regarded him coldly. 'We have to start it,' he said, almost stamping his foot. 'We must . . .'

'Change partners quick!' said Matchek. 'Now, Stefan!'

'Is for me to start . . .' began Stefan again, glaring around him.

'Dance with Ischia,' said Matchek, smiling sweetly. Matchek's pretty Polish girl slipped into Stefan's arms, the orchestra took courage and struck up a whole bar, and then swept into the full tune. Matchek picked Tessa up bodily, lifting her right off her feet, and began to dance with her clutched to his chest as a child holds a teddy bear. The mazurka seemed to be a folk dance with rows and changes of places, and the dancers weaving in and out, and Matchek picked Tessa up and put her down, and the girl now dancing with Stefan seized her hand and tugged her round her moves, and then pushed her smartly in the small of the back, and sent her lurching across a gap in the lines towards Matchek again, who picked her up and went leaping joyfully around with her to the wildly rhythmic beat of the dance.

On the final chords he put her down gently behind a pillar in the aisles of the hall. She leaned against him, head spinning, laughing jubilantly at the thrill of being whirled around, at the sudden rescue . . .

'You must not be cross with Stefan,' Matchek said to her disjointedly, between gasps for breath. Tall and strong as he was, carting Tessa around at a gallop had been quite a challenge.

'Why not?' she said, feeling cross again at once.

'He doesn't understand things very well,' said Matchek. 'Not about England.'

'But why not? And whoever is he?'

'He is special to Poles,' said Matchek. 'I don't know quite what you would call it in English – he is Prince, perhaps. His mother is very aristocratic lady. She has brought Stefan up to return one day to Poland and have castles and be Prince. This is very difficult for him, you must see.'

'Do you have to follow him round all the time, getting him out of fixes?'

'That's my privilege,' said Matchek, smiling. 'I am his friend.'

'Oh, friendship,' said Tessa. 'That's different from Princedoms. All right, I'll forgive him.'

'I'll take you back to him,' said Matchek, leading her from behind the pillar into the limelight again.

The music struck up again. Matchek rejoined his own partner, and whirled away from Tessa in the patterns of the dance. She stood glumly beside Stefan, who was silent. Then, 'What can you dance?' he asked. A little discussion between them established that she might manage a waltz or a polka. 'Very well,' said Stefan, 'when is waltz or polka we will dance. Till then we must eat.'

There was, certainly, in an adjacent room, enough food laid out to occupy a considerable number of exotic dances. This room was full of all the middle-aged and elderly participants, who had clearly made a bee-line for the buffet tables and were giving only very desultory attention to talking. Tessa realized she was famished, and found some fragile wafer-like things, coated in icing-sugar and delicately spiced, of which she consumed so many that she felt for shame she had better conceal the nearly empty dish. Stefan seemed more interested in cold meats and bright red chilled soup, laid out at the other end of the line of white-clothed tables, so she was separated from him. When the notes of a waltz penetrated to her she looked for him, and found him so deep in conversation with a pair of grey-haired, distinguished-looking people, that she thought better of it, and returned to find more delicate things to eat. Then in due course she thought some polka music was playing, and she looked for Stefan again and found him dancing already, his partner a laughing child of about twelve with a band of flowers in her hair. At last she realized that Stefan honestly didn't need her any more, and with an up-surge of intense relief she went down the sweep of stairs, and through the main doors. It was now raining dismally outside. She had come, of course, wrapped up in Stefan's cloak, and she hardly liked to claim that from the cloakroom attendant. It really didn't seem fair to walk home in the rain in Barbara's taffeta; Tessa had a nasty feeling that material like that might show water marks for ever after. And she hadn't money enough for a taxi.

She stood in the shelter of the portico, waiting for the

rain to stop, and gradually freezing to the bone. Being Stefan's friend, she thought bitterly, is a kind of virtue I do not aspire to; I must propose it to Hubert instead of a grade-three hair shirt . . .

A voice said, 'Tessa? What are you doing there? Aren't you too cold?'

Father Theodore was standing in the street at the foot of the steps. When she tried to answer him her teeth chattered – not as a figure of speech, but actually enough to chop up her words. He took off his black jacket and ran up the stairs to put it round her shoulders. 'Come with me,' he said. 'It's only a step to the Chaplaincy, and there'll be a fire in Father Max's study.

'What has happened to you?' he asked, an arm round her shoulder, holding his jacket in place and hurrying her along the street. 'Has someone stood you up?'

She thought, to her amazement, that he was angry at the thought. But when, seated by a roaring fire, drinking hot toddy concocted by Father Max, and comfortable in the knowledge that Father Max would lend Father Theodore his car to drive her home by and by, she told them what had happened to her, they both laughed very merrily at it.

Stefan, it turned out, had a lot of friends. For quite a while after the Polish Dance, impeccably English-sounding undergraduates with Polish names hailed Tessa from bikes, or whispered to her in the library, claiming aquaintance with her on account of the dreadful mazurka. It seemed for a dizzy week or so that every Pole in Oxford wanted to stand her a coffee in the Tackley.

Vladek, who worked in the Bodleian, even insisted she must be a Pole herself.

'Whyever?' asked Tessa in the sore-throat whisper that was *de rigueur* in the library. 'I'd have thought you would know I *couldn't* be.'

'Well, we all guessed what must have happened, and we knew, that could not have happened to you, unless you had been being kind to Stefan.'

'Couldn't an English person be kind to Stefan?' Tessa wondered.

Vladek considered. 'Possible. But then also you are a Catholic.'

'But Vladek,' she said. 'Not all Catholics are Poles, after all.'

'Irish Catholics we know about,' he said, 'and Italian Catholics, though not many in Oxford; and English who are *caatholics*, and go *orphan* to *Maas*. But common English are not Catholics. They are Church of England, or Quakers, or something. So common English Catholic is maybe Pole who lies low . . .'

Tessa laughed, loudly enough to bring disapproving glances and indignant shushing sounds upon her. 'Well, not me I'm afraid,' she resumed in a whisper, 'I just *am* common English and Catholic.'

'OK, so you are not Polish at all,' he said, grinning. 'But you would come with me to Polish society meeting?'

'Just once, I would,' said Tessa. 'Out of curiosity.'

One thing which Tessa learned from encounters with Poles was that Vladek had a point about common English. It was true that common English were not Catholic; indeed no English, uncommon or not, could be Catholic as Poles could be. Or as Irish could, or Italians. The Oxford Poles were full of passion; they walked about with all their raw nerve ends uncovered.

She realized, for example, sitting with Vladek through a meeting of the Polish society, with gradually deepening dismay, that the real reason for the gathering, and doubtless for the other impressive meetings on the Society's programme for the term, all addressed by public figures who had visited the Eastern Bloc – Poland if possible, but somewhere else at a pinch – was not really in the least to hear about Polish politics. Certainly at this meeting, she heard a courteous and distinguished man discoursing on Polish affairs. In particular, on the budgetary crisis. He finished to a gratifying storm of applause. Then there were one or two normal questions, provided by Matchek and Vladek. But then someone stood up, wringing his hands, and asked in a voice full of anguish if it was safe and possible to send food parcels to Poland. The real reason for the whole paraphernalia of an undergraduate society, it seemed to Tessa, was to ask these few unanswerable questions: is my family starving? If I send a parcel, will it reach them? If it reaches them, will the authorities take a horrible revenge on them because of it?

The speaker coped with perfect kindness. He must, she supposed, have realized that they hadn't wanted his actual address at all, but he showed nothing but concern.

'Nobody there is actually starving,' he told them, over and over.

'When I was last at home,' said a middle-aged man from the back of the hall, 'when they last let me in, things were terrible, terrible. No milk for babies, no medicines.'

'There is a major economic crisis,' the speaker said. 'But things are better than they were.'

'We read in the papers . . .' someone called out.

'And we don't know anything,' the man continued. 'We are told this, or told that. Only we know what we saw when we last were there.'

'Poland is changing,' said the speaker, gently. 'Has changed.'

'What can we know for certain?' the man said, with tears in his eyes.

But the passion that surfaced at the meeting didn't on superficial appearances go also into religion. The Polish undergraduates all turned up at the Polish Mass every third Sunday; otherwise they were very relaxed about missing Mass. Matchek once remarked idly in the course of some discussion that he had not been to confession since he was nine. But of course Poles just *were* Catholic; if Matchek didn't practise his religion that didn't make him not a Catholic, any more than it made him not a Pole. He could be a bad Catholic. 'God will forgive,' he said, smiling.

But if you were common English you couldn't be so light-hearted. The only way of being a common English Catholic was to be a good one; once you stopped being a good one you would simply stop being one at all. And while you were a good one you would be always swimming against the tide. You would always be not English but Roman. You would always belong in the corrugated iron shed at the village end; in the hideous concrete building, or the scout hall on freezing every-second-Sunday mornings, while in every place the lovely ancient stones of the English Church, spires and towers and aisles and clerestories proclaimed the exile of your faith from the fabric of your country.

> Oh, Rome, my country, City of the Soul,
> The orphans of the heart must turn to Thee,

poor exiled Byron had written; but Tessa, though she knew of course she was English only for life, and could be Catholic for eternity, was in all respects other than her church warmly a lover of her country, and she did not feel like an orphan; more like a foster child whose temporary parents disagreed with her permanent ones.

Of such a disagreement as that Tessa did indeed have knowledge. Not that she was really a foster child. She had a loving mother and grandparents alive and well and living in North Finchley; but like so many others of her precise generation she had been an evacuee. She had a dream-like memory of the train journey, going on and on, and a crystal-clear memory of the train stopping for hours and hours in a cutting, a flowering cutting with strange glossy bushes growing on the banks. She watched a bee flying on the tiny pink flowers of the bushes, and hardly listened to a long diatribe from Miss O'Neill about what would happen, and what they ought to do. A little girl of five is better at dreaming than at listening; she could come to no harm, she was labelled with a cardboard tie-on label round her neck. She remembered the cry of 'St Erth for St Ives!' echoing in the darkness, and waking her up. And another train; every child half asleep or more, stumbling about, crying, doing the wrong things. The sharp chill of the clean-smelling air on the platform, after the comforting, familiar smell of urine in the warmth of the train. And then being wide awake, staring into the moon-glare on bulbous faint cloud. She remembered seeing the lighthouse winking and signalling to her before she even got off the train. She could not at all remember the scenes on the station, the desperate chaos, and the way in which she had come into the care of Cornish Grandad. He told her the story often enough and she could remember him telling her, that was all. So that if she recalled this episode she saw herself from the outside, and above, as he had seen her – a pale, stumpy creature, looking lost, crying as much as all the others, but silently, a blue bow-shaped slide in her blond hair, just waiting.

'I can't do with a mite that ought to be still with its mother,' Grandad had said. 'I'm a single man, and have never had to do with a child.'

'There's been a mistake,' the WVS lady said. 'We have mostly mites, and hardly any older boys. You'd best take a boy quickly, or there'll be nobody left but tiny girls.'

'I'll perhaps take nobody,' he said. But he felt uneasy, and he glanced at small Tessa. She was standing staring out to sea; the sea unseen, but softly splashing and sighing in the dark.

'You're down to take one,' the lady said. 'You've got the room, and many haven't. You know that. What about that one? She looks a bit older, and sensible.' The lady pointed, Grandad always said, at someone who looked like the three ugly sisters all rolled into one. He stepped up to Tessa, quick. 'Would you like to stop with me?' he asked her. He more than half thought she would say no, looking at his tanned face, and his sweater stained with salt, and his bushy eyebrows.

'Can I see the flashing moon from your house?' she asked.

'The what? The what did you say?'

'The flashing moon. There's one that keeps on shining, and a lovely one that's going on and off. I'd like to watch it.'

'The lighthouse. You mean the lighthouse. Yes, you can see that from my house. Water's edge, I am; the sea will bump your bedroom window, when it blows north-easterly.'

'It's bedtime,' small Tessa had said. 'My clothes are getting heavy on me.'

'Yes it is,' he had said, and signed for her, and then he had picked her up bodily and taken her home.

She had woken in heaven. Or so it seemed. Outside the window a soft repeated sighing, and sharp cries, the sound of the sea, and the gulls like noisy children, making a playground of the sky. Tessa's room was full of shimmering nets of gold, all over the walls and ceiling and the glossy brown scumbled door, and even on Tessa's face and hands, reticulated glory like the wings of Michael, the scales of Lucifer in a holy picture. She was lying under a worn and faded quilt, with all her clothes still on her. She remembered with visionary clarity the beauty in the room, and the crumpled, heavy feel of being dressed in bed. She got up, and went to the window.

The sea lapped at the wall below, and swept away, far away, to the horizon. Where sea met sky, far out, was a shadowy island, and on the island was a white tower.

Then she saw that the window was a door with a panel of glass in the top half. She opened it, half thinking that she was dreaming, that the sea would wash into the room. But the door opened to a balcony made of scoured planks, between the cracks of which the seaweed-stained green depths of water glinted. The house was standing on the last rock of a bluff jutting into the harbour; the curving town-clad slopes all visible from it, as well as the open sea, the distant green hills beyond the bay, the lovely island. From the wooden balcony a stair descended; but it was, on that first morning, high tide. Tessa sat down on the cool wood, gritty with sand, and watched the jade and moonstone water, polished by the morning light, uncurl the treads from its shining fingers and relinquish them one by one. Little by little she moved down after it, though the lower stairs were slimy with long green floating tresses, and little by little as it lost ground, the water grew quiet, and showed her a flock of little fishes swimming half-way down to the coggled green-gold floor. The fishes too were bathed in the light of angels' wings; they swam in the golden nets as though the sun were trawling for them.

Tessa had heard talk of heaven, and never any of the sea. She waited for God, or an angel, to appear and tell her what to do. God did not come; but by and by Cornish Grandad appeared, not like a common grown-up, from within the house, but in a white-painted rowing boat, standing, sculling himself towards her across the harbour. He tied his boat to the massive newel post at the foot of the stair; and then he said to her, looking up, blinking at the sky behind her, 'Mackerel for breakfast, girl. Take'n, while I bring my box . . .'

He handed her a pair of blue-black, shining fishes in a little loop of string, and she took them; and then they flapped and twitched, and thumped against her shin.

She dropped them; and they drummed their strong bright tails upon the boards. And then she saw that her legs were freshly freckled with tiny gouts of mackerel blood; the string had printed a line of blood across her four fingers. The wet patch on her leg where the fish had slapped her was drying tight in the smart breeze off the water, leaving her with a dragon-patch, leaving her scaly, each tiny transparent meniscus gleaming pearly like the sequins on her mother's evening dress. But Tessa knew that nothing in heaven would bleed and so, in spite of appearances, she knew she had not died and gone to heaven.

Later, when her questing conscience went fishing through her memory for sins with which to supply the voracious demands of the confessional, she was to think of the gusto with which she had eaten the poor mackerel, so recently so pitifully alive, as the first self-proof she had of fallen nature.

Later again she was to reflect with astonishment on the apparently accidental nature of things which have shaping power. If she had not landed in heaven at so young an age, then surely she would not have been swept away with enchantment by *To the Lighthouse* at the tender age of fourteen. The house the Stephens rented for the summers stood behind Cornish Grandad's house, and a little to the east of it; but the book itself pretends to be set in Skye, and Tessa did not know for many years the source of the powerful enchantment it cast over her. So, if she had not liked Virginia Woolf at an age which surprised Sister Mary Winifred, who taught English; if she had never been led to think she might be unusually good at English; then she would not have tried Oxford . . . nor achieved it, with all that that would entail; so that in the beauty of the dream morning the first time she saw the sea, her life lay coiled up, hidden, like a winkle in a shell.

Cornish Grandad almost certainly did not know that he lived just below the Stephens' house, and was pleased when his new charge ate the carefully filleted strips of mackerel he put before her, and asked for more. Almost certainly, Cornish Grandad's idea of sin would have been refusing good fish rather than hard-heartedly eating it. Indeed their first day together went astonishingly well. The falling tide revealed a golden strip of sand at the foot of the stairs outside the blue balcony door, on which Grandad's rowing boat came to rest and tipped over slightly, so that it was easy to climb in and out of. Tessa simply played on the beach. Grandad found her a wooden spoon for a spade and a brown glazed jar for a bucket, but the best game was just sitting so quietly that the sand-pipers came back and walked around near you, or, when the sea changed its mind and began to creep home for supper time, writing scribbles and watching the leap-frogging waves erase them. At dusk she was visited by another of those moments – we cannot tell at the time which they are – which will be durable for a lifetime in our retrospective minds: for the flashing moon re-appeared, while there was still enough light left in the lilac dusk to let her see that it shone from the top of the white tower on the far island. The lighthouse. Grandfather named it, Godrevy . . . she thought he said 'Good-dreamy'.

Names gave them their only trouble with each other all day. Tessa had never been able to get her tongue properly round Theresa, and Grandad seemed curiously unwilling to find it out by reading her luggage label. Any odd name was possible, he said, for up-country folk naming their children were capable of anything. The nearest they could get was 'Tress', and 'Little Tress' she was, all settled on, before anybody arriving to check up on the billeting arrangements could tell him any different.

It was at bed time that their mutual satisfaction came unstuck. Tessa's clothes were full of scratchy sand; so while Grandad's back was turned, she took them off and demanded a bath. Grandad flushed deeply when he turned round and saw her standing naked with her thumb in her mouth. 'Cover yourself, girl!' he roared, and Tessa, well used to London, and misunderstanding him, dived at once under the table and said, from behind the hanging heavy, rust velvet tablecloth, 'I didn't hear the siren go. You come in here too, Grandad.'

'Suffering seamen!' said Grandad. 'Now what do I do?'

What he did, Tessa gathered later from Granny Nan, was to thrust his hands through the tablecloth under the table and catch Tessa up in it, and take her to bed wrapped up in fringed velour.

She didn't, but for Nan's telling her, remember that. But she remembered how he took her by the hand one morning – the next morning, probably, what seemed very early, with a lemon sky behind the dunes at Lelant, and walked her up the steep street into the town. They walked on and on, right through the town's windy streets, always climbing, until they came out on a height, with a wide view of the bay, by a row of little cottages. Every window in every one turned its back on the view and looked instead at a neat little garden, no longer than it could be to have the cottages giving lee of the wind. There was a thin, birdlike woman, wearing a faded cross-over flowery apron in one of the cottages, and she gave them tea, with lovely scones so well risen Tessa could hardly open wide enough to bite them . . . She half heard the talk, but was more interested in a fascinating noise coming from the kitchen. Soon she wandered off and found the source of it – a discontented parrot, moulting in a wicker cage. 'Watcher doing, watcher doing now!' it said.

'I'm an evacuee,' said Tessa, and added, for it seemed to be waiting for more, 'sir.'

'That's nice,' it said. 'Give us a bite, then!'

Tessa retreated. The conversation in the parlour was over, and Grandad was getting up to go.

He had been very silent walking up the town; but as

they walked down he talked to her. 'She's always said I didn't need a woman to look after me, and at my age I shouldn't need her for anything else. She wasn't moving in to no pin neat place, she said, to have the neighbours nudging and winking. So I said to her, "Here's Little Tress now; and isn't that reason enough for a woman in a house?"'

'Do you mean she's coming to live with us?'

'Soon. As soon as we can fix it. She thinks it takes time to get wed.'

'Will she bring her birdy?' asked Tessa.

'Holy mackerel!' he said. 'She might, she might. On the other hand, perhaps that belongs to her son. She's a-living with her married son. Did you like the parrot?'

'No,' said Tessa, 'it wanted to bite me.'

'Can't have that,' he said, laughing. He skipped along home so fast Tessa couldn't keep up, and he couldn't bear to linger so in the end he heaved her up high on his shoulders and carried her back.

It was only three days, in the end, till Nan appeared with three large wooden boxes on the back of a van, and a hat with purple flowers on the brim. It hadn't taken so long to fix, after the night of the storm. The maroon had gone up for the lifeboat, and Grandad had put on his oilskins and gone out in the dark of the night. Tessa had woken when the sea thumped on the windows and gone wandering round the house, frightened and alone, and then slept on the hearth before the stove, so that when he came in at dawn he had found her freezing cold by the dying fire, with muted sobs still shaking her in her sleep. She remembered nothing of it; but he told her that it had happened. 'And that was a hard night, that service,' he said. 'And if I'd not come back . . . I told the Minister to wed us within the hour, or she'd move in with me unwed.' Tessa had slept through the wedding, making up for the disturbed night; she woke to the bustle of Nan's boxes arriving, and Nan in the flowered hat with a faded ribbon. An old hat, not a new one.

It didn't look like a love-match; in that dissimulation they had indeed succeeded; and Tessa was an adult before it occurred to her that the matrix of her own happiness had been theirs. They laughed a lot; they called each other very rude names – Boneshanks, she to him; Hagbag, he to her. She brought a rocking-chair with her all in pieces, and Grandad at once set about glueing and cramping and mending it, and soon she sat rocking by the fire, knitting a thick little sweater for Tessa and a great hairy pair of socks for Grandad, to keep his seaboots lined. And, the adult Tessa would remember, smiling, there was no more getting up early for mackerel. They lay late in bed together, while she wandered the beach picking up pretty shells, and called her in at last to breakfast on fish caught yesterday. Nan kept her bathed, in a big tin bath in front of the fire, at moments when Grandad was out 'on the rampage', as Nan said.

Every week Nan bought a postcard for Tessa to write to her mother, and added a postscript of her own in tiny, neatly formed letters, ringing all round the edges of the card to find room when Tessa filled the middle with large shaky letters spelling a love she no longer felt. She had forgotten everything except the present, and every place but that one.

It was months before the Catholic priest in the town found out that he had a claim on her. When he did, he accosted Grandad in the street, as he walked on the quays, holding Tessa by the hand, on the way to Laity's to buy some mysterious goods for Nan's splendid cooking. Tessa could always dredge out of memory the tall, black shape of the priest looming over her, and the tight grip of Grandad's hand on hers. She remembered the sense of threat in the encounter, like a bruise in her mind, though all she could recall having happened was that the black figure leaned towards her and asked her if she would like to go to Catechism, and she said no. She would have said no to anything coming from him.

'There you are, then,' Grandad said. 'You keep off us and let us be.'

'I shall write to her parents,' said the priest.

'He says she is a Papist,' Grandad told Nan. His dislike and anger clouded the feel of the day as vividly as foul weather.

'She can't be,' Nan had said. 'She's too young to be wicked.'

'He says we've to take her along to his church and his Sunday School, every Sunday, or else. Do you think we must?'

'Wait on,' said Nan. 'It's her mother we'll harken, not *him*.'

Tessa's mother, full of relief at the stream of happy postcards from the seaside, and with other things on her mind, felt disinclined to fuss about church-going. Whatever she wrote to Nan put Grandad's mind at rest, and hardened him to ignore several more sharp exchanges in the street with the roving priest, and to keep Tessa away from the hated looming church and the idolatrous worship.

And so for some time Tessa's heaven went along as heaven ought to do – cruising timelessly in an indefinite prospect of continuance.

It was Grandad who put an end to it, though it was the last thing he intended to bring about. There was a boat being built for him. He took Tessa nearly every day to see it, standing on the stocks in the builders' shed on the quayside, all freshly cut and sweetly smelling of timber. Jake and Thomas, both unbelievably old, worked on it; their hundredth, give or take a few. It was to have an engine, though Grandad had never had an engine before. A little turretlike wheelhouse, of course, and a mizzen mast, with a rust-red sail, to allow it to head into the wind and go steady. Tessa liked the words, though she did not understand them. Once the boat was launched Grandad would catch more fish, though the real money was taking parties of trippers round the bay and letting them do the catching. When the war was over, trippers would be back. Tessa liked the boat best when it was empty: a shell, a ribbed curving shell, into which Grandad lowered her to stand upon the keel inside, and feel the comfort of the shape.

'What shape is this?' she asked.

'Shipshape,' said Jake.

'No – what is it called?' she persisted. 'Not circle, not square, not tirangle, what?' Her early schooling in the emergency nursery in the Town Hall was going to her head.

'That's sea-kindly, that is,' said Thomas, and smiled.

Tessa never thought the boat improved by all the things that went into the perfect shape later; least of all by the stout decking that covered it in.

'Just look at it from the outside, girl,' said Grandad, but it wasn't as good.

The only time that both Grandad and Nan abandoned her to her own devices was for the hour on Sunday mornings when they went to the service in the Seaman's Mission on the quay. For that time they left her playing along the harbour shore in the exceptionally quiet town. They had no idea how conspicuous she was – the only child free on Sunday – or that anyone bothered to notice her.

Disaster struck because on the Sunday when the finished boat was to be blessed, they took her with them to chapel.

And because someone was watching, someone knew.

Tessa herself enjoyed it. The preacher was a man with a warm Cornish voice, and a wide, sea-tanned face. He praised Christ for His skill at calming stormy waters, and His uncanny knowledge of where to cast nets for fish. These were particular attributes of God that Tessa had never before heard singled out for glory. 'To carpenters and fishermen,' the preacher said, 'God's Kingdom came first – to men of just our kind. And let's never forget it!' And then everyone sang very heartily, and it was a good song, Tessa thought:

> Oh hear us when we call to Thee,
> For those in peril on the Sea!

Then everyone trooped out along the quay, and there was Grandad's new boat, tied up shining in spanking new blue paint, alongside the steep stone steps. The preacher blessed the boat. He blessed it with a wish of safety in storms and holiness in conduct, and with a hope of enormous catches and another hope that there would never be any foul language spoken aboard her, not whatever happened. The boat's name, he said, was under covers for the moment, until somebody's birthday next week, but he had spoken the name in his heart and blessed it as good and thoroughly as though he had called it to the winds of the world. The winds of the world were blowing chill and cheerful and buffeting his congregation as he spoke; but they stood their ground long enough for the Salvation Army band to march out to join them, playing stoutly. The harbour master blew the foghorn three times, and then they all went home for dinner.

A week later came the letter from Tessa's mother. She would come on the following Friday to take her daughter home.

Nan grieved silently. Grandad sat by the fire and wept. They resolved to argue for keeping Tessa, but they knew they would lose. They kept looking at her, anxious to tell each other how well she looked, how she had grown. Her nursery school reports, all praise, were propped on the mantelpiece clock in readiness. So great was their penitence they even, on the single intervening Sunday, took Tessa up the road to the

Catholic church, and left her on the steps. A lady with a white veil all over her head took Tessa's hand and led her in.

The sermon wasn't nearly as good as the one in the Mission. Tessa didn't understand it. But she liked the sound of Latin, the shining candles and the white clothes and silver chalice. The hated priest looked less fearful clad in the creamy silk vestments. And here too there was a good song: 'Virgin most pure, Star of the Sea, Pray for the mariner, pray for me!'

The prayers seemed long and puzzling. What, for example, was petrol light, that everyone was asking to shine upon them? There was electric light in London; gaslight in Grandad's house, oil-lamps in the lighthouse. Somewhere there must be petrol lights, even though petrol was rationed.

Best of all was the song that was sung as the priest finished and left. Everyone stood up and sang; Tessa stood up and listened.

> Dark night has come down on this rough-spoken
>   world,
> And the banners of Darkness are boldly unfurled,
> And the tempest-tossed Church, all her eyes are on
>   Thee!
> They look to Thy shining, Sweet Star of the Sea!

The Star of the Sea, Tessa thought, must be Godrevy Light. And it was true; everyone looked to its shining. Then as she left, the priest, who was standing on the steps saying goodbye to people, stopped her and gave her a little silver pendant, like a sixpence on a chain. It had a lady on it with the moon and stars. He told her to wear it, and to remember always to be like the Virgin Mary.

'But I don't want to be like the Virgin Mary,' Tessa told Nan. 'I want to be like myself!'

'And what's the betting you'll do that,' said Nan, with considerable satisfaction.

The day before Tessa's mother came was her birthday, though she had lost all count of time and quite forgotten about it. Nan made a cake, somehow, with scrounged and hoarded sugar and eggs. It sank in the middle, so that the icing sat on it like water in a duck-pond and made them laugh. And then Nan put on her coat and came out walking with Tessa and Grandad, a thing she had not been known to do. A lot of Grandad's friends were standing around, and giving good-day to them brightly, as though they thought something was about to happen; people were standing about all along Smeaton's Quay. The new boat was at anchor, and there were Jake and Thomas rowing around the stern in Grandad's rowing boat. Tessa stood between Nan and Grandad, and watched while Thomas stood up and pulled the canvas off the stern. In lovely fairground letters Grandad's boat was labelled LITTLE TRESS.

'There, girl,' said Grandad gruffly. 'You'll know that you're remembered when you'm gone back.'

'But Grandad,' said Tessa, who had not understood anything, 'the war's still happening. I'm not going anywhere . . .'

But Tessa's mother was unrelenting, and she was.

Years later, when Tessa began to notice in her mother's talk a less than fervent attitude to the Church, she thought to ask her why, if that was how she felt, she had taken Tessa home on the strength of just one attendance at a Protestant service; just because of blessing the boat.

'I thought your father would want it. I had promised you would be brought up in the Faith. And he wasn't there to discuss it . . .'

'But surely . . .'

'And that dreadful priest kept writing to me . . . the truth is, I was missing you. I wanted you with me.'

'Oh!' said Tessa. 'I always thought I was nothing but a nuisance to you then!'

'Silly,' said her mother, touching her hand lightly.

You cannot blame your mother for missing you. And there are things that cannot be said; you cannot tell your mother that you were happier with strangers than ever again since, than ever at home. Nor, in the long run, can you erase the powerful confusions of childhood from their hiding places in the memory, or blunt their shaping power in life. Tessa would never, now, lose the impression that tenure of heaven was inextricably connected with exactly which church one stood in, praying down mercy on men at sea.

In the short run, in London, she pined. Caged in the daytime garden, frightened by things going bump in the night, jealous and irritable at the antics of her younger brother – all her brick towers toppled, all her drawings crumpled and torn – whom she had last known safely cradled and unthreatening, Tessa spent long hours in her room alone, and sad. There was nothing to spend time on except reading. Tessa still could not write; the nuns would not allow anyone to hold a pen left handed. And she would never, life-long, achieve spelling, but she had somehow absorbed reading like breathing, and could do it. Understanding was a long way ahead, but actually reading, swimming along the surface of the words, she could and did do all day long.

The books were her real grandfather's. Uniformly bound rows of the classics adorned his glass-fronted shelves. In spite of the glass, the books were dusty and made Tessa cough. He had them in sets, and in alphabetical order of author, and the delight and relief of the marathon reader when A gave way to B and the *Orestiea* was succeeded by *Jane Eyre*, gave Tessa another push in the direction of English at Oxford. Not that *Jane Eyre* is a cheering book, and in any case it was confiscated swiftly by a nun who thought it unsuitable for a child of Tessa's age. Religion is full of mysteries: what, exactly, was unsuitable about *Jane Eyre*? Even in her most devout period, Tessa could not have told.

The day came when Tessa reached Keats, and read:

> What little town by river or sea shore,
> Or mountain built with peaceful citadel,
> Is emptied of its folk, this pious morn?
> And, little town, thy streets for evermore
> Will silent be, and not a soul to tell
> Why thou art desolate, can e'er return.

Reading, she began to cry, silently at first and then with uncontrollable sobbing so that people came – the charlady, and her mother, with kindly tutting and questions. And Tessa simply couldn't stop. She went on for hours, till she ached all over her chest and her eyes felt like two bee-stings, and the flow of tears was palpable down the back of her throat, and lurching in her stomach like the water that gets into you when you dive. She couldn't explain. Her mother called the doctor. And then sat on the end of the bed, in which Tessa lay pinned by the immaculate sheets, still heaving at lengthening intervals and drowsing off to sleep, and said softly, 'Darling tell me. Tell Mummy . . .'

'The sea,' said Tessa at last, 'I miss the sea so much . . . ' and slept.

Tessa was a much-loved child. Grandfather – her real grandfather – somehow scrounged petrol, wrote to someone, gave a reason of some kind, got the canvas covers off the Sunbeam in the garage, got the battery recharged, somehow got it going. Mother made a picnic lunch. And they took off for a day by the sea. Not, of course, to the western shores, not from North Finchley. They went to Frinton.

'Well, then,' said Grandpa, driving them back, gloriously late. 'What did you think of that?'

'It was lovely, Grandpa,' she said, wriggling in the back seat under the weight of her lolling, sleeping brother, 'but . . .'

'But what?' he said, contented, though, at her first answer. A nestful of unremarkable pebbles, each chosen lovingly from among millions, lay in her lap.

She wondered how to tell him. Her mind compared the golden plains of sea-scoured beach and the glassy clarity of the enormous rolling breakers with the Frinton beach, partitioned by all those half-buried groins, stony as well as sandy, and the grey-green occluded water, that had, certainly, arched and danced and frothed very nicely.

'It was a different sea,' she said.

'A different beach,' he told her, 'but there is only one sea. It goes round the whole world, Tessa, infinite, the same sea on every shore.'

'What's infinite?' she asked, chinking her pebbles together.

'What's the largest number?' he said.

'A million million?' she tried.

'What about a million million plus one?'

'Oh, don't be tricky, Bertie!' protested Gran, in the front seat. Gran, for reasons good enough, associated thinking with distasteful conduct.

'Then there's no end to counting!' said Tessa, astonished.

'That's what infinite means,' said Grandpa, in a satisfied tone.

Tessa's mother must have known, really, that Frinton was not the complete answer. A week or two later, she took her now always quiet daughter on a trip in to 'town' for the day. They went to Paddington first. And there, wearing his Sunday clothes and looking smaller, they found Cornish Grandad, and took him out to lunch. Grandad, it seemed, had never been to London before. Mother walked him round Piccadilly Circus and Trafalgar Square, and down Whitehall to see the Houses of Parliament. Then they wandered into St James's Park, Grandad holding Tessa by the hand all the while. In the park they found a bench to sit on, beside the lake. Mother suddenly said she had some shopping to do, and she would return in an hour or so; and left them. 'I'll be back in lots of time to get you to Paddington for your train,' she said.

'Are you going home the same day you came?' said Tessa.

'On the night train,' he said. 'To catch the morning tide.'

'Won't you be sleepy?'

'There's a bed on the train.'

'There can't be! There wouldn't be room!' said Tessa, delighted at the thought.

'A bunk. And a tiny washbasin. Better quarters than on many a ship at sea. I would have done with a seat, Little Tress, but your mother bought the ticket.'

'She didn't tell me. I didn't know it would be you.'

'Yes. Well, Nan sends her love. And she's knitted you a fancy hat, to keep the wind off your topknot. Here.'

From a brown paper bag he produced a knitted Fair Isle hat with a blue bobble on top. Tessa pulled it on at once. They stared together at the ducks on the flat grey water.

'Your mother says you're fretting after the sea,' said Grandad in a while.

'Could I come back to your house until the war has gone?' she asked.

'You can come whenever you've a mind, once you're older,' he said. 'The hat's from Nan, and this is from me, look.'

He fumbled in his bag, and brought out a huge shell. It was pearly orangy pink. A twisted, pointed cone all tricked out into spikes. In one end a shining orifice, with lips rolled back from the edges, and of lascivious smoothness, led further in by far than fingers could reach.

'Did you find it on the beach, Grandad?' she asked, caressing it.

'I trawled it from somewhere,' he said evasively. 'It's got the sea in it. To remind you.'

'It couldn't have!' she said, smiling at him, poised between disbelief and hope of something marvellous.

'Not all of it,' he said. 'We couldn't have it all. There's got to be some left in the harbour. Can't have the *Little Tress* grounded at high tide, and the fish all dry and dying. But there's enough in there for you to hear it. Listen.'

He held the glistening opening to her ear.

And she did hear it. Very far away and breaking softly, like an ebbing tide. The sound brought visions with it, visions of bay, and beach, and shining shore.

On the way back to Paddington, Grandad fixed with mother some kind of holiday for Tessa, a visit in the summer. But she never made the visit, for Grandad and *Little Tress* fell foul of a floating mine in the channel in a fog one morning, seven miles south-west of Land's End. Nan let them know on a postcard with a picture of Godrevy Light.

Tessa kept the shell, 'for ever', though her real Grandad said darkly that for ever was a very long time.

It sat in the middle of the mantelpiece over the shilling-in-a-slot gas fire in her undergraduate room. It was still there long after she had understood its gimcrack nature, its cheap exoticism, when she knew that Cornish Grandad must have trawled it from a souvenir shop. She kept it still, long after she had understood also the nature of the ocean it contained.

When Tessa got into Oxford, the nuns offered a Mass for her soul. They had always seen her cleverness as putting her in peril. Thinking was a dangerous habit, an occasion of sin. Blessed are the meek, for they shall inherit the earth; the girl who keeps passing exams compromises her meekness. Tessa didn't really understand this. She didn't strut about boasting of her marks, she didn't preen herself. She had long tried not to argue in religion lessons but the nature of her offences against meekness escaped her, as the nature of impure thoughts had done when she was younger.

It is a major difficulty in the practice of the Catholic confessional that those who are innocent of a sin will have trouble recognizing it. Impurity was a cause of the profoundest bafflement in Tessa's group of friends. Their religion everywhere enjoined love, yet the nuns were tight-lipped and condemnatory about everything to do with sex and that the two things were in any way at all connected was forbidden knowledge. Tessa, who could not find in her anxious self-examinations – conducted on her knees before the altar – the smallest rational ground for accusing herself of impurity, had, naturally, like any growing girl, experienced sexual feeling. She had not recognized the disturbingly vivid hot-rod sensation between navel and crotch – accompanied by a glow between the shoulder blades and a sharpened awareness of lips and palms and nipples – as a form of impure thought, because it had come over her almost always while making the Stations of the Cross, though occasionally while contemplating the martyrdom of some especially attractive saint. Moreover, she had been taught it, and by those very nuns whose horror of impurity was so emphatically expressed.

The contemplation of the suffering of Christ was a major element in the devout life, as taught by the nuns. Intense love of the Redeemer came first; then calling His image into your mind, you rehearsed repeatedly the blows and the wounds inflicted on the beloved, while accusing yourself of every one, for it was sin which had caused the terrible torments of the Saviour. Appalling accounts of the precise manner in which death occurred in a crucified body, or in a racked, burned or crushed one, were everyday fare in religion lessons, and the victims were always offered for love and veneration. A curious hierarchy of sanctity was one result: Sister Mary Imelda, whose eyes and brow grew moist and shining as she spoke of poor Edmund Campion, hanged, drawn and quartered for being a priest, could never work up quite the same enthusiasm for Thomas More – a more important saint politically, but whose death had been disappointingly quick and clean; and Thomas Aquinas, who had crept into the number of the Blessed without apparently having to suffer at all, got short shrift indeed. You could pray for his intercession if you liked, merely.

What effect all this had on any young soul with the smallest disposition to cruelty Tessa would later shudder to think; into her own heart it poured a lethal cocktail of pathological feeling, in which love was contaminated by pity, desire linked to the apprehension of suffering, and sanctity to pain. Natural feeling survived under a cloud of suspicion labelled Lust and Impurity; and dutifully trying to be good, Tessa had barricaded herself, by the time she was seventeen, into a curious hedge of thorns in which pity was the weakest point and the intellect was her only unguarded erogenous zone.

All the time, of course, genuinely innocent of self-knowledge, she could not find herself guilty of impurity; and since the nuns appeared to think it impossible that anyone could wholly escape it, she had a highly developed habit of confessing it 'just in case', a sort of divine all-risks policy which could easily be extended to manage also the matter of meekness; she just added a confession of pride to her weekly tariff of sins.

When it came to meekness, she was, in fact, the victim of a conflict of expectations. Her grandfather, the one who took her to Frinton, was a clever, argumentative man, who had struggled up the social ladder, educating himself on the way. Nothing had been given to him; even his first job behind a desk, from which he had risen to dizzy ultimate heights, had been won because somebody high up had spotted the uniformed message boy reading Plato in the lift. Some time or other in his career of single-handed thought, he had convinced himself of the truth of Catholicism and swept his children into the Church, thus causing, eventually, Tessa to be brought up a Catholic. His wife, whom he had met when they were both Sunday School teachers for the Methodists, would not budge. It did not seem to her that questions of religion could decently be settled by thinking. She was a Methodist because her parents were. She was Methodist in the same way as Poles were Catholic, and though she stopped going to chapel, she would not otherwise shift an inch, and her attitude to cleverness of every kind, which she called 'being tricky', strongly resembled that of the nuns whom she so fervently detested.

But Tessa's grandfather adored and encouraged her. He taught her chess and lent her hard and serious books. He wrote little essays for her on the difference between Plato and Aristotle, he tried to pass on his dislike of 'modern poetry', by which he meant anything after Tennyson. He said to her so often, 'Be clever sweet maid, and let who can be good!' that Tessa thought it was really that way round, and was startled when she first heard it correctly quoted. When, stung by some rebuke at school, Tessa told him of her trouble with meekness, he replied that there ought to have been a Beatitude: 'Blessed are the brainy, for they shall have some chance of rightly understanding the teaching of the Church.' Tessa had more sense than to repeat that at school.

Tessa was standing outside the classroom, in disgrace, when the new headmistress arrived. Tessa's misdemeanour was having doubted the Proof from Design. There are five proofs of the existence of God in St Thomas; individually they may be flawed, but collectively they are supposed to overwhelm doubt. Sister Alphega enquired of Tessa what she had done, and when Tessa, much in awe of the new eminence and trying to be meek about it, told her, she laughed. 'What do you want to do?' she asked.

'I want to read English at Oxford,' said Tessa, very daring.

'What are your A-levels to be?'

'I'm just starting. English, Latin and French.'

'Not history?'

'Miss Murphy teaches English and history. I thought . . .'

'Does she now? Then, Tessa, you are not to go to any more English lessons. Spend the time in the library, and spend it reading. I'll look in on you from time to time.'

Everybody looked in on Tessa from time to time. Making any kind of an exception of someone, especially of Tessa, was disapproved of strongly by the longer-established nuns. They made sure she was really reading and not idling about committing sins against meekness. Sister Alphega came in now and then, and took odd books off the shelves and read passages aloud. She had a good reading voice.

> Ring out ye crystal spheres!
> Once bless our human ears,
> If ye have power to touch our senses so . . .

she read, and Tessa eagerly gobbled up Milton. Then Marvell, then Campion, then Pope.

'Don't bother with critics. Just texts,' Sister Alphega said. Tessa felt, of course, neglected and lonely under this treatment. She didn't see the nature of tricky cleverness coming from so unexpected a quarter as a nun. But at her Oxford interview a puzzled don said to her, 'You very obviously haven't studied Milton, Miss Brownlaw. Why have you read so much of him?' Tessa, with complete candour, said that she had loved the sound of his prosody from the moment she first heard a few lines of his read . . .

'And Bacon? You equally obviously have not studied him. Your opinions on him are naïve and ill-informed. Were you carried away on the sound of that too?'

'Oh, no,' said Tessa. 'Not the sound, the thought. He opens so well. You always think he's about to get something really profound into a neat nutshell.'

'And does he, according to you?'

'Not really. He frets his thought away into the sand, somehow.'

In short, whatever Tessa sounded like in interviews, she didn't sound like Miss Murphy. They gave her a place.

The telegram came on Monday morning. She rang her Grandpa to tell him, and so missed the bus. Then she came late into the school building, and in her joy ran, breaking the eternal commandment against running in the corridors, all the way to the headmistress's room. The door stood ajar. The mosaic marble floor gleamed with polish, for devout elbow-grease was never lacking in a school run by nuns. She could not stop in time. She simply skidded at high speed, crashed through the door and stumbled, nearly falling across the carpet within. Sister Alphega was conferring with Reverend Mother.

'*What* is the meaning of this?' she demanded, standing up abruptly from behind her desk.

Tessa, out of breath and horrified at her precipitation, just stood there.

Sister Alphega's eyes lit on the telegram.

'You didn't? You didn't? You did! Oh, glory!' she said, and she rushed at Tessa almost as extravagantly as Tessa had rushed at her, and hugged her. She was only the headmistress of the school, though, not the Reverend Mother. She couldn't stop the community from offering a Mass for Tessa's soul. They were still convinced that passing exams was fraught with spiritual danger, and that Oxford was a den of iniquity which would sweep her out of the Church.

Chapter Two

LAPSING : CANON

'My child, when you say you try to be a good Catholic, am I to understand that you find it hard? That you sometimes fail in the attempt?'

'Yes, Father, I do. It is hard, Father.'

'In what way is it hard for you? How do you fail Our Blessed Lord, do you think?'

'I lack faith, perhaps. Certainly I am not meek.'

'You are a student?'

'Yes.'

'A very clever one?'

'Oh, no. Not nearly clever enough. But . . .'

'But someone has persuaded you that you displease God by thinking too much? On the contrary, if God has given you any talent you are under an obligation to use it.'

'But thinking seems so easily to lead into . . .'

'Heresy? Is that what you are afraid of?'

'Pride.'

'Tell me about this other matter which you mentioned. Is it connected with your sin of pride?'

'I don't think so, Father. I really don't.'

Tessa had come up to Oxford, after all, deeply committed to the view that there was no conflict between being clever and being Catholic. Not that the question could not give her occasional unease. There was the matter of her clever uncle, for example, a high-powered doctor at the Radcliffe Hospital who lived at

Steeple Aston, some distance out of Oxford. Tessa had stayed with him for a fortnight in the Easter vac of her first year to look after her baby cousins while her aunt escaped to Ireland. The first Sunday she spent there, Uncle got out of bed in time for a leisurely breakfast and a drive into Oxford for twelve o'clock Mass at what he curiously called 'Alley-woggers'. It was a well-sung High Mass, and Tessa enjoyed it.

The second Sunday of her visit, Uncle declared that they did not have to go to Mass and he proposed to sleep in until lunch time. Questioned by an anxious Tessa – there was no bus from the village on Sunday, and without his little sports car she certainly could not get there herself – he offered a complete explanation. It seemed that on every third Sunday there was a Mass in the village. A priest came round on a motorbike, with the sacrament in his panniers, and said Mass in the scout hall. However, this happened at five-thirty in the morning as the priest had dozens of villages to get round – and clever Uncle had no intention of getting out of bed at so brutal an hour. But if there was a Mass in the village, it was a mortal sin not to attend Mass that Sunday. So on days when the priest came to Steeple Aston, Uncle got up mid-morning, and drove himself into Oxford to church. But, on Sundays when there was no Mass in the village there was no obligation either, for the duty to attend Mass, on pain of mortal sin, did not apply at a distance of more than ten miles. So on those Sundays the trip into Oxford was not obligatory, and was not made. Uncle assured Tessa that she, too, would be free of sin, and told her that if she did not believe him she could ask the Jesuit friend who was coming to dinner that night, and who was a great expert, but she would find his theology was correct. And so it was; or at least, the Jesuit thought so too. The trouble was that Tessa was not absolutely sure that God could accept as virtue quite so blatant an example of what Gran would call 'trickiness'.

At Oxford, naturally, cleverness, whatever one thought of it, was not in short supply, even among Catholics. Tessa found herself on many matters, especially in the endless discussion of philosophy in which nearly everyone was engrossed, in the unfamiliar position of group dunce. She didn't mind that; what was odder was finding herself among the very devout. But the secular air of the university, the constant mixing in with others of very different views, the gentle mockery with which Oxford at large received any statement of religious affiliation – for it was politics, not theology which quickened the pulse of the majority of her generation – had a perverse effect on Tessa. So that the more she saw it was perfectly possible to live without religion, the more intent she became on the practice of her own. Oxford was full of contrary behaviour, of course; in being quirky she was being the fully authentic Oxford character. A certain history professor, for example, delivered notoriously rabid anti-Catholic lectures, blaming everything from the Black Death to the activities of the mole in Hampton Court park (which had unseated a Protestant monarch) on the machinations of Roman devilry. This at once bored almost everyone and fascinated Catholics, so that by half-term the composition of his audience was a special case of preaching to the converted. It was a tonic to flagging faith to have its enemy so eloquently bearing testimony to its universal power and importance; it wore a groove, almost, in the pavement, between the history schools and the nearest Catholic altar.

When it came to her own, increasingly fervid devotions, Tessa had a choice of altars: she could hear Mass with the nuns in the little vulgarly baroque chapel at St Winifred's, or she could walk through the heart of the city in which, at a pristine morning hour, the loudest sounds by far were ubiquitous crows, to the Nissen-hut Chaplaincy, where Mass would be said to a very sparse congregation by Father

Theodore or Father Max, or sometimes by both at once, one of them using the Lady Altar.

Tessa liked Father Max; he was really Monsignor Max, a fact which caused him some difficulty since he loved the purple cummerbund and bright cloak it entitled him to wear, but also liked to flaunt his modesty and so insisted on being called plain 'Father' by his flock. He was a fatherly kind of man, full of gravitas, and full also of a consuming anxiety that there might be Catholics whom he had not heard of, had not kept an eye on, lurking somewhere. A terrible thought; he had a card index, colour-coded for each year of the ephemeral undergraduate triad, and to keep him happy you had to attend one, or more, of his Sunday tea-parties. Here he held court and his flock consumed vast trays of lardy cake, provided by the Irish housekeeper, dripping with sugar and real lard – not for her any truck with the English practice of making the stuff with butter; and even when washed down with gallons of brown tea from a real samovar, brought from Leningrad by young Father Max, this was weighty food, and removed the need for the expense of supper. Indeed it made supper almost impossible, except for Matchek, whose vast frame could take it and who had to be stoked, rather than fed. Father Max, on hearing a name mentioned or catching sight of a face at a Chaplaincy Dance, would cry in pitiable anxiety, 'But do I know her? Is she one of mine? Have I got a card for her?' He had even, half-way through Tessa's first term – her year were on pink cards – announced from the pulpit, just after news of a Campion Hall retreat and a visit by the choir to Kidlington Parish Church, 'Will any fresh woman who has not yet filled out a pink slip *please* come to tea in my room!'

The gales of laughter that greeted this announcement took him entirely by surprise; he tutted faintly, and with a pained glance at the altar demanded a seemly hush.

But if Tessa's year caused Father Max concern, Tessa was, in return, not always quite sure about *him*; what could one make, for example, of a priest who preached to undergraduates the need to use the years at Oxford to cultivate friends who would be useful in later life? What should she make of a priest who told her gently, after she had heard morning Mass on a weekday for a fortnight together, to be less serious and spend more of her time among non-Catholics? When she confessed gluttony to Father Max, and, being pressed for detail, admitted to a whole half-pound bar of milk chocolate, he roared with laughter, audibly, which was deeply embarrassing. Of course, he could not see who was in the confessional, and should not know it was her, but she had to leave the box in front of the startled gaze of six or seven others kneeling in a queue waiting their turn.

And Father Max, like the nuns, was given to boasting discreetly of a wicked youth; he, like them, had truly lived, had known all about the world before renouncing it, he would have you believe. The trouble was that this claim, wildly implausible and faintly pathetic coming from Sister Alphega, was very easy to believe of Father Max. Nor was Father Max's renunciation anything like as complete as that of a nun: he lived in considerable prosperity and comfort, and talked a good deal about food and wine to the right kind of young man among his charges. Theodore said, in surprise at some comment she made about it, that after all the secular clergy had not made a vow of poverty. Tessa had not known that they hadn't; such an aura of total sacrifice surrounded priests in her mind.

Nevertheless, at the beginning of that climactic second year at Oxford, Tessa's membership of the cell led her to want to do still more, and her mind turned, not towards hair shirts, but to the practice of having a spiritual adviser. Confessing always to the same priest and letting him know who you were, so that he could monitor progress, and give real advice, seemed thrillingly risky and self-exposing, – designed to defeat the arrangements for privacy in sin which the confessional normally ensures. Deciding to take this fateful step, Tessa thought naturally, not of Father Max, but of Father Theodore.

They had spent the hour from eleven to noon in a cell meeting, discussing worldliness. It had been a good meeting; talk had warmed up nicely. Was it, for example, unworldly to be so intent on prayer as to forget to pay one's taxes? To be so wrapped up in the study of mathematics that one had no time for one's family? Or no time for prayer? Ben, who was a mathematics lecturer, tried for a while to maintain that neglecting all else for mathematics *was* unworldly, while trying at the same time to argue that neglecting all else for politics, was, on the contrary, the quintessence of worldliness. He was soundly routed from this position by a consensus of the others and then rescued by Father Theodore, who thought that maths and philosophy had rather more title to unworldliness than other subjects. That seemed to Tessa, who couldn't do either, plain unfair, and she said so. Eventually they reached a distinction between unworldliness and other-worldliness, and decided that there could be no virtue in being absent-minded or neglectful of this world for any reason other than absorption in consideration of the next. Ben then claimed that doing mathematics was, almost, a form of prayer.

'The Pythagorean Heresy,' said Tessa, catching the sharp immediate gaze of Father Theodore, who had obviously not expected her to know enough to make the joke.

'But why should one not do maths for the glory of God, as much as any other thing?' said Ben eagerly. 'We glorify God in doing what He gave us talent to do; being what He made us.'

'But not all our talents or capacities are equally blessed,' said Alison. 'Aren't we supposed to sacrifice ourselves in this world for the sake of heaven: that *would* be unworldly, wouldn't it?'

'And it's so odd!' Tessa exclaimed. 'I've never understood it. God makes this amazing, incredible, marvellous world full of delight and invites us all, as to a party; and then, we are told, is best pleased with those who refuse to enjoy anything and leave it all untouched. I must say, if I were giving two parties in succession, on earth and in heaven, I would invite to the second one the people who laughed and danced and ate most at the first!'

'As long as they said "thank you" nicely!' said Ben, laughing at her.

'Well, *of course* we should say thank you,' said Tessa.

'But what would you make of a guest who elbowed others aside and took more than his share?' asked Father Theodore. 'Or who ate so much they were sick? Even supposing God would like us to enjoy ourselves, it doesn't mean anything goes. There is still a place for sin.'

'There always is,' said Hubert. 'Surely all the pleasure and beauty is put there just to test our resolve. We are supposed to refrain, not wallow in it.'

'Hubert, if we see you wallowing in anything except self-denial, you can trust us to tell you!' said Tessa.

'Well let's be wickedly worldly right now, and go and have some lunch,' said Alison.

They spilled out of the Chaplaincy and along the row to the Bookshop, where among tomes of piety and theology virtuous vegetarian salads full of grey-green beans were served. The golden glowing autumn weather, which had lasted since the beginning of term, was still bright and warm, and after lunch they went across the meadow to see if by any divine gesture of perfect hospitality God had arranged for there still to be punts available at Magdalen Bridge. It had to be hoped that these delights *were* intended for enjoyment and not for temptation because there were indeed a few punts still in the water in deference to the unseasonable summer, and they took two and began a procession up-river, with Ben and Hubert punting and Tessa and Alison lying side by side, in the foremost punt, facing Hubert, and trailing fingers in the cool dappled water. Theodore had detached himself and withdrawn from the party when they embarked.

They were not surprised, for they did not expect a priest to spend time sharing their idleness; but when half an hour later, having punted past the entire water walks of Magdalen's secretive gardens and hauled the punts over the runners above Parson's Pleasure – Tessa and Alison walked decorously round, though surely it was on the cold side for naked bathing even by the most wildly eccentric dons – when they glided, poles dripping silver, under the Rainbow Bridge, there, leaning over at the crest of the arc and waiting for them, was Father Theodore with a basket.

The basket contained a mountain of left-over lardy cake provided by Father Max's housekeeper and a bottle of white Chianti, which, with elaborate care, he attached to the mooring chain at the back of the punt so that it would trail submerged and cooling in the river.

'Supplies! Supplies!' cried Alison. 'We are provisioned to go as far as Islip, or the Pole!'

Later, one will be able to remember every face in the circle except one's own. In Tessa's memory the afternoon will vividly contain the others: Ben punting sturdily and skilfully so that the lazy Cherwell chuckled under the front of the punt; Theodore rolling up his sleeves to punt, his forearms as freckled as his face and covered in a coppery down – he is a man coloured like a harvest-field; and the second punt coming along behind propelled by Hubert with willowy grace, and somewhat uncertain direction. The sun shone; the willow trees launched a thousand yellow boat-shaped leaves on the surface of the water. Clusters of swallows thronged in flight.

But it was the unlooked-for presence of Theodore which gave the afternoon its life-long quality. It was a mark of the innocence of their pleasures that he should share them; a mark of some special status that he should choose them as his companions. They played up to him, talking and laughing, trying to win his laughter, wishing to deserve the privilege. And he played back; the barely subdued excitement sparked between them. For he too, she would realize later, felt privileged; that for once he could join in, could get close to the carefree young, and they would let him. They would go on playing with him among them, instead of meeting his every approach by freezing at once into self-consciousness and putting up a wall of either reverence or embarrassment. Just for an hour or two, just for once, he was a young man among his friends.

'Father, what did you think of that Vint lecture?' Alison asked. 'I saw you there.'

'Oh, but don't call me that when I'm in mufti,' he said. 'Just Theodore.'

And from teasing him about what degree of difference the lack of a dog-collar made, they fell into mock-earnest discussion about whether the nature of the swans they were passing – one of which directed attention to its nature by hissing and flapping wings at Theodore while he took his turn punting – had been changed when black swans were discovered in Australia. Theodore and Ben maintained stoutly that it had, for after all the definition of a swan had altered radically: what had before been of the essential nature of swans – whiteness – became suddenly a mere accident; one had to hope it hadn't hurt!

But the others all rejected so loony a proposition. After all, Tessa pointed out, if you put side by side an English swan from before the discovery and an English swan after the discovery, you would be unable to find any difference at all. Whereupon Theodore outraged them by saying that people like themselves, who believed in transubstantiation, should have no trouble at all with that . . .

They had drunk all the cool Chianti and eaten all the lardy cake when they got as far as the Vicky Arms; and the Vicky Arms kept odd hours, being far off the beaten track, so they landed and bought pork pies and pints of bitter and carried their plates and glasses into the little boxtree bowers in the garden.

Tessa sat opposite Ben; his gaze was directed often at her, and he appeared calm, and in a distant fashion happy, as though his mind were occupied in some serene mathematical calculation. He looked often also at the priest sitting beside her, a trace of concern on his face as he did so. He talked with Theodore about Austria, about expeditions in the Tyrol and eating places and the quality of baroque churches; or rather, Theodore talked to him. Ben seemed a laconic sort of conversationalist.

It was dusk before they found themselves returning past the boathouse at Bardwell Road. Alison had digs there, very close, and they stopped again while she dashed home for an armful of sweaters – Indian-summer evenings cool rapidly. She also brought two candles in jam-jars, and her guitar. So in the chill twilight they glided homeward, shivering, huddled in old sweaters, with a candlelight burning on the prow of each boat.

Tessa and Theodore were punting now, he a few yards ahead, and seeing his russet head threatened by a low branch, she called unthinkingly, 'Father! Look out!' and caught then a startled stare from two late walkers in Lady Margaret's gardens.

'Please don't call me that,' said Theodore, in a voice that struck her – but she must have been wrong – as full of misery.

Alison thrummed at her guitar, and they began to sing.

Oh you canna getta heaven,
In a Cambridge punt,
Cos a Cambridge punt,
Goes back to front!
Oh you canna getta heaven in a Cambridge punt,
Cos a Cambridge punt goes back to front,
I ainta gonna grieve my Lord no more!

Ben offered,

You canna getta heaven,
In purple socks,
Like Father Max,
Or Ronnie Knox!

Hubert's verse went,

You canna getta heaven
Without a gown;
There are proctors there
To send you down!

Tessa's,

If you canna getta heaven,
With a fourth and last,
Then fail the lot,
And don't get classed!

And Theodore, getting the hang of it, offered in a remarkably tuneless voice – but then all they had ever heard him sing before were the words from the altar, *Credo in Unum Deum* –

And if you can't get to heaven at all,
There's a back way in by Campion Hall,
I ainta gonna grieve my Lord no more!

It was dark, they had sung themselves into silence,

and the candles were guttering in their jars by the time they had returned the punts to base. The boatman had long gone home, and they had lost the deposit on the boats. They were light-headed, in spite of lardy cake and pork pies.

They went up the High together, Ben leaving them at Catte Street and Hubert at Brasenose. The rest departed up the Turl. Alison and Tessa walked on with Theodore. Up the Cornmarket, by the Martyrs' Memorial, Theodore insisted on putting Alison into a taxi for Bardwell Road – a long way, late with a guitar – then he walked on with Tessa. She supposed he must, with a touch of worldly gallantry be taking her to the hostel gate.

'Father . . . Theodore, I've been thinking,' she said, half-way up the Broad. 'I think I should have a spiritual adviser. Will you be that for me?'

'No!' he exclaimed. 'Oh, no! You are the last person . . . I couldn't . . . You must ask someone else . . .'

She stopped in her tracks, appalled. It had not occurred to her that she might be refused. And he, saying 'Good night' in a choked-off voice, turned at once and half-ran, half-walked away from her, southwards down the Broad, leaving her standing as though she were the devil behind him, and he feared to be followed.

But how absurd. How absurd and pretentious she was! Obviously for her to ask for a spiritual adviser was just like Hubert asking for a hair shirt. Perhaps this was what the nuns had sensed in her as lack of meekness. And had she, perhaps, been far too hasty in condemning Father Max as worldly? Was this what he meant by telling her not to be so serious and to spend some time among non-Catholics? Not being serious appeared very hard; it went against the grain of Tessa. But the other half of the advice was easy. Tessa, flinching inwardly with agonies of embarrassment at the thought of how she must appear to Theodore –

thank God nobody else knew! – took down from her mantelpiece a gilt-edged invitation card which had been propped against the shell; it was from Richard, for a party that night. Nice, non-Catholic Richard. She had met him in Forfar's Old Northumbrian Remains lecture. Well, met was an understatement – he had leant across the dented boards of the tables in Merton dining hall, where the lecture was taking place, and murmured, 'Angel Face . . .' at her, so that she missed hearing whether they were talking of Long Ash One or Long Ash Two, and became extremely cross. 'Non Angla, sed Angela?' he tried later.

'Tessa,' she hissed. 'Shut up!'

For a terrible moment she thought Forfar had heard them; he was frowning in their direction from above his hopsack tie, which had unravelled as far as the knot and hung in strands so that it amazed Tessa that it was possible to get it on and off. Perhaps he just slid the knot down far enough to get it over his close-cropped head, and then put it back again and tightened it like a hangman's noose . . . a pleasing analogy, really. Every single student of Anglo-Saxon who did not command enough German to read the great Luike in the original was compelled to attend every one of Forfar's lectures until such time as he liked to publish a book. And he made the most of it. Tessa was rescued from the wrath to come upon those who whispered in a lecture by the arrival of two late-comers. 'Ah!' said Forfar with satisfaction. He had noticed at once the absence of two of his statutory band. 'I had just said . . .'

The hapless two scrabbled for their notebooks and pencils – it did, after all, matter desperately whether the lecture was about Long Ash One or Long Ash Two—

'. . . that I would wait till the late-comers had arrived,' said Forfar gleefully to the poised pens. 'I have just met Professor Wrenn in the corridor,' he added, unusually chatty. 'And he said to me, "Not many people for Old Northumbrian Remains today, Mr Forfar, I shouldn't wonder . . ."' for it had been indeed a golden day, in the height of summer, when river and meadows took on their most irresistible charm, '. . . and I said to him, "People always come to my lectures, Professor Wrenn!"' He gazed around, full of satisfaction at the captive faces, relishing their hatred before proceeding to analyse Caedmon's song. Not of course its astonishing lyric beauty – the first voice in English poetry, enraptured by nature like any nineteenth-century romantic, making the stiff and formal rules of ancient Germanic prosody sing the song of Christendom. Tessa's heart lifted at it; she still thought a song thrush offered a better refutation of doubt than any of the Five Ways; but Mr Forfar directed their attention only to those words in the song that were of distinctively Northumbrian form, and those he tracked backwards and forwards in the history of English sounds until the very angels, had any been present, would have fallen asleep.

At almost every lecture since, Tessa had resisted playful approaches from Richard. The most ground she had given to him was to have coffee with him in the Tackley, which had just set itself up to serve Espresso. She had nothing against him, except a strong feeling that it was only fair to keep clear of a non-Catholic who fancied you; since marrying him would be out of the question, letting him give you dinner was dubious. A party, however, should be all right. Having, as usual, nothing remotely suitable to wear, and not wishing to appear again in Barbara's toffee-coloured taffeta, Tessa set out in search of Anna who had just bought the very newest thing – a sack dress, deliberately so shapeless that it would fit perfectly on anyone along the whole corridor.

Richard had rooms on the south face of Merton, overlooking the meadows. They were very crowded, with people spilling out on to the landings and sitting on the narrow stairs. Tessa eased her way through, and somehow got into the sitting room. She was greeted by a thin lanky youth with ash-blond hair and pallid complexion who put a glass of champagne into her hand and said, 'Do you believe in God?'

'Not at parties,' said Tessa firmly.

'Ah! Do you play the flute? I do,' he said smugly.

Tessa stared uneasily. 'Are you in a book by Evelyn Waugh?' she tried.

'No!' he said gleefully, 'are you?'

Tessa was rescued by Richard elbowing his way through his guests and greeting her. 'Tessa! I didn't expect to see you!'

'Well don't look too surprised. You did invite me.'

'I know I did. But you keep giving me the brush-off. Does this mean you are relenting at last, or is it just that you are at a loose end this evening?'

'Oh, Richard,' said Tessa penitently. 'Look, this won't do. I'll explain properly next time we have a quiet coffee together. But not here!' She was shouting but even so, if he heard her it could only be by an unusual effort at differential listening.

'It's better in the bedroom,' said Richard, taking her elbow and shoving her through the scrum to the door in the far corner of the room. The bedroom, too, was full of people sitting all over the bed and floor, and well supplied with drink and glasses, but their conversation was decibels softer, and they had the heavy antique door shut between them and the racket beyond. Richard tugged his pillows from under a lolling friend and set them on the floor against the wall to settle Tessa on them. Then he squatted down beside her, looking pleased.

But Tessa's attention was immediately diverted by a huge stack of gramophone records sitting in the wastepaper basket against which she found herself wedged. Beethoven's Symphonies.

'Hey, Richard, you'd better rescue these,' she said.

'Your party will cost more than the drink if you don't keep an eye out.'

'Oh those,' he said. 'Don't fret, Tessa, I chucked them. I've just bought myself the Klemperer ones; terrific!'

'You *chucked* them!' cried Tessa. 'But Richard, you can't! They're worth a fortune; somebody wants them.'

'You?'

'I haven't even got a gramophone. But somebody. People go without dinner to buy records; you must be able to give them to somebody.'

'Well, I hadn't thought of it,' he said, 'but I don't know that it's as easy as you say. I mean, if I don't want them, why should anyone else?'

'Because not everyone is rich. Not everyone can just buy the new ones.'

'So I go up to some poor fellow, and I say, "Have these; I don't want them" . . . Hmph. At least the wastepaper basket isn't insulted, Tessa. But I don't feel dog-in-the-manger; if you want them, or if you have a deserving friend, you take them. And now let's . . .'

But someone was shouting for him in the other room, loudly enough to penetrate the closed door. 'Sorry,' he said, standing up. 'Back soon.'

Left alone for a moment, Tessa began to listen to the conversation going on, somewhat above her level, on the bed.

'What we really need is some intellectual heavy-weight to give the thing conviction,' a girl was saying. 'I mean, all this fuzzy waffle about how awful the damn things are doesn't get us very far. We need to *prove* the case against.'

'Well I think we are getting reinforcements in that quarter,' someone replied. 'I just heard Theodore Wytham is in Oxford.'

'The one who wrote those marvellous discussion papers? Where is he? Can we hear him lecture?'

'He isn't lecturing. He's doing a D.Phil. at one of those Catholic fringe colleges. He's in a Roman religious order of some kind. Ravenna Fathers. Something wild like that.'

'Why doesn't he come to meetings?'

'Perhaps he doesn't know about us. I've written to invite him.'

'Are Romans allowed to get political?' the girl asked.

'Well, if I understand his stuff correctly, according to him Romans are morally bound to oppose the Bomb; that just *is* political, as I see it.'

'If so, their hierarchy keeps very quiet about it,' said a man leaning on the wall beside Tessa's ground-level seat. Not quieter than Tessa, who sat still as a mouse, astonished. Two things about it amazed her: that Theodore should be known outside the Church, and famous; and rather more mind-boggling, she was learning for the first time that her faith entailed opposition to the Bomb. Mind you, one couldn't trust non-Catholics to get things right – half of them thought you worshipped the Virgin Mary and wanted to burn heretics – but just the same, she would have to ask Theodore at the first opportunity.

She would have gone on listening, but someone sitting on the floor facing her, a blond and handsome man, said, 'Haven't I seen you at the Chaplaincy?'

'You could have. I'm sorry, I don't remember you.'

'I don't go there. Not for the likes of me. I don't go to this kind of party either,' he added.

'Well no wonder I haven't met you yet!' she said. He didn't smile. 'What do you mean about the likes of you?'

'The Chaplaincy is hopping with swanks,' he said. 'Too posh for me. I'm just a grammar school boy. My father's a coalminer. I'm only here because of the noise,' he added.

'The noise?'

'I'm on this staircase. Richard always invites me to his parties; people don't fuss about the noise if they're at the damn things themselves. He doesn't actually know anybody like me.'

'Well, I'm a grammar school girl, and my father was an engineer,' said Tessa. 'And he knows me.'

'Girls are different,' came the rejoinder.

'Why are girls different?'

'Well, you're the quarry, aren't you? Girls are status, whatever they're like.'

'Do you mind my saying that you have an extraordinarily sour viewpoint?' she said.

'It's all right for you to say that. Do you have any idea what it's like to be nobody in particular and bloody hard up, with the Richards of this world around?'

'Well, I might have, actually. How much money do you get?'

Being on a full grant, he got, of course, more than she did. She was just about, with malice, to try to connect him, to his own benefit, with the contents of the wastepaper basket, when Richard came back, pulled her to her feet and took her into the now much clearer outer room. He had borrowed the room opposite across the staircase, and the party had spread out and turned to dancing in the newly colonized space. 'Angel Face!' Richard said. 'Fair one! Dance with me, do.'

Tessa let herself be gathered into his tight embrace and propelled gently round the floor. The black satin sack made the contact between them so glossy and slippery that Tessa was mildly alarmed by it. 'What were you going to explain to me?' he murmured in her left ear.

'Why I wouldn't let you take me out to dinner, was it?'

'Don't explain; just let me . . .'

'The thing is, Richard, I can't get serious about you. I'm a Catholic, and I don't approve of mixed marriages . . .'

'Good God, girl!' said Richard. 'I haven't asked you to marry me!'

Tessa blushed. 'I don't think it's fair to let you take me out and then suddenly spring it on you, that's all,' she said.

'Ah,' he said. 'I get the drift. But if I knew you would never marry me and I still wanted to take you out to dinner, you would come?'

'Well, if you did still want to, I suppose . . .' said Tessa dubiously. Something about Richard made her think he had designs of a rather more dangerous nature.

'You see, Tessa,' said Richard, 'a light-hearted, won't-get-serious relationship is just what I need. I am engaged to a girl at home; I couldn't get tangled up with anyone else. But it's a bit much never being able to go out. Someone who would come out with me and have fun and not mistake me in any way is just who I am looking for. Why don't we have a pact together, Angel Face?'

'What's she called?' asked Tessa.

'What's who? . . . Cynthia. She is called Cynthia. She is a brunette. I only go for brunettes. You can see how well you would suit me!'

An enormous relief was sweeping over Tessa. It *would* be fun to go around with Richard; fun with safety was a totally unlooked-for opportunity. She treated him to a radiant smile.

'Done!' she said.

Cell meetings began with prayers in the Nissen-hut chapel and continued in 'The Newman Rooms' – a dusty adjacent room equipped with a few chairs and a grand piano. There was also a lopsided bookshelf containing works of piety, three missals, six Westminster Hymnals and the minute books of the Newman Society, to which in theory all Catholic undergraduates automatically belonged. These books contained dozens of entries, all signed by the secretaries, except for one puzzling batch simply marked 'Oxford' at the foot of the pages. Tessa, having arrived late for prayers and not wanting to interrupt, leafed through the minute book while waiting for the others to come in, with a flicker of curiosity about the unsigned entries, until she found the earliest one in that handwriting. That was signed, 'Oxford and Asquith'.

Matchek joined her, smiled, and seating himself at the piano played a flourish of Chopin.

'Hullo, Matchek. I thought you'd stopped coming to meetings. How's Stefan?' The music irresistibly reminded Tessa.

'Very poorly. In hospital.'

'Oh, I'm so sorry! What's wrong? I must visit him.'

'Everything is wrong. No visitors.'

'But Matchek . . .'

'He is in the Warneford, Tessa. I will tell you when they let friends come. But now they don't. Not even me.'

At this moment the others arrived, and with another flourish of agonized, ecstatic notes, Matchek got up, lowered the piano lid and came to join them. Theodore averted his eyes from Tessa the moment she looked at him – but surely he had been looking at her until that moment? The memory of her discomfiture brought a warmth to her cheeks; nevertheless she plucked up courage to say, when the opening formalities were over, 'Shouldn't we, sometime, talk about the Bomb?'

'What about the Bomb,' asked Hubert, 'in particular?'

'Well, whether it's all right, I suppose . . . what must we think about it . . .'

'Does the Church have a line on it at all?' said Alison. 'I've never heard a sermon on it.'

'Perhaps not,' said Father Theodore. 'But there isn't any doubt about it nevertheless. The Church has a well-worked out dogma going back to Saint Thomas about just and unjust wars, and it leads one ineluctably to a view about the Bomb.'

'But what view?' asked Tessa.

So Theodore expounded. The Church was not pacifist: there *was* such a thing as a just war. Pacifism was a deadly trap. If first you condemned all war as wrong and all weapons as wicked, you ended up saying that it could never be right to protect yourself, and there was no important difference between bows and arrows and nuclear weapons. Because this view was hopelessly unacceptable in a sinful world it merely encouraged people to reject attempts to distinguish right from wrong. By saying that bows and arrows were as evil as nuclear bombs you invited people to conclude that bombs were no worse than bows and arrows.

There were various well-known conditions for a just war: a just cause; no other way to obtain justice; a reasonable likelihood of obtaining it by fighting; and waging war only by just means. One of the conditions for just means was that non-combatants were not to be killed deliberately. Of course, they were often killed accidentally. Yet there had to be a proportion; it would not do to use a nuclear bomb to wipe out a whole city because it contained a munitions factory – the mortality among non-combatants, which was an illegitimate aim, was out of proportion to the legitimate military aim. Deliberately to kill non-combatants as an aim of war was plain, simple murder.

And our defence policy apparently envisaged wholesale murder as a fixed policy in case of war. No Catholic, no Christian, could possibly have anything to do with it; indeed our duty was in all ways possible to oppose it. Theodore taught them; but they did not greatly like what he said.

Alison said, 'But, Father, if it comes to killing non-combatants, what about the Blitz? What about the Allied bombing of Dresden? Surely those actions were wrong, according to you: no proportionality.'

'Not according to me, Alison, according to God's law.'

'And they used only TNT; in huge amounts, but only TNT? So why not also preach against TNT? Isn't it equally wrong to sit here armed with that?'

'There is a very important difference. The unique

problem with nuclear weapons is that they are so vast and so wholesale that it is impossible to imagine any just use for them, so the person who has them – unlike the person who has ordinary TNT and bombs and tanks – must be contemplating the commission of wholesale murder.'

'But there must surely be some possible just use for nuclear bombs too,' said Paul.

'Such as?' asked Father Theodore.

'Well, what if the Russians used one first?'

'Oh, no Paul. There are some things one must not do in any circumstances no matter who else has done it first, and murder is one of those things.'

'Some conceivable military target exists, surely,' said Dominic.

'Like what? A fleet in the middle of the ocean? A tank formation in the desert? Christians are not supposed to be fools, you know. Could we believe that all this weaponry is being mustered at vast expense just in case an enemy ever masses his fleet in the ocean, or his tanks in the desert? We know quite well that the bombs are wanted to threaten the mass murder of civilians.'

In argument Theodore's countenance shone with animation and he looked round the circle with a questing eagerness. Tessa kept her eyes on her Bible, lying open in her lap. 'To threaten it, Father. But not to do it,' she said. 'We have to have the things, because if we didn't we would be defenceless against the Russians. But we have them so that we *won't* need to use them; they will never be used. Surely it isn't wicked simply to keep them, and say in effect "Don't attack us, or else." '

'Or else we *will* use them. That's how threats work, Tessa. There are a lot of Catholics who think like you. Just hope against hope that our leaders, although they say they would use the Bomb against an attacker, actually would not do so when it came to the point. They're just bluffing. But how can we be sure of that?'

'Well, we couldn't be sure,' she said. 'If we knew they wouldn't really use them, then the Russians would know too and the threat wouldn't work.'

'So although it is just bluff, nobody must know that. And to make the threat credible we have to have soldiers who would carry out the orders to drop them if those orders ever came, and who think that the orders might come; we have to employ willing potential murderers. Just that fact alone should be enough to show us that we cannot support the Government's policy with clean hands. When you think about it, anybody here – well, not the girls, I suppose, but any of the men – might have been forced to commit mass murder while doing National Service, on pain of being court martialled for treason. A policy that could lead to that must be particularly wicked; but in general it seems to me that it must be wrong to intend to do conditionally – if attacked by the Russians for example – what it would be wicked actually to do; and it must be wrong to threaten to do something if it would be wrong to carry out the threat.'

Tessa felt a great extra load rolling on to her shoulders. She didn't argue with him; being a priest he was an authority on what she believed.

But Matchek exploded with wrath. 'A very Christian theory, Father,' he said, 'that will leave us fighting big bombs with little ones. Just like poor Poland, fighting tanks with cavalry. What will happen to the Church if Christians fight atheism with cavalry? Yes, yes, I hear you say it is wicked to threaten bad things; but not very wicked just to threaten, you know. All they must do is hands off us, and nothing happens to them. So we make a wicked threat and we go to confession and we keep the Bomb. Is very safe in England, and there is enough to eat, and we go to Church any time we want; if Poland had the Bomb Catholics would be safe there too!'

'It's the last dreadful trap we are led into,' said Theodore quietly, 'to think that because we are on the side of the good, the Church, democracy, freedom, and because our enemies are very evil and cruel, tyrannical, atheistic, we are justified in doing wrong. Using the Bomb is murder; it is against the law of God. If it is our only alternative to being crushed by the Russians, then we must steel ourselves to endure being crushed by the Russians.'

'Better Red than dead, you mean,' said Alison.

'Better Red than being a murderer, certainly,' he said.

'You should be ashamed of yourselves!' said Matchek wildly. 'You say you would not fight for your country? What kind of people are you? Here are lots of Poles because they came to fight against the Germans, and no nonsense about we fight, but not with bombs that will win. If we have to fight for the Church we should use anything we have.'

'To save the Church?'

'Why are there soldier saints? Doesn't God want us to fight for the Faith?'

'The Church will not go under. We have been promised that. The gates of hell shall not prevail against it.'

'Well maybe when God said that He thought He could have a little help from the faithful!'

'Matchek, would you stand at the Judgement Seat and say to God, "We could not keep your commandments because we did not believe your promises?" '

'I have heard enough of this,' said Matchek. 'I am going and not coming back. Goodbye.'

'Oh, Matchek!' cried Tessa, as he precipitated himself down the stairs. 'Don't go, we're only talking!'

'Were you only talking, Tessa?' said Father Theodore. He directed at her a steady gaze of strange intensity, so that she turned aside her eyes at once, not wishing him to see that this was hard for her.

It *was* hard. Walking home with Paul and Ben she was silent, thinking it over with a troubled mind. In the first place it shook one of her firmest ideas – that religion was a private matter. It concerned how you lived behind closed doors, how you prayed, which church you attended. It did not enter into matters such as how you voted. But if Theodore was right, it would. It would make being a Christian entail voting Labour. Joining CND. Perhaps even the Committee of 100. Perhaps even breaking the law.

'So were you really nearly a mass murderer, Ben?' Paul asked as they strolled up Logic Lane, bound for the Turl Tavern and points north.

'Well, not personally,' said Ben, grinning. 'I didn't get called up. Flat feet.'

'Me neither, as it happens,' said Paul. 'Short sight. Phew! Close shave, that. I'd have pressed buttons with the best of them, given a chance, I'm afraid.'

'And now?'

'Well, obviously I wouldn't now . . . after this morning.'

All this made Tessa deeply unhappy. The tentacles of belief crept about everywhere, and left one very little area for free choice. And Tessa still could not really see what was so terribly wicked about threatening a use one would never enact. If the threat worked. And it seemed to be working. Tessa was absolutely certain that England needed weapons only for defence; England would never be the aggressor. Of some things, after all, one could be sure beyond possible doubt.

Even the amazing blazing autumn colours of the leaves glowing against the grey ancient stones did not lift her heart.

But dinner with Richard did. Richard came to collect her for dinner – he insisted on it – at ten in the morning on Saturday.

At that unlikely hour there were no nuns to see him and be impressed by him; instead he could simply enter the hostel and find Tessa's room. He came with a huge fur coat on his arm, and a green army balaclava helmet, both of which he offered to Tessa. Tessa, at last alerted to the need for clothes, had bought, and was sporting, a grey jersey sack and a string of pink bubble-beads; determined to do the thing properly if at all she had a pearly string to substitute for the pink ones when day modulated into evening, and she had bought a pair of very plain black shoes with high heels and pointed toes. She was reluctant to engulf her new unfamiliarly intentional appearance in the massive fur Richard offered. And the sun was shining outside. From her window the autumn Parks were blazing in gold and rust, with one stately cedar of Lebanon holding hard to green.

'You'd better, though. You'll see why,' said Richard, putting the coat round Tessa's shoulders. He himself was wearing a khaki army overcoat, his college scarf, and heavy lace-up boots. At the door she saw. Parked beside the 'No Parking' sign in the drive was a white Aston Martin convertible, with red leather seats, and the hood down. Richard opened the passenger side door for her, and recommended the balaclava helmet and a pair of goggles she would find in the glove compartment.

'Should reassure Cynthia, anyway,' said Tessa, muffled in wool as she pulled on the helmet.

'What? Oh, yes,' he said, starting up, and roaring the engine. 'What would reassure her?'

'Getting me togged up as Mr Toad before we go a mile,' she said, happily. 'Where are we going, Richard? Do we have an exeat?'

'I must speak to you very severely about this,' he said as they purred up the Woodstock Road. 'It's all right being a Roman Catholic. Even all right being a pious one. I mean, what is Oxford for if not for the ripening of eccentricity? It's even all right being a virgin. Since you're a girl. But being a pious Roman Catholic virgin who worries about college regulations is too much, just too much. Learn where to draw the line, OK?'

Tessa had no breath to answer by this time. Richard dealt with the normal suburban impedimenta like ladies with prams, shoppers, bicycles, other cars, by speeding up and driving round them, fast. Long before they reached the by-pass she was more worried about the police than about college bylaws.

When they got to the by-pass Richard turned north-west and speeded up. 'Where did you say we were going?' she asked.

'Wait and see,' he said.

And before they got anywhere, she was more worried about survival than the police.

They went first to Fairford. Richard took her into the church, to see the glass. By some quirk of history Fairford has a full complement which escaped being smashed up in the Reformation, or by Cromwell, and at the western end, a magnificent rose window, with green and blue devils administering fanciful torments to the damned, beneath the feet of Christ in majesty.

Tessa was well able to contemplate the torments of the damned with equanimity; it was the torments of the blessed that made her feel queasy – feeling which she had latterly begun to regard with the profoundest suspicion, and avoid whenever possible – but she exclaimed with delight over the rose window.

'I thought you'd like this,' said Richard.

Next they went to Wooton Courtney, where they giggled at the stacked up Fettiplaces, propped up on their elbows in case they missed anything; the only known instance, Richard said, of the dead waiting for the last trump in bunk-beds.

Tessa laughed. 'They look as if they thought they might sleep through it if they didn't keep wide awake,' she said.

'And, Angel Face, I am to take it that you really think they *will* be wanted again, at some future eschatological moment? They will present themselves for the taking of an account?'

'Well, yes,' she said. 'I do.'

'The dead shall live, the living die,' he said, 'and music shall untune the sky. You know, I think I could easily accept the rules of Papistry, even the batty ones like no contraception. It's the preposterous cosmology I gag on.'

They wandered into the churchyard, reading the picturesque and pathetic inscriptions on the rows of leaning headstones, and soon sat down on the plinth of a tomb shaped like Noah's Ark, leaning back against Enoch Goodenough, RIP, departed this life, in a far corner beyond the yews. Richard leaned over and kissed her. They lost balance, and tumbled full length on the lichen-blotched stone. Tessa was not alarmed by being kissed, and it was some moments before she realized that Richard's body, pressed against her, was taut from top to toe. A sort of *rigor vitae* had seized him, and his hands were frantically groping at her seamless and buttonless dress. She rolled over abruptly, and tipped him off into the damp grass.

'I'm sorry,' he said, sighing. 'Unmannerly of me. I promise to wait to be invited, henceforward. OK?'

'So I should think!' she said, annoyed at him for confirming so promptly the warning about the morals of non-Catholics about which she had been so often, so ludicrously, warned. And instantly, of course, it occurred to her that it was probably at least partly her own fault.

'Richard?'

'Angel Face?' He looked at her ruefully from a sitting position, propped on the adjacent slab – Enoch's Relict, Hilda, who for a little tried to live without him . . .

'Richard, what do I do? I mean what is it about me that . . .'

'Entangles people? Drives them mad with desire?'

'Don't mock. Tell me what.'

'Why?'

'Because if I knew what it is that I do that entangles people, I would be glad to stop.'

'It isn't anything you could stop.'

'It must be something. Because I don't mean it; I don't mean it at all. I really didn't mean to lead you on. I must have momentarily driven Cynthia right out of your mind. And I don't know how I do it. Really.'

'I see you don't,' he said, pulling a face. 'And you are quite right, I *had* forgotten Cynthia! Well, you are very good-looking, you know. All that shiny hair twisted up at the back of your head, and the curls escaping round your face. You look like a girl in an Italian master.'

'Oh, rot, Richard! I should have known better than to ask you . . .'

'It's the expression on your face,' he said, looking away from her. 'A sort of eagerness . . . hopefulness. You always look as if you expected something marvellous to happen . . . it's irresistible. I want to make it come true for you.'

'And you thought deflowering me in a graveyard would be a marvellous thing to happen?'

'Well, it would have been lovely for me,' he said, grinning. 'I probably underestimated your attachment to those rules. Am I forgiven?'

'Oh, really!' she said. 'It isn't ten minutes since you were claiming to prefer the rules to the cosmology. Yes – I forgive you. It's my Christian duty!'

'Enough of this,' he said. 'Lunch. Urgently.'

They had lunch at the Rose Revived at Newbridge, finding that the kit they had donned for keeping warm in the car made the river-bank garden just about tolerable, though all the other customers preferred the fireside indoors.

And then, Richard having declined coffee, they drove off down a very narrow lane, tightly winding, with a tumbled overgrowth of late flowers and grasses, not yet cut back by frost, brushing the car on either side, and turned suddenly between white gates down a gravel drive, under lime trees, turning butter-yellow, and scattering the ground with fairy coin. Down the drive was a Victorian battlemented house, with a colonnade of gothic arches along the front. A low, square, handsome house, standing in lawns, and twined over with wisteria. 'Ma will give us coffee,' Richard said, braking suddenly in loudly crunching gravel at the front door, and tooting on the horn.

A grey-haired woman appeared almost at once at the door. 'Oh, there you are,' she said. 'How long can you stay?'

'Back for dindin,' he said.

'But it's Saturday, Richard. Couldn't you stay till tomorrow?'

'Women's colleges have draconian regulations, Ma. This is Tessa. She needs coffee; and you wouldn't believe what will happen to her if I keep her out after midnight.'

'Hmph,' said Mrs Mercer. 'I never know when that boy is fooling, Tessa. Do you?' and she suddenly smiled at Tessa.

They had coffee in a square handsome room, with a log fire burning in a white, classical fireplace. An elaborate needlepoint panel lay half worked beside a chair. Mrs Mercer wondered what Richard thought might be going on in the Middle East; something about shares in oil. Tessa didn't listen, but wandered round the room, looking at good furniture and browsing along a line of splendid books.

'Would you like to see the house, Tessa?' Mrs Mercer asked. Tessa was glad to see it. It was lovely all through. Then Richard walked her round the garden, a stable block, a paddock, and a farmyard, full of thrusting crowds of cows, come home for the night. He talked briefly to a man whose accent was so thick and remarks so technical on the subject of cows that Tessa was lost completely, and then took her back to the house.

'What a pity you can't stay longer,' said Mrs Mercer, over tea poured from a silver teapot into translucent cups, but accompanied by lumpy lopsided scones that looked like emergency cooking. 'I like young faces round the place.'

'Lucky Cynthia!' said Tessa.

'Who, dear?' said Mrs Mercer, setting down the teapot and picking up her needlework. Richard frowned.

'Well, yes, of course she is,' said Mrs Mercer, biting a strand of wool off very precisely with well-groomed teeth. 'Find my scissors for me, will you, Richard? Well naturally, Tessa, like other mothers I think whoever catches my son will be lucky. He is both sweet-tempered and good-looking, don't you think?'

'Yes,' said Tessa, 'I do.'

Richard blushed and said it was time to go.

Tessa asked for the lavatory before they set out, and swapped her beads over in the prettily tiled bathroom. Coming downstairs she overheard a scrap of talk between mother and son.

'. . . not bother you?' Richard was saying.

'My dear, brains and beauty have always been an acceptable substitute. And a nice, affectionate nature does wonders. Unless you were serious about the Foreign Office, Richard. It wouldn't do then.'

'Fuck the Foreign Office!' Richard said; or at least Tessa thought that was what he said. He couldn't have.

For Tessa overhearing was indelicate, though involuntary, like belching at table; to think about what one had overheard and try to decode it was just plain vulgar. She didn't.

Richard took her at high speed back to Oxford in the dark, and to dinner at the Elizabeth. She enjoyed herself vastly, confidently sure that pearly bubble-beads against grey jersey must look wonderful by candlelight, except for the moment when, just as she had a curl of Sole Véronique balanced, grape and all upon her fork, half-way to her mouth, Richard said, 'You know, Tessa, you have the most beautiful teeth!' and froze her, mouth tight shut, while the grape pulled loose from its moorings, and splashed into the sauce on her plate.

Richard began to talk about the philology lectures. He appeared to have a perfectly serious scholar concealed beneath his frivolous exterior. They wondered together if knowing the history of the words helped you to use them accurately. They wondered all through dessert, and coffee, and a fast short drive home to St Winnie's just before twelve o'clock and curfew.

The Victorian eminence who had built St Winifred's as a palatial house, long before it was bought by the nuns, had laid out a shrubbery around the side approaches which led to the students' door. A bosky darkness was therefore cast around the last few steps home which was seldom uninhabited at a late hour. The lock-up nun would lean out of the door and rattle her huge bunch of keys furiously for a minute. Shadowy figures would then emerge from the bushes and stampede for the door; the penalty for failing to reach it and getting locked out being at least a fine, and worst, worse. Moments later a dishevelled band of young men would troop out of hiding and tramp away down South Parks Road to the various walls, drainpipes, bribeable porters or wakeful sea-green landladies which lay between them and bed.

Richard had got Tessa home in good time. She had, of course, no intention of inviting him into the bushes to await the jangling keys. But they slowed their steps as they moved down the path to the door. They were talking now on the question whether a person who doesn't know Old English might be able to learn enough Middle English to understand Chaucer – not just superficially, but with the real inwardness and accuracy that they themselves commanded.

Tessa was not of course surprised to hear various rustlings and heavy breathings from the shrubbery; but when someone stepped out of the darkness across her path and touched her arm she jumped half out of her skin, and fell back against Richard. Richard, who was not forewarned about the shrubbery, spun Tessa round behind him at great speed and with fists up said, 'Get off and leave her alone!'

Tessa's assailant stepped backwards, and was engulfed by the dark foliage of the laurel bush beside the path. 'Tessa!' he said, 'I wanted to speak to you. I'm sorry, I thought you'd be alone.'

'Is this someone you know?' said Richard.

'Who is it?' said Tessa, peering in the gloom. Just then a dim illumination was cast by the nun within switching on the blue-hooded lamp above the door.

'Father!' exclaimed Tessa in amazement, recognizing Theodore.

'Oh, don't be ridiculous!' said Richard.

And the scuffle, and the light, drew a group of onlookers at once out of the branches, curiosity overcoming passion.

'Ho! A lovers' fight!' said a young man gleefully, who had Anna leaning on his arm.

'Christ!' said Tessa – three Hail Marys a day for a week at least for that when she next went to confession – 'Not so. Let me introduce everybody. Father Theodore, Richard Mercer, engaged to a girl called Celia. Sorry, Cynthia.' The keys began to jangle at the door. 'And several women undergraduates with their attendant lords. Not sure I know many of them by name.'

'Tessa, I must speak to you,' said Theodore, his voice sounding odd.

'At this time of night?' said Richard. 'A religious matter, I suppose, that can't wait till morning?'

'Richard, it's all right,' said Tessa. 'Honestly it is.' The keys jangled loudly, and reluctant young women tore themselves away from the fun, and trooped through the door. Their escorts were still standing around staring with unconcealed delight.

'Oh well, if you say so,' said Richard, and taking Tessa firmly in his arms he kissed her with shameless efficiency while the nun tutted fiercely at enormous decibels in the door.

'But what about Cynthia?' said Tessa, emerging from the embrace. 'I've got to go. Come and see me tomorrow, Father.'

'Fuck Cynthia,' said Richard, disappearing down the path – or at least that's what Tessa thought he said. But the keys by now were dancing and clanging like a peal of church bells. He couldn't have. Before the furious nun closed the great oak doors and banged the bolts across, Tessa, looking back, caught a glimpse of Theodore, white-faced, staring after her.

In her room she found a note from Reverend Mother. Father Theodore was trying urgently to contact her, had called three times. Would she telephone the Chaplaincy if she got home before ten? Beneath it on her rug another – Father Max was trying to contact her; would she get in touch as soon as possible? Tessa stared at these notes. Her first instinct was to suppose that she had committed some nameless sin – the offence against meekness, or some such, without knowing it. But then Tessa had not been educated by nuns without learning that the worst sins are the ones you commit without knowing it. The priests were seeking to deliver a timely rebuke. An urgent one, evidently. What could she have been doing?

But she knew perfectly well she hadn't been doing anything so awful that Theodore could need to wait for her outside the door at midnight. She fell asleep mystified, with no more reflection to give to Richard's embraces than the passing thought that that Cynthia ought to watch out.

Theodore knocked on her door at ten o'clock the next morning. 'Come in!' she called. When nobody came she went to the door, opened it, smiled at Theodore and repeated, 'Come in.'

He almost flinched. 'Will you be so kind as to walk around the Parks with me for a few minutes, Tessa?' he said.

'Unless you'd rather come and sit down and let me make you some coffee.'

'No. Please.'

She got her coat, and they sallied forth into a misty chill morning in which the grass of the Parks was iced with frost and the golden leaves shone dimly through the white fog banks rolling off the river. They walked in silence for some way. At last they stood together on the crest of the Rainbow Bridge, looking at the dark hasty water.

'I have been in terrible agony of mind, wondering what you must think of me,' he said.

She stared at him.

'I was cruelly rude to you the other day. And since then you have barely met my eyes. I brutally refused your request, and you do not know why.'

'But I didn't think . . .'

'You took me by surprise, you see. I really thought I could just walk you to the gate, just walk with you alone for a few moments . . . but you see I can't be your spiritual adviser, or risk having coffee alone with you in your room. I am in love with you. I was trying to protect myself. I probably shouldn't be telling you about it, but I must keep away from you. I couldn't – forgive me Tessa! – I can't bear for you not to know why. For you not to know . . . for you to think . . .'

Tessa was looking at Theodore as if for the first time. She saw a thin, slight man, older than Richard, or Hubert, or Ben – beyond the age of playing – with very dark eyes, red hair greying at the temples, and sharp, intelligent face sunken in misery. '. . . for you to think,' he was saying, 'that I was avoiding you from dislike . . .'

'Poor Theodore,' she said. She instinctively reached

out a hand towards him, and then sharply withdrew it.

'It's all right,' she said. 'Quite all right. I wasn't offended, truly. And don't worry about it now. I'll keep away from you.'

He seemed to flinch again. There were tears round the rims of his eyes; but then it was fiercely cold.

'You need never see me again,' she said gently, and put her words into practice by running off the bridge and striding homewards through the mist, which was brightening now, gleaming with diffused sunlight.

Did Theodore answer? She was quickly out of earshot, and she did not look back.

When she thought about it in her room she was thunderstruck. What had she done? What a dreadful thing to do! Poor, poor Theodore! But wait; what had she done, really? Had she enticed Theodore? Had she lusted after him in her heart? Had she glanced, smiled . . . no, no, of course she hadn't! She knew she hadn't. It had never occurred to her to think of Theodore as a man; and in any case, however often she confessed to impure thoughts, just in case, even if she *had* thought of him as a man, it wouldn't have amounted to three Hail Marys' worth of temptation. She simply *hadn't* intended to tempt Theodore.

Then had she, perhaps, done it unwittingly? Had she dressed provocatively, without regard to the possible effect on him? Not even Tessa, try though she might to find a foothold for guilt, could accuse herself of dressing provocatively! Nevertheless, though there didn't seem to be a sin to cover the situation, she had, somehow, caused this disaster. Manslaughter rather than murder – or perhaps not even manslaughter, just plain accident, but still she had brought it about. A sort of awe lay on her at what she had done. Well, in a manner of speaking done . . .

But also, like the sea breaking through, irresistibly, the sand-dams she had dug across the shore, came joy.

Theodore was by far the most excellent person she had ever known. He was brilliant, admired by all around, the cleverest of the clever; he had a clarity and tenderness of mind when he taught them . . . and he had aspired to perfection – he had left his father and mother to follow Christ, he had sought holiness, and paid the fearful price of it. And, Tessa thought, this marvellous person loves me, loves me, me!

How dreadful, she thought next. She was very sorry for it. Sorry for Theodore; it must be agony for him. There was only one thing she could do for him – she would have done anything for him, from the first moment she understood his declaration – but the only thing she could do was to keep away from him, to minimize his pain, and that she would do at any cost to herself. No more cell meetings, then. That was a bad thought – she would miss them. And she would need to think up a phoney reason to give people, for they would certainly ask. Unable to sit still with such turbulent thoughts, she put on her coat again and walked once more into the Parks. She returned to the now sunlit bridge, but Theodore had, of course, gone. Then she felt a powerful need to pray – not at the Chaplaincy, where Theodore too might be on a like errand, not St Aloysius, but Blackfriars, where the bleak cool austere chapel might somehow calm her. She prayed for strength to carry out her purpose; she tried to pray, and partly managed it, that Theodore would get over her at once. And she had this so much on her mind all day that she was in bed and falling asleep before she remembered that Father Max had been trying to get in touch with her too.

Father Max did not want to make declarations. The ludicrous thought had occurred to Tessa and made her giggle as she wobbled on her battered bike towards the Chaplaincy. But he wanted her because he had a job for her. It seemed he was a member of some committee for intercultural understanding, which had fixed a visit for thirteen Russians, all student teachers, and he wanted to find somebody to show them round Oxford for a fortnight. The committee had produced two communist undergraduates, who would escort the visitors for half their time; he, Father Max, had arranged for two Catholics to look after them for the remaining time. Now one of them was ill, and he hoped Tessa would do it. Tessa demurred a little on account of work in term time; Father Max told her he had already got permission from her tutor, who would change her tutorial if necessary, and expect her to make up any missed work in the vacation. He added that he had invited Ben as he supposed they would get on well together, being members of the same cell. 'I have given Ben a programme of the visit, and all the details, as well as some money,' he added.

'I'll do my best,' said Tessa, 'but . . .'

'Well, well, Ben will put you in the picture, Tessa. Come to me if any troubles arise, dear girl.' He steered her towards the door, patting her gently on the shoulder.

Ben's room was comfortable and plain. He had put very little of his own in it – a row of mathematical texts in battered Victorian editions, an antique crucifix with a crazed ivory figure, a photograph of his mother in a silver frame. In one corner a cello was propped. On his desk stood an amazing object: a helical slide-rule a foot in circumference and eighteen inches high.

'I hoped it would be you,' he said. 'I'll make some coffee while you look at this.'

'Goodness!' said Tessa, looking at the programme. 'Will there be time for it all?'

'We'll have to sprint,' said Ben.

The Russians were accompanied by a Party Member, one Catherina, who insisted on starting with a briefing, opening in Russian and modulating into English in courtesy to Tessa and Ben, or, possibly, by way of passing some propaganda to a pair of English young. The briefing session astonished Tessa. For every destination – the Bodleian, Christ Church Cathedral, Stratford – Catherina doled out a quotation from Marx, Lenin, or some other Russian worthy, and all around the ring the visitors chimed in, adding words of agreement, with quotations of their own. This gave a dismal impression of conformity, and reminded Tessa of stories about brain-washing.

Walking them round, however, quickly gave a different idea. Catherina physically could not be within constant earshot of every little cluster into which the group separated as they strolled round frosty quadrangles. As long as you were with a sub-group not within earshot of Catherina, the conversation was relaxed and pleasant, and all in remarkably good English. Tessa quickly found herself liking Rosa, an astonishingly slight and small person from Alma Atta, who had a notebook, and on being told anything at all about Oxford cried joyfully, 'Quaint folk custom!' and wrote it down. When Ben was explaining that the term was called Michaelmas, because of a saint's day, and the following term would be called Hilary for the same reason, she so far forgot herself as to cry, 'Quaint folk custom of decadent society!' as she scribbled. She seemed inseparable from Nicholai, a huge blond fellow, whose reaction to almost everything was 'This, we do not have this in Russia', and from Ivan, who bristled with rage on being called Russian, proudly claimed to be Ukrainian, and asserted that his country had perfect freedom within the family of Soviet Socialist Republics.

They spent the whole day walking; not only through colleges, though it turned out they could skip the churches, because the Russians (and the Ukrainian) were deeply reluctant to go inside them, and it was all Tessa and Ben could do to talk them into going up the spire of St Mary to contemplate the view. When once they reached the parapet below the spire, they all said,

'Is very nice,' and trooped down again at once. The view from the Sheldonian Theatre was more of a success, a secular high spot seeming much more acceptable to them, and when Ben put on his MA gown, so that he could take them in without paying the small fee to tourists, they were in positive raptures. Wearing gowns was a marvellously quaint folk custom; 'that they did not have that in Russia', and what they really wanted was each in turn to put the gown on, and be photographed under the ironical eroded gazes of the Twelve Caesars outside. The front window of Blackwell's bookshop, opposite, was entirely filled with a display of a book called *Marxist Economics – A Flawed System*, which Tessa hoped they would not notice.

The photographs taken, Catherina demanded that they see 'houses of ordinary poor workers'. Ben and Tessa consulted together and got everyone on to a bus to Cowley. But the Cowley estates were not at all what Catherina had in mind. She had read, they had all read, about workers' lives under capitalism; they wanted to see the slums.

'Things have changed a bit since Dickens,' murmured Tessa.

'I like, no, I love *David Copperfield*,' said Ivan surprisingly. Getting off the bus again at Carfax, they took their ragged crocodile into Jericho; that seemed nearer what was wanted. It seemed that Catherina still thought they were covering up; down some side street, if only they had known which one, the full glorious disgrace of housing like a Doré engraving would be revealed. But she had to be content with delivering a long monologue on the provision of housing to Russian workers, which she continued all the way back to the obscure hostel on the Banbury Road which they were using as a base camp.

Back at the base there was a considerable uproar. The Committee for Intercultural Exchange had billeted the Russians in the homes of individual families, to give them a glimpse of English family life. The trouble was they had been billeted singly, and when they understood this they flatly refused to go. Catherina talked to them heatedly in Russian; they stood adamantly sullen, refusing.

'We sleep here on floor,' said Rosa at one point. In the end a harassed don, who seemed to be in charge, had to telephone all the host families to ask if they could accept two students instead of one. By and by he was left with just Rosa; Tessa offered to take charge of Rosa herself, since there was a perfectly good guest room in St Winifred's. An outburst of horrified refusal from Rosa put paid to that. The harassed don managed to find a family who could commute the expected one student to three without too much difficulty; the only problem was that there was only one room, though a camp bed could be put in it to take the third person; but if two were young men and the third was a woman . . .

The Russians seemed to find this problem comic when it was put to them; Rosa went off happily enough to share an unprivate night with Ivan and Nicholai.

Exhausted, and far too late for hall dinner, Tessa and Ben strolled homewards down St Giles. At the doors of the Randolph, Ben asked Tessa out to dinner. They exchanged opinions on it all, by candlelight. 'They're spying on each other,' Ben said. 'That's why they can't go anywhere alone; they've got to keep a tail on someone twenty-four hours a day.'

'But do you really think so? How disgusting! And they seem quite nice, really.'

'Well what else can all that just now have been about?' said Ben. 'You know what, though, Tess. I enjoyed today a lot . . .'

'So did I!' said Tessa, almost to her own surprise. Ben had been very good at the job, she realized, keeping calm and amiable all day. She smiled at him. 'We'd best get back, though,' she said. 'If tomorrow is going to be like today . . .'

He paid the bill, waving aside her democratic offer to go Dutch, and they strode out through the coffee lounge to the hotel lobby.

A pair of clerics were ensconced in the far corner of the lounge with a pot of coffee on the table between them, deep in talk. The one who looked up briefly as Ben took Tessa's elbow and steered her through the heavy glass and mahogany door was Theodore.

Time with the Russians rapidly took on the characteristics of a disorderly dream. England seen through their eyes was fantastic, transformed for Tessa. It was beautiful, but without a time dimension; Ivan, who was interested in architecture, could not see the difference between Victorian gothic and the real thing; Tessa spent several hours trying to teach him. In the end she convinced him that the Broad Street front of Balliol was hideous; but it wasn't all one way; he convinced her that Keble was beautiful, an opinion that Ben persisted in finding eccentric. 'There are *no* beautiful buildings wearing Fair Isle sweaters,' he said with finality.

Attempts to take Russians with diverse interests on different outings continued to be thwarted; they would not break down into less than pairs. Attempts to show them 'Real English Life' – the object in which they expressed the most persistent interest, kept turning disconcerting. Lunch in The Welsh Pony, for example – surely a pub was a good sample of English Life? – went wrong when they all refused to drink. 'You can't visit England without tasting beer!' said Ben, outraged. But it appeared that the Party Leaders in Moscow were leading a campaign against drink, and had all gone teetotal, at least in public. Not one drop of alcohol was going to pass the lips of any Russian, not even in the interests of researching the life of the worker in a capitalist state.

'It's only the beer that keeps people happy,' said Ben

coaxingly. 'Without it there'd have been a Red Revolution here years ago!'

'This is pub,' said Nicholai. 'This, we do not have this in Russia.'

'So if you had just one drink here it could hardly begin a habit you would continue back at home,' said Tessa, but in vain. Ben had to elbow his way through a packed throng of undergraduates, and order twelve ploughman's lunches, two pints of bitter, and ten lemonades.

'Ten *lemonades*!' bellowed the publican. 'This is a pissing pub, not an effing café!'

'Hush,' said Ben. 'We'll have an international incident in a minute. They're all Russian visitors. Please.'

The publican brought the orders and dumped them on the tables where they sat saying bitterly, 'Ten fucking Russian lemonades . . .'

Within minutes Nicholai had mistaken Tessa's glass for his own, and swigged a quarter of a pint of her beer. Catherina's attention was temporarily diverted by the fruit machine in the corner, and she was holding forth on the evils of gambling, and the connection between capitalist morality and the urge for a flutter. 'Ah,' he said. 'Factory workers can afford this, Tessa?'

'Easily,' she said.

'Keeps workers happy?'

'Students, peasants and workers, all alike,' she said. 'Drink up, big sister isn't looking.'

This seemed to put Nicholai in a good mood. He smiled broadly, and began in an astonishingly low and vibrant voice to sing something to her which made Rosa titter. It also brought Catherina's frown to bear on Tessa's empty beer glass, and Nicholai's untouched lemonade.

They spilled out on to the pavement later, all laughing, Ben with an arm round Tessa, and Nicholai still singing soft and low – if you don't drink, does it make you abnormally responsive when you do? wondered Tessa – just at the moment when Theodore was passing.

He had a positive gift for being bumped into. Every time she saw him Tessa's heart lurched. Or perhaps it was her stomach? Something did.

They took the Russians to hear Michael Young lecture on Meritocracy, a lecture which troubled Tessa. He seemed to be saying that scholarships like hers to Oxford would remove all the leaders from the working class; would educate them into the middle classes. Did he mean the brainy poor should be left where they were for the sake of the team? That that boy Mark at Richard's party, for example, should not have had a scholarship, but been sent down the mine to become a future Aneurin Bevan if he could? What would Ivan and Rosa think of that? Nicholai had no comment to offer; he had, quite simply, not understood a single word. 'Difficult English,' he said.

Since Blackwell's was their next stop, while they inspected the degree of availability of Marx, Lenin and Engels for the English reader, Tessa bought a copy of Michael Young's book and presented it to Nicholai. He seemed alarmed rather than pleased.

The trip to Stratford to see *All's Well That Ends Well* was almost ruined by the Stratford bookshop, which was displaying *Marxist Economics – A Flawed System* as prominently as Blackwell's had been. Catherina gathered her flock around her and delivered some sharp remarks on the government propaganda machine. Ben explained patiently that even if the Government had wanted everyone to read the book, which was doubtful, they couldn't have contrived its appearance in every bookshop window; the machinery for doing such a thing simply didn't exist.

'So who does decide?' asked Ivan.

'The bookshop manager.'

'And who tells him?'

'Nobody. Each bookshop manager guesses what he will be able to sell, and stocks that. Sometimes he guesses wrong, and has to sell the books off cheaply to get rid of them.'

'So how do they know what to print? Who says how many?' asked Nicholai.

'Nobody says. The publisher guesses how many copies the bookshops will take, and prints enough . . .'

Ivan laughed. 'Pull the other one!' he said. 'Is good English? Pull the other one?'

'Very good English,' said Tessa. 'But Ben isn't pulling your leg, he's telling you how things work.'

'But we are not silly!' said Rosa. 'We know that couldn't work.'

'What a muddle there would be!' said Ivan. 'Tell us properly now.'

'Well. I suppose it does make a muddle,' said Ben, 'but it is how things get done here.'

'But . . .' said Ivan.

'Comrades, it is quite clear that our young friends are not trying to pull the wool,' said Catherina. 'They tell us what they have been told. Just like the workers' housing. They showed us what they knew.'

'In your country,' said Nicholai, like an actor responding a second late to a prompt, 'the workers are fed with lies, and bribed with material consumer goods. In ours everyone knows the truth and one works willingly for all.'

'Quite right, Comrade,' said Catherina, but she was looking at Nicholai with an expression of sharp suspicion.

Compared to this, the play was a relief. Admittedly it was in modern dress, and somewhat disconcerting. But the Russians seemed to be enjoying themselves. Half-way through the first act Nicholai leaned across Rosa to Tessa and whispered hoarsely, 'Please – what is virginity?'

'This, you do not have this in Russia!' said Tessa, in a choked giggle; and saw at once from his struggle not to laugh that he knew the word perfectly.

As they drove home, late and happy, Ben at the wheel of Father Max's car, Rosa in the front seat, and Tessa wedged firmly between Ivan and Nicholai in the back, Catherina and the others in cars driven by the dons on the Intercultural Committee, the Russians at last saw something they really liked in England – cats' eyes. They exclaimed how marvellous, how good for safety, wonderful! Then Nicholai said sadly that Russia could never afford such an extravagant use of power.

'But they're not electric!' Tessa told him. 'They just reflect.'

'So bright? They must be electric!'

So Ben stopped the car, and switched the headlights on and off, and then when they were still fascinated, produced a penknife and extracted one from its rubbery seating and offered it as a souvenir.

The Russians certainly made you think. Lying in a hot bath, Tessa meditated on them and their ways. She and Ben had got it wrong at first. They were not spying on each other, they were backing each other up. If none of them was ever alone with a westerner, then any accusation that they had heard or spoken treason or dissent could be denied, with a witness. Catherina was the one who was dangerous to them; but they had Catherina sewn up. When she briefed them with great chunks of orthodoxy and quoted Bulganin at them, they all agreed and quoted back – Lenin, Marx, anybody permitted to be correct. But every single time they took it in turns round the ring from left to right, like a party game, and as the turns ran round the offered quotations got less and less relevant, and soon wildly off the point; Catherina served, and they lobbed the ball into the bushes, every time. Yet what could she accuse them of? Quoting Lenin? Tessa smiled.

Had they really disbelieved Ben's explanation of a free market? Hard to tell. Their salvation was not taking Catherina too seriously; the extravagance of their assent concealed dissent. Hidden laughter was their form of moderation.

Suddenly she found herself comparing their briefing sessions with the cell discussion on nuclear weapons.

She compared the Russians' mocking quotations with the compelling force, in her own mind, of anything – however unwelcome to her – which was the teaching of the Church. Could it possibly be that she, freeborn westerner as she was, was less well adapted to life in an orthodoxy than the poor brain-washed Russian? Then she shook herself, hugged herself into a towel, and recollected that it made all the difference whether the orthodoxy was true or false.

Could laughter co-exist with belief? Did Father Max really say I took Catholicism too seriously? She promised herself intense attention at the briefing session the next morning. She would watch them all like a hawk!

But that she did not do, because the next morning the Russians had disappeared. They simply weren't there for the briefing; the day's programme never even began. They had climbed into coaches and driven off very early in the morning, leaving no word. The organizers were baffled; one of the dons more than baffled, rather alarmed. 'It's got to be politics,' he said. 'Something must be happening, but I don't know what. I think I'll go and ring the Foreign Office.'

Unexpectedly at a loose end, Ben and Tessa wandered back to St Winifred's for coffee. A large parcel wrapped in brown paper, addressed to Tessa in scrawled handwriting, was waiting by the pigeon-holes. Tessa took it upstairs to her room. Tearing off the paper, she found a thickly cloth-bound volume, the title, author, title page, letters all in an alien script. A card fell out as she flicked through the pages, looking in amazement at page after page of poetry. 'The complete works of Chevchenko,' said the card, 'not even in Russian, but in Ukrainian. The book you give me will take me weeks and weeks to read, but that I give you you will read never! We will not forget you, but do not write to any of us. N.'

Tessa pushed her shell along the mantelshelf, and

stood the complete works of Chevchenko in the middle.

'Very curious,' she said, smiling.

'A bit off, really,' said Ben. 'Rude to the organizers. And to us, too. But we might get to the cell meeting after all, if we drink up our coffee and go.'

'Not me,' said Tessa quickly. 'I'm going to give it a miss. But you go, Ben.' She poured him coffee in a chipped white mug. 'I haven't any biscuits. I was expecting to be out all day today.'

'I know,' said Ben. 'Won't you really come to the group? I always thought you . . . I thought . . . you seemed pretty serious about it.'

'I am,' said Tessa. 'I was. But not today, Ben. Don't let me stop you.'

'What will you do?'

'There's plenty to do!' she said, smiling. 'A Shakespeare essay for one dragoness, and a passage of Bede for another.'

'Well, all right, but I think I will go,' said Ben, slowly putting on his scarf. 'Tessa? I hope we can spend more time together . . . I mean I hope it wasn't just the Russians . . .'

'Of course we can,' she said. 'Of course not.'

He brightened a little, and gave her a light kiss on the cheek. 'I'm off then.'

'Yes,' she said, 'though . . .'

'Though?'

'I wonder . . . aren't there any groups for graduates? We must all seem very salad green to you . . .'

'It's the only group with Theodore,' he said, closing her door gently behind him.

She opened her desk, took the list of Sonnets set for discussion, and the book, to the window seat.

The expense of spirit in a waste of shame
Is lust in action; and till action, lust

Is perjur'd, murderous, bloody, full of blame, . . .

she read.

. . . Mad in pursuit, and in possession so;
Had, having, and in quest to have, extreme;
A bliss in proof, – and prov'd, a very woe;
Before, a joy propos'd; behind, a dream . . .

and Tessa, as always on encountering a description of a sin, examined her conscience to discover if she herself was guilty of it. A reasonably diligent Catholic can almost always discover a touch of guilt under almost any heading of account; but she couldn't do it this time. The fact is, she told herself, I haven't the slightest idea what he's on about. He sounds off his head. Shakespeare off his head? That didn't seem likely to get a good mark in an essay. 'Bear in mind,' Tessa's tutor had said, 'that new observations on Shakespeare are wrong.'

But I really don't understand it, she thought, and turned to the next sonnet on her list.

Love is my sin, and thy dear virtue hate,
Hate of my sin, grounded on sinful loving . . .

She struggled on. But she felt restless. She should have been on a coach taking the Russians to the Science Museum. Her state of mind hadn't caught up with the change of plan.

Let me not to the marriage of true minds
Admit impediment. Love is not love
Which alters when it alteration finds . . .

That one seemed easier. But she left it half read, and stared out of the window at the autumnal Parks and remembered Theodore standing on the Rainbow Bridge. With a powerful sensation that was neither of pleasure nor pain, her memory delivered a replay of every step towards the bridge, and away from it again, and an image of Theodore's face so vivid it made her blink at the empty lawns below her window.

All this the world well knows; yet none knows well
To shun the heaven that leads men to this hell.

her mind said to her, like a late footnote.

'If I can't work, I'd better go out,' she said aloud, and put on her coat.

Outside was a sharp bright late autumn day. The sky was of luminous pallor; a light of diffuse clarity etched the intricate towers of Oxford against it. Inked in the soot of centuries, every detail looked crisply printed. Tessa was to be astonished and not entirely pleased, revisiting years later, to find Oxford cleaned up, and apparently cut in Madeira cake. The coolness of the still-uncleaned stone offset a final blaze of russet and golden trees which were divesting themselves now, analysing themselves into underlying structural forms, turning from paintings in a pointilliste manner into fine prints, black on a hand-tinted sky. Down Longwall Street an undergraduate, glimpsed in a long scholars' gown, harmoniously asserted the monochrome.

Tessa wandered on to Magdalen Bridge and leaned over the balustrade. As green and deep as any waters to be found in Cambridge the stream mysteriously glided beneath.

'Green as a dream and deep as death,' said Tessa.

'I beg your pardon?' said a lady passing close behind her with a shopping basket.

'Lovely day!' said Tessa.

'All right if you're young,' said the lady. 'You have a good time while you can, ducks. I would.'

'I am,' said Tessa. 'I am.'

For she had shaken off her worries entirely.

It was quite illogical, of course, to suppose that she need not work today anyway because if the Russians had stayed on she would have been unable to; but that was how it felt. And Oxford was safe. She would not round a corner and catch a glimpse of Theodore; no lurching, disturbing, narrowly avoided meetings threatened; he was with the group, safely tied up for two hours, and Oxford was all hers.

She gloated at its beauty. And took herself into the Botanical Gardens to sit on a damp cold stone bench and stare at the slowly emerging vision of the Lily Tower, appearing through the thinning veils of the Botanic trees. A mild warmth from the enfeebled sun just touched the nape of her neck. She sat very still. And then slowly there came to her, faintly at first, and then with blazing force, a sensation of the presence of God. She knew the word for what she experienced: 'immanence'. As she knew also that it was not something to be had by taking thought. Belief in God did not always bring it – hardly ever brought it. But at a moment such as this the darkness of the glass through which we see thinned out, lifted for a moment, and let through the glory beyond. So that the presence of God in every aspect of His creation became accessible to the senses as it always was to the eye of faith, and the blessing that He rained upon humanity in every leaf, every wing, every pulse of light or particle of dust, every atom of earth, air, fire or water suddenly blazed incandescent to the eye. The light of heaven fell into the Botanic Garden, and a child running past appeared in the visionary likeness of an angel. It was suddenly apparent to Tessa, as a thing felt, not a thing known, what a work of the devil it is to make us despise and mistrust material things. The things of the spirit are not opposed to the things of the body, for God made all. He not only made the material world, in all its dazzling multiplicity, but inheres in it. He did not remain outside the tangible world He had made, and into which He had sent mankind; he was incarnate, made flesh like us, dwelt in the world in the simple sense in which we do. He ate and drank; all food, all drink are bread and wine now, have become God to us. The priest in the Mass takes simply one example, to stand in for the whole universe, of what an incarnate God has done for His creation. In everything we see, we touch, we feel, in everything we reach for in any human need God bears down upon us. All pain is redemption, all death is resurrection, all action is holiness, God's purpose works through every atom of infinity . . . If we despise the material we shall cut ourselves off at our own roots and die. For we are ourselves transubstantial, a magical fusion of spirit and clay. And our flesh too bears witness to us of the nature of the divine.

She could not have told how long this perception lasted. But in a while she got up and gathered a bunch of sweetly aromatic twigs – lavender and bay and rosemary and escallonia – recklessly, as though the garden belonged to her, and wandered off with it towards an altar: Blackfriars, her favourite altar these days, going up St Giles with the scent of herbs on her hands, and the vision fading and lingering in her like a long summer dusk. She put the herbs on the altar rail and knelt in such confusion that for an hour she could not pray at all, but only exhale her own emotion, until at last God smiled on her, and led her mind into an old formula, words worn by centuries of use . . . '*Gratias agimus tibi propter magnam gloriam tuam* . . .'

She went on praying in these words only till at last the radiance departed, and she found herself surprised that she was repeating the Gloria.

For a moment she was desolate. She felt forsaken. But she knew she would never be that. For all those moments when the vision is beyond our mortal view, God has left us the kind of thing we can always see and lean upon. There is always the Church. We need never be at a loss. God's mercy embraces the worst things we could do in our blindness, as it embraces the malaria fly; nothing is irretrievable except deliberate refusal of grace. Only leaving the Church would be outside the tolerance of God, and as Tessa had no intention – could not even imagine an intention – of doing that, she could hope for mercy on any other thing she did, even if the vision had faded and she was again in the dark.

She got up, surprised to find herself stiff from kneeling too long, and went out, signing the cross upon herself with fingers dipped in holy water as she went. Out into a real darkness, for the shortening afternoon was long over, and into an uproar in the street.

Some kind of demonstration was taking place in the lower end of St Giles, round the Martyrs' Memorial. There was a mass of people and a noise of shouting. Someone with a loud-hailer was addressing the seething throng. There were a lot of scrawled posters. From an upstairs side window of Balliol buckets of water were being emptied on the crowd. A man rushed past Tessa, waving a banner which said 'Smash the Wogs!' She heard the ugly growl of the crowd turning nasty as he reached the edge of the mêlée, and thought she could see blows struck. Behind her a fleet of police cars, driving side by side, advanced steadily. High and dry in the mass of people were a number of coaches and there seemed to be fighting to get into them, and to stop people getting into them.

Tessa stood stock still, dazed. In the uproar fragments of the words of the speaker reached her. 'Imperial . . . aggression . . . unprovoked . . . Nasser . . . Americans . . . Jews . . .' She could make no sense of it. 'Canal!' she heard, 'Canal!' The speaker was holding his right hand above his head and shouting. The crowd were shouting too. 'We hate Ruskin!' and, was it 'We want war!'? Someone struck up 'Rule Britannia!' and was joined by other voices, shortly drowned in howls of wrath. Obviously she would not easily get home through all that. She wondered about slipping into Balliol by the back gate, and through to the Broad that way, but the gates seemed to be closed. Someone pushed a leaflet into her hand as she stood undecided. Behind her a considerable number of policemen were advancing on foot. She scurried for the Lamb and Flag Passage, and away from the riot.

On the back stair of St Winnie's she met Barbara, and said to her lightly, 'What's going on? There's bedlam in St Giles.'

'A protest, I should think,' said Barbara. 'We have invaded Egypt.'

'Oh, but we couldn't have!' said Tessa.

'Everyone is watching the news on Reverend Mother's television set in the common room, if you want to confirm it,' said Barbara dryly.

'BRITAIN'S AGGRESSION: WE STAND CONDEMNED' said the leaflet in Tessa's hand.

Of course, in the fifties people did not know that they were in the fifties; they did not know, that is, that the sixties were coming next. They thought that pop music was Bill Haley and the Comets; they thought that casual chic was tying a scarf round your neck while wearing an open-necked gingham shirt. They thought that undergraduate scruff was buying a duffle coat from Alkit's instead of a college blazer. Tessa's generation at Oxford guffawed at the vulgar liking for Liberace, and had pin-up posters of James Dean instead. They queued for hours to see Audrey Hepburn and Mel Ferrer in *War and Peace*. Their idea of cocking a snook at offensively paternal authority was not to protest at college regulations and attempt to overthrow them, but to climb in. When a medieval wall at Exeter College collapsed, leaving room to get a cart-horse through, the college authorities put a notice in the gap: 'Will gentlemen please not avail themselves of this facility.' Gentlemen didn't – they climbed over, as before, perilously up a drainpipe three yards from the gap.

They thought they were in the vanguard of post-war change. They didn't know their every ace would be trumped by those coming just after, that they would be almost instantly antediluvians, for the next generation would be certain that the fifties had preceded every interesting change; and that Tessa's generation were the last of the frumps, not the first of the free. They, of course, thought they *were* liberated; but what they thought they were liberated from, was Hitler, and the rigours of war and the late, very late survival of rationing and utility furniture. When the *Isis* leader-writer, apropos of Suez, wrote 'for the first time in our own lives we are unable to speak with an open conscience to a member of any other country' he marked at once a remarkable innocence about the past, and the end of innocent patriotism for the future. What Vietnam would one day do for America, Suez had done for him and his like.

The night of the Suez news, Tessa, unable to sleep, wandered the corridors of St Winifred's carrying a tin of cocoa to the gas rings to make herself a good night drink. She was deeply agitated.

The defence she had made, to herself and in the cell meeting, of keeping the Bomb and never using it now appeared to her very foolish. Of course she had thought that her England would never do wrong: never attack another country, never use power to bully and exploit a weaker nation. She had assumed that the appalling weapon would be safe in English hands; it now appeared to her that the line she had taken was about as reasonable as defending the giving of an axe to a toddler . . . if we could attack Egypt, we could do anything. If we could do anything, we could not be trusted with a Bomb, and Theodore had been right. Of course Theodore was right. He was a brilliant man with long training in moral thought, – how could she ever have supposed otherwise? So, inexorably, it followed that her Catholicism demanded of her allegiance to a cause; the marching and the civil disobedience against the Bomb would have to have her support . . .

'God, Tess, you look awful,' said Patsy, arriving at the gas ring with a kettle, and wrapped in a black satin dressing-gown. 'Some of us are having a nightcap in Anna's room. Come along – do you good.'

'I'm making myself a nightcap already,' said Tessa.

'Christ, not chocolate!' said Patsy, retreating with her kettle.

Tessa ambled down the corridor to Anna's room. A babble of voices, far too loud for the time of night, leaked from the door. Inside, Anna in pink pyjamas lay smoking on her bed. All round the bed other occupants of St Winnie's sat on the floor amid tooth-glasses and bottles of whisky.

'Tessa can't sleep,' said Patsy, kneeling down with her hot kettle, and beginning to pour it over instant coffee in paper cups.

'None of us can,' said Anna amiably. 'We're making too much noise.'

'OK, OK,' said Patsy, 'what have I missed? Where has the discussion got to?'

'Love kisses,' said Anna. 'Val doesn't think she could ever, possibly, bring herself to, and Barbara on the other hand thinks she might.'

'And what, for gawdsake, is a love kiss?' said Patsy, handing cups slippery with melted wax, brimming with coffee which glistened on the surface.

'You tell her,' said Anna.

'No, you!'

'I'll tell her,' said Val. 'It's kissing a man's . . . er . . . whatsit. Yuck.'

'And Barbara thinks . . . ?' said Patsy, gleefully, turning to Barbara.

'Now, look here,' said Barbara. 'I only said I didn't see that it was any more repulsive in prospect than sexual intercourse of the normal kind. I deduce that some earth-shattering change in one's usual disgust mechanism must intervene at some point, to make the whole thing possible. It is, after all, quite widely found possible.'

'And isn't it ridiculous,' said Marcia, from somewhere behind the bedside table, 'that in the middle of the twentieth century you can fill a room with intelligent and adult young women who don't know anything about it? We just stink of virginity!'

Tessa sat dazed. She leaned back against Cathy, and sipped coffee which slipped down leaving her tongue coated with a taste of candles.

'Speak for yourself, Marcia,' said Anna. 'Some of us know more than others.'

Cries of 'Wow!' ensued, followed immediately by indignant thumping on the wall from the unfortunate occupant of the next room.

'Well, come on, Anna, tell us! What is it like?' demanded Patsy.

'I don't think I should,' said Anna smugly.

'Oh, do tell us. Go on. Is it really so marvellous?'

Anna looked down and shook a veil of her long brown hair across her face. 'No,' she said. 'It isn't much. It's a bit pathetic, really. They need it so much, like it so much, and you can let them if you like, or not let them – it doesn't matter which. It makes you feel important, the way they come after it.'

'But isn't it thrilling at all?' asked Val.

'It feels nice. It isn't what it's cracked up to be.'

'What about the first time? Did it hurt the first time?'

'No. Not a bit. Look, you know what I think? I think it's all a con. Everyone making a huge fuss about it as though it was absolutely the most important thing, and really it's just a normal sort of a thing to do, like eating, or sleeping. Nothing much to it.'

'What if you got pregnant?' said Barbara.

'Don't be daft. I make bloody sure.'

'But that's a sin,' said Tessa suddenly. She had,

without really noticing herself doing it, swallowed large amounts of whisky to wash the wax away, and her head was humming away on its own.

Everybody laughed. More thumps on the wall, more laughter. 'Fornication is a sin anyway,' said Anna. 'Fornicating with contraceptives isn't any worse than fornicating without them; in fact it's better.'

'How do you know?' demanded Val.

'Well, that's what they tell you in confession,' said Anna.

'I should have thought that two sins were always twice as bad as one,' said Marcia.

'Try confessing to Father Max, if you don't believe me,' said Anna. 'Though it's more fun confessing to Father Theodore.'

Tessa felt suddenly very sick. She lurched to her feet.

'Why? Why is he more fun?' Patsy was demanding.

Anna giggled and tossed back her hair, revealing a deeply flushed complexion. Tessa got up and left. She collided in the corridor with an infuriated Susan, who pushed past her and began to shout at the uproarious room.

Cathy turned out to have come with her, and putting an arm round Tessa said, 'Are you all right?'

'What a vile conversation,' said Tessa. They were whispering, in delayed consideration for the sleepers behind the row of doors.

Cathy said, 'Anna has it wrong, you know, Tessa. She doesn't know much; she doesn't know anything by the sound of her. Don't take any notice of her.'

'But Cathy, do you mean . . . ?'

'She's just wrong, Tessa. Good night.'

Tessa lay awake a long time, miserable, thinking about sex and Suez, and nuclear weapons, and how she couldn't rejoin the group with her new-found fervent agreement that it was wicked for us to have the Bomb; she had promised Theodore he wouldn't have to see her.

In the morning she got up early, extricated herself with difficulty from twisted sheets, dressed hastily and walked to the newsagent in Holywell for a morning paper. Oxford in autumn fire burned dully through the misty halation of the rivers. She was expecting to read about Suez, and there was plenty about it in the paper; but the word that leapt out of every damp front page on the wire rack was Hungary.

You could, of course, do something about Hungary: there would be refugees, many of them students, needing money, clothing, places to stay, courses of study. An undergraduate appeal campaign was setting itself up in somebody's rooms in Balliol. Although Tessa's usefulness was confined to addressing envelopes, she could, and did, diligently help.

It was far from thrilling in itself, addressing envelopes all afternoon, till the looming darkness closed down abruptly and she cycled back to hall dinner in St Winifred's with faintly flickering and dubiously legal cycle lamps. But the campaign *did* raise money; various colleges offered places to students, to allow them to complete degrees begun in Hungary; there was a heady sense of action and importance in the appeal committee rooms, and darkly self-righteous remarks flew around about senior members of the University, whose contribution consisted of writing pompous leaders in the *Oxford Magazine*. One or two younger dons *did* appear one Friday afternoon; to Tessa's mild surprise they included one of the two who had organized the Russian visit.

Seeing Tessa, he came across and perched on the corner of the table at which she was writing. 'Doesn't it beggar belief?' he said. 'However do they think we can continue with a cultural exchange programme when they do this sort of thing?'

Tessa looked up and blinked at him. Pinned up all over the wall behind him were newspapers showing photographs of people running in the city streets, and fighting tanks. In one, a young man lay face down on the cobbles in the foreground with a dark smudge spreading from his head. She had a sudden ludicrous image of a Russian leader fully prepared to unleash all that, saying, 'Hang about chaps, what about our visits to Oxford?'

She was rescued from the need to reply, however, by the arrival of a committee member, who enquired tartly if the visitor had come to help address envelopes. It seemed he had wanted to help, but had had in mind some less menial function. He was told that addressing envelopes was the only help of which the committee was short, and he disappeared hastily.

Though Tessa was spending all her time on the Hungary appeal, she knew quite well what the cell would be discussing, what they would be thinking. She knew without Ben to tell her, though Ben arrived and took her out to dinner one night and told her at great length.

Even without Ben's reminders, Tessa could not forget about Suez with Richard to worry about.

Richard had appeared in her room early one morning. She had come up the echoing spiral stair laughing, with Cathy on her heels. Cathy, who sang in the Oxford Choral Society, had been humming a phrase of Bach to herself as they waited in a line at the sideboard to serve themselves with softly oozing bacon and congealed scrambled eggs, and Tessa had joined in. Sister-Mary-Dining-Hall had rounded on them, furious. 'Singing in the dining hall! And you call yourselves Catholics!'

They came laughing and singing to Tessa's door, and found it open, and Richard in a khaki greatcoat standing, hands in the huge pockets, looking out of the window over the Parks. Cathy slipped tactfully away, and Tessa, embarrassed at there being nowhere to sit except on her unmade bed, offered to go out for a cup of coffee.

'I just need to talk to you a minute, Angel Face,' he said. 'I haven't got long. I've come to say goodbye.'

'Where are you going, Richard?' she said with foreboding.

She thought he would say 'To war', but he said, 'To prison, I think,' and sat down on the crumpled bed.

'Prison! What have you done?'

'It's what I won't do, Tess love. I don't approve of this war. I shall refuse military orders, rather than fight. That will mean prison. I have come to tell you I'm going; I have to be at Aldershot tonight. And to ask you . . . to hope you won't cast me off if I turn into a convict. Tess?'

'But surely, Richard . . . they won't send everybody into battle will they? They seem to be having such trouble getting people to Egypt at all . . .'

'I'm on priority reserve, you see. I learned Arabic during my National Service. I think I will be sent forward at once.'

'So you will have to be a conscientious objector. What happens to them?'

'You can't be a conscientious objector to the war of your choice, Tess. You can object to any fighting whatever; but if willing to fight one war you can't suddenly object to another. The name for what I shall be is coward and traitor.'

'No,' she said.

'Not to you?'

'Not to me, ever.'

'Well thank goodness for that!' he said, and offered her an uncertain smile.

'Surely you didn't think I'd hold it against you if you followed your conscience? How could you imagine that? I'll think you a hero!'

'You will? You're so bloody respectable; I can't imagine you consorting with a jailbird.'

'I'm not your mother, Richard.'

'That was sharp of you. How did you know?'

'Know what?'

'How dreadfully Mother will mind if I am disgraced and court martialled.'

'Not hard to guess.'

'I suppose not. But I shan't lose my chances with you?'

'I shan't mind.'

'In addition to being a jailbird, love, I shall be a non-graduate; you won't mind that either?'

Tessa realized with a shock that she would mind that much more, in the context Richard was speaking of.

'Why that? Wouldn't they let you come back and finish?'

'I'm sure they'll take the heroes back. I'm less sure about those discharged without honour. Possibly not. One had better face the worst.'

'Well the very worst . . .' she stopped herself.

'Would be being a poor immoral brutal slob willing to fight in a grotesquely wicked cause in the wogs' own country, and as a result getting killed. I know. All I needed to know was how you felt.'

'But, Richard . . . what is all this about chances? I like you immensely; if you stick to your beliefs I shall admire you too. I should go on liking you anyway. But . . .'

'But as for chances, I can't lose what I haven't got?'

'You can't lose my friendship. You always knew there wouldn't be anything more. And anyway, Richard, what about Cynthia? What does she think? Shouldn't you be worried about her?'

'My dear, I only made her up as camouflage. A protective covering to quiet your alarm while I wheedled closer. No such girl. Didn't you guess?'

'No! Well, though, I suppose I must have, in a way, or I wouldn't have let you talk like this. How beastly of you, Richard!'

'It worked. I must go; I have to see the Senior Tutor

at eleven. I'll let you know what's happening if I can. It may be difficult.'

'I'll worry.'

'Good.'

'Do you want to kiss me goodbye?'

'No thank you, Tess. I'm in deadly earnest you know; I shan't want to kiss you again until you want to kiss me. See you.'

She stood listening to the clatter of his footfall down the stone stair, and the bang of the heavy door behind him.

Dear Richard. Poor man. Though the sonnets were opaque to her, Tessa had learned from *Much Ado About Nothing* that it was possible to be swept off balance, to fall deeply in love merely on the supposition that one is loved by another; the Benedick effect. And knowing how Richard felt simply didn't produce it. She was full of feeling for him, full of tenderness and concern – so full, in fact, that she might have mistaken this feeling for love had not the Benedick effect already engulfed her; and the author of it was Theodore, with whom she had not exchanged a single private word since the day of his declaration.

With Richard gone she felt sickeningly lonely. She was cut off from the group; when she bumped into Alison she was treated with a touch of reproach, for leaving the group inevitably seemed to the faithful to indicate slackness. She was so far from wishing to leave that she was quite unable to think up convincing alibis, and Alison was distinctly cool. Tessa wandered about the college library, trying to concentrate on the problem plays, with her mind full of problems of the non-theatrical kind. She even biked out to the Warneford to try to visit Stefan, thinking shamefacedly that he too must be lonely, stuck in there. She had not realized that it was a mental hospital until she got there and she was relieved, really, at not being allowed to see him. She understood from the ward sister that visits might be allowed in a week or so; he was getting better.

'Poor Stefan,' she said. 'His work must be weeks behind. How will he manage?'

'His tutor brings him books,' the nurse said. 'You'd be amazed. We get more Firsts in here than any college, you know!'

'Tell him I came,' said Tessa.

A note from Ben lay in her pigeonhole. He would be glad to take her to dinner if she was free. She cheered up at once. The loneliness vanished like Oxford mist at noon.

Ben took her to the Roebuck and in scented candle-light they sat, knees jammed together under a tiny table, and ate beautiful food. Ben ordered three different wines to go with it, providing Tessa with her first experience of that kind of appropriateness. She would have enjoyed it more had he not seemed so ill at ease; he seemed, she thought, for ever on the brink of saying something, and then drawing back. Perhaps because, with tables placed so close in the crowded room, one could certainly not count on not being overheard.

'There's a concert in Merton I thought we might go to; we'll be only a little late,' he said at last, drawing a thick pink napkin across the bill in case she saw it. 'Have you time?'

'Lovely. What is it?'

'Schubert. A quartet. One-six-one, I think.'

'I don't know it.'

'It's a fairly popular piece. Shall we give it a try then?'

'Fine,' she said. 'Let's.'

A college concert has a particular atmosphere. Many of those who listen, shifting on unsuitable chairs, their eyes meeting the self-satisfied eyes of ancient worthies hanging on more ancient walls, can also play, can also sing. The music professors who turn out dutifully to hear their pupils know the music note by note. The whole affair has a provisional feel, like a rehearsal in which, should the violinist be taken ill, someone in the second row could come forward and complete the piece. Although posters all over the town have recruited – even begged for – an outside audience, those few John Citizens who have accepted the offer, at a ticket price less than a pint of beer, are certain to feel like intruders. Not a note is being played for them; the performance is not for the sake of the audience at all.

At first the music seemed very ordinary to Tessa and she had difficulty paying attention to it. Instead she looked into the dimly lit recesses of the roof, and at the curious texture of stained-glass windows without benefit of external light. A faint smell of ancient cabbage mixed with that of a stand of wax candles adorning the High Table, pushed back against the panelling on the dais on which the four cherubic and improbably young maestros sat with their music stands and played. An undertow of sadness in the movement they were hearing steered her thought to Richard, his predicament; and then to Stefan, his even worse one, and so, with a suffocating combination of joy and pain to Theodore. She felt guilty at her selfishness in being all right. In being comfortable, and particularly well-fed, and warm and safe . . . At the end of the movement she fidgeted in the outburst of shifting chairs, coughing, sighing, whispering which the audience seized the chance for. She didn't fidget as much as Ben; he stretched, frowned, turned to her and asked if she was enjoying it . . .

Her answer was silenced by a tuning scrape or two on the cello followed by the next movement, and she was lost in the music. It was nervous, fidgeting like the audience. It was sharp, like a handful of needles, like a range of a thousand pointed rocks. It was drily agitated, parched with anxiety. And suddenly there flowed through it a clear tune of extreme sweetness, which just as suddenly was gone, had lost itself in the roughness and dryness again. She listened, bereaved, longing for the lost fluid tune; and it did return, just as briefly, and changed, as though it knew itself now impermanent, and then was lost again.

And as the rough sounds reappeared, suddenly there was a twang and the quartet faltered into silence. A buzz of voices rose all round her. The cellist had broken a string. The musicians consulted together. 'Ladies and gentlemen,' said the lead violinist, standing up, 'we apologize for the interruption. We will take the interval now and play the last movement of the quartet after the interval. Thank you.'

The sweet tune ran on in Tessa's head. She could hear the sound of a faintly chiming bell ringing in it. Ben put a hand on her arm to draw her attention.

'Sorry about this,' he said. 'Hullo, here's Hubert.'

Hubert was making his way towards them through the now standing and chattering throng.

'Bit of a disaster,' he said to Ben, reaching them.

'Yes, and how!' said Ben.

'Are you staying? I don't think I will,' said Hubert. Tessa, listening with her head full of roughness and sweetness, gradually realized that they weren't talking about the music at all, but about the performance. She gathered, as she could never have gathered for herself, that the performance was dreadful.

'I'll stay if Tessa wants to,' Ben was saying.

'What do you think?' Hubert asked her. 'Are you enjoying it?'

'I think it's lovely!' she said.

'Well, perhaps I'm a bit spoilt,' said Hubert. 'Perhaps one gets hypercritical. But the fact is, I'm only really interested in the last few Beethoven quartets these days, and then only in one or two choice performances.'

'But how terrible, Hubert! Do you mean you don't enjoy music any more at all? I'm glad I know so little about it!'

'There is, after all, a happy medium,' said Ben, 'between late Beethoven played by – let me guess – the Amadeus – and this.'

The musicians were coming back and reclaiming their chairs. 'Shall we go?' said Ben, taking Tessa's arm. 'Tell you what, Tessa, I'll buy you a record of this thing done properly.'

Tessa just stopped herself telling him she hadn't anything to play records on, and submitted, since otherwise he couldn't decently make his own escape.

They walked out into the night with the sounds of the last movement diminishing behind them, and found the great tower and the great tree alike dimly delineated by a bright moon. It had rained; every surface gleamed with muted sheen like tarnished silver. They turned right and strolled down Merton Street, the two men discussing the mortal sins and heinous crimes of the cellist. At the bottom of Logic Lane, Hubert asked them to come back to his rooms for coffee and brandy.

Tessa would have said yes, but Ben said, 'Thank you. Another time,' before she got it out. 'There's something I have to talk to Tessa about,' he added ominously.

'Oh, I see,' said Hubert, obviously seeing far more than was there. 'Well, don't let me cramp your style. Good night, good night . . .' and with a swaggering phoney wave he disappeared up the narrow lane.

Whatever it was, Ben was obviously finding difficulty with it, for they walked on in silence for some way, first into the High and then down Rose Walk and out on to the moon-flooded meadow. The city wall and the view back to Magdalen Tower were standing in the mist of the faint light. The invisible carpet of leaves sounded like water falling round their feet. And in her head the recollection of strings playing songs and bells ran on.

At last he said, 'Tessa, could you bring yourself to be kinder to Theodore?'

She stopped short. 'I am doing the only thing I can,' she said.

'And what is that?'

'I am avoiding him.'

'You couldn't manage to see him now and then, and be kind?' She was dumb.

'He is so miserable,' Ben went on, 'he is in such deep trouble. I am afraid for him, I think he may crack up. And he has, you know, nobody: no brother or sister, and his mother is dead.'

'I didn't know that. But Ben, why are you asking this? How do you know about it? Did Theodore send you?'

'No,' he said hastily. And then, 'Not exactly.'

'You had better explain,' she said.

'He came to me, and asked my permission to try to see you now and then. The present state of affairs is torment to him.'

'But why ask you? What do you mean, permission! What right do you have . . .'

'Naturally you are angry. Theodore has got hold of the wrong end of the stick. He has repeatedly seen us together, over the last few weeks, and he assumed . . .'

'So you told him it wasn't true.'

'No I didn't. I told him I would ask you to see him. I told him I wouldn't mind.'

'But Ben, how could you! How dare you? Why didn't you tell him it wasn't, it isn't true?'

'I thought it would be the best thing all round if I talked to you first. And, of course, I wish it was true.'

She lurched suddenly off to sit down on a damp bench beside the Broadwalk. 'This is ridiculous!' she said, her voice shaking now as well as her hands. As though she had received a physical shock, not merely words . . . 'What do you wish was true?'

'That you were engaged to me,' he said.

'You want me to be engaged to you, and you want me to be kind to Theodore?'

'You are trembling. Are you well? I must take you home.'

'Yes,' she said, getting up. He took her arm, and they walked out of the light and open meadow into the thickly dark lanes.

A little way up Merton Lane Ben began to talk to her. Marriage, he told her, was a great sacrament, but it was not meant to enclose people, to entitle them to turn their backs on the world. It was a sacrament for those who stayed in the world; a secular calling. It could not be right for the married to become a sort of mutual selfishness society, locked in each other. A marriage should be a refuge, a house with a welcome always ready for the less fortunate, for those in need of kindness, help, comfort.

As they passed the great baroque doorway of Saint Mary the Virgin, in lamplit chiaroscuro he told her that he was in a position to marry; his research fellowship was sufficiently paid, and would bring a college house if he needed one.

In Radcliffe Square he told her that, married, they could be the brother and sister that Theodore needed, they could make a home for him as well as each other. As they passed the looming mass of the Bodleian he remembered that she was an undergraduate, not allowed to marry, and so the whole design would have to wait a while . . . and as they walked the leaf-piled, muffled pavement of Parks Road he told her how in the Orthodox Church they put upon the brows of bride and groom in the middle of the marriage ceremony, a martyrs' crown, that they might well understand what path they had chosen.

At the doors of St Winifred's they paused, the blue light over the door tinting their tense faces a macabre hue, as of the risen at the last trump.

'I'm sorry Ben,' she said. 'I can't answer. I can't think. I need time to think.'

'Of course,' he said. 'Take all the time you need. But what shall I tell Theodore?'

'Tell him yes,' she said.

Very early in the morning, just after Theodore had celebrated six o'clock Mass, Tessa set off with him, biking down the Botley Road, to carry out her mission to be kind. It was overcast as they set out, but a brisk wind was sweeping up the sky and by the time they reached the little lane to Wytham woods a thin sunshine managed to cast faint shadows, though not to cast off the cold. They left their bikes leaning on the churchyard wall and walked in the woods. At their feet the whole woodland floor lay thick in golden leaves; the bare branches overhead supported still here and there lonely transformed leaves, like single souls in glory. And they walked at first in silence, hardly knowing what to say.

At length the path they were following led out to the edge of the trees, to a gate beyond which the sun shone on an open field. They walked to the gate and leaned over it, carefully apart. Outside the wood the sun shone on a slope of pasture sweeping down to the pewter gleam of the Thames, and the level meadows beyond. The frost had been sharp overnight, and though the sun had now rendered every patch it had touched emerald and brilliantly sequined with melted beads of dew, the white encrustation lingered in every shadow, down every hedgerow, under every tree.

'How did this happen?' Tessa asked.

'I could tell you, given time enough, how things have happened to me,' he said, 'supposing you were interested. But to you? Has anything happened to you?'

'Yes,' she said. 'Oh, yes.'

He dropped his head in his hands for a minute. Then he looked up and turned towards her with so desperate an expression of distress that she turned her own glance aside from his instantly.

'My dear, my dear,' he said, 'what are you telling me? What have I done? If I had any hope of salvation, I would sacrifice it without hesitation, I would suffer anything in this world, rather than do you any harm, lead you into any sin . . .'

'But you haven't done me any harm! How could it harm me to love a person like you?'

'You don't know me, Tessa. I am not what you think.'

'And are we led into sin? What sin are we committing?'

'We have come here alone together. We are certainly not avoiding occasions of sin; we are certainly not avoiding temptation.'

'Well, you know more theology than I, Theodore; but is love, the simple fact of feeling love, for each other a sin? How can it be? Did we intend it? It feels, to me, as involuntary as breathing.'

'Love pure and simple cannot be a sin,' he said, 'but . . .'

'Well then, cheer up!' she said, smiling at him.

As though reluctantly at first, he smiled back at her. They turned from the gate and walked another path through the wood.

'We should not be here,' he said. 'I did not know – it never occurred to me – you could have any feeling for me. If I had known I would not have risked bringing you here alone. We can never do this again.'

'How dramatic you are! Do you feel yourself to be in danger?'

'Well, aren't we in any danger? I mean, my dear, is it perfectly all right, do you think, for us to be alone?'

'Yes. I am in complete command of myself. Are you afraid I might go berserk and fling myself at you?'

She spoke laughing; but the amusement died at once when she saw the deep flush that flooded his face, and the flinching vexation in his eyes.

'Am I being absurd?' he said. 'Yes, I see that I am. But I can't help it, Tessa. I'm older than you, but I don't know anything . . . I just don't know about normal, ordinary things. Help me understand. You see, we were always being taught about irresistible temptation overwhelming people . . . the moment they were unguarded, and . . . how could you care for me . . . ? But if you do . . . Oh, God, I think I sound as if I am saying that I think myself a temptation to your appetite . . . Tessa, I know I could never be that . . . but . . .'

'For heaven's sake, Theodore, calm down!' she said. 'Stand still a moment.' She stopped the restless walking, and leant against a tree trunk and waited while he did the same, leaning facing her, and hungrily and intently returning her gaze. The depth of his misery, and its entangled nature appalled her. Her instinctive urge to put her arms round him to comfort him was getting in the way of thinking what to say. She overcame it.

'But truly, love,' she said, smiling at him, 'love makes people want to walk together, and talk, and read the same books, and all sorts of things. I can't see why what we may never do should prevent us doing what we may. Unless, of course, you find it so painful that it would be loving in me to avoid you. As I thought at first . . .'

'I can't get you out of my mind,' he said. 'When you avoid me I am in hell.'

'Well, then, we must love each other chastely. People do. All sorts of people, engaged people . . .'

'Perhaps less often than you think,' he said. 'It must be very hard.'

'Theodore, believe me, I love you too much to let you come to any harm from me – promise! We shall walk and talk affectionately together, and nothing will occur to disturb the angels of which this wood is full. They will not have a single wing feather ruffled . . .'

At last he smiled.

'You are kind,' he said, 'and your kindness is like dry clothes and a warm fire when one is drenched and frozen. I must make the most of every moment of it, because, Tessa, it will not last when you know what I am really like. I go under false pretences in the world. The truth is that I am wicked and contemptible.'

'You cannot be,' she said.

'If you knew . . .'

'You can tell me your life story, when you want to, and I will tell you if you seem wicked to me,' she said. 'But in any case, you make love sound like a good-conduct award. One doesn't deserve it, you know. One just gets it – or not as the case may be.'

'Or loses it?'

'Oh, no! It is an ever-fixed mark . . .'

'Ah. A marriage of true minds, you mean?'

'Isn't that what we might manage, without sin?'

'But do you really mean it, Tessa?' he asked. They were walking on again. 'Are you really offering to love me? What about Ben? Doesn't loving him prevent you?'

Tessa thought for an instant about Ben. She felt a glow of affection for him: dear steady sensible Ben, who had correctly seen how to make it all right for her to help Theodore. Who magnanimously thought of marriage as including refuge and affection for others . . . 'It isn't true that one can love only one person at a time,' she said. 'One can only love a person in the way they need, and another person's needs may not conflict.'

'You mean, if Ben were hurt to think of us seeing each other, you would have to choose which of us to care for . . .'

'But as he asked me to look after you, no choice arises. Yes.'

They reached the end of this second, longer path, and once more stood looking across mistily sunlit fields.

'Tell me how, and when, you first started to care for me,' he said, softly.

'Why, on the Rainbow Bridge, of course, in the moment when you told me you loved me. The Benedick effect!'

He laughed, softly. 'Beatrice,' he said. 'Be my Beatrice; the perfect alias for the worshipped platonic she. Can we really manage this?'

'Yes!' she said, turning from the gate across the path, and leading the way back into the wood.

They found their bicycles leaning into the ivy on the churchyard wall as though intending to grow into the landscape. Leaving them a little longer they walked into the church. A plain enough church; they dated its parts to each other, and checked against the printed guide glued to a wooden board found leaning against the font. Golden chrysanthemums, artfully arranged, filled brass vases at each side of the choir. The place smelt of damp, and dying flowers. Tessa picked up a warped and foxed copy of the *Book of Common Prayer*. It reminded her suddenly of Cornish Grandad. And the sea. As she was holding it Theodore came up beside her and gently put an arm around her shoulders.

She looked round at him in amazement; she was very startled.

And as her eyes met his she saw him flinch away. He withdrew his touch at once. 'Not that, then,' he said, sadly, and without another word they left the church, and began the ride back.

At Carfax they parted, she for Forfar's lecture, he for the road to his digs.

She dreamed right through the Vespasian Psalter Gloss, word after word passing over her while she thought only of the words that had passed between her and Theodore. Had he said that he knew he could never be a physical temptation to her? What a funny thing to say; was it becase he thought she was engaged to Ben? With a sudden leap of understanding she saw what it was: it was connected with all that talk about how wicked he was, and so she must help him, she must heal his mangled self-esteem if she possibly could.

As the lecture ended Tessa suddenly came to herself

and stared with dismay at her empty notebook. And whose could she borrow to copy, with Richard far away?

As though her thought had produced it, there was news of Richard waiting in her pigeonhole when she got back to St Winnie's for lunch: a neat, deckle-edged letter on deep blue thick writing paper from Richard's mother. The absurd boy was well and cheerful doing some kind of training course in Yorkshire, which involved rock-climbing; were there rocks on the way to Cairo, one wondered? He had asked her specially to tell Tessa that he was not, after all, likely to be court martialled, but not to lose faith in him, it wasn't his fault; he had tried. 'Is he joking?' the note enquired. 'I can never understand the child. Can you?'

Tessa smiled. She also realized that not only could she not crib Richard's notes for the lost lecture, but that very likely he would reappear hoping to crib hers. She rode off straight after lunch to visit Sheila, miles and miles up the Banbury Road, who was boring and diligent and would have very full and accurate notes and be only grudgingly willing to lend them. She was full of virtue that afternoon.

When she returned there were flowers in her room. For a moment she thought joyfully of Theodore, but with them was a note from Ben, asking her out to dinner. It occurred to her that he wanted a report; that she would be very loath to make one.

He did indeed want to talk to her about the morning's expedition, but not in the way she expected. How had she found Theodore? was what he wanted to know. Did she too think he was in a fragile state of mind? And yes, she did. She didn't mind telling Ben that she thought Theodore was in a desperate state of some kind; that something was terribly wrong, and he needed all the friendship he could get.

* * *

Tessa sat in her window seat, with the rain beating against the cool glass inches from her cheek. The heavy conifers which bordered the Park along St Winnie's garden fence lumbered about in the wind. A scatter of dead leaves ripped across the muddy grass beyond. Spread out around her lay books for the week's essay – Joan Bennett's *Four Metaphysical Poets* and the slender blue-bound Oxford Donne.

> Dull sublunary lovers love
> (Whose soul is sense) cannot admit
> Absence, because it doth remove
> Those things which elemented it
>
> But we by a love, so much refin'd,
> That ourselves know not what it is,
> Inter-assurèd of the mind,
> Care lesse, eyes, lips, and hands to misse.

She read, and copied the page and line reference on a card to Theodore, to be sent by the afternoon messenger. Surely Donne was describing something which he had experienced himself. There really *had* been platonic love in the world; others had felt and acted as she and Theodore now felt, and were constrained to act. The ghosts of every lover who had needed not to touch surrounded her and comforted her against the fear that it was impossible so to love Theodore as to do him no harm. If God was a God of love, then virtuous love had to be possible. And then, on the analogy with the fall of sparrows, it must be God's doing, after all.

Doubtless He had created Tessa on purpose for Theodore's need. Well, mostly for that; but she did have other functions. She returned to her essay on metaphysicals.

But when, after supper, she walked out into the Parks and met Theodore under a shadowy tree to walk for an hour in the damp and dark with him, he said sadly that the words she had sent him, which Donne applied to the absence of lovers, applied for them to their presence, face to face.

In the last weeks of the term there were repeated sharp frosts. Morning after morning the view from Tessa's window was silvered and decorated like a Woolworth's Christmas card. The shillings eaten by her gas fire ran away with the money for books, and she read long hours in the library with a rug wrapped round her knees, saving on both kinds of expenditure at once. At nine, when the library closed, she went back to her room and lit the fire to work by till bedtime. It seemed that she was often making cocoa at eleven when Cathy came in; she took to making a mugful for Cathy as well as a matter of course. Cathy came in dreamlike, with distended pupils that shrank only gradually in the lamplight. Cathy came straight from the shrubbery outside the side door and though she was not a girl for pouring forth her soul abroad on such matters, Tessa knew she was in love. Her happiness came in with her, like her freezing hands and feet – courtship in the open air exacts a price in frostbite as the Michaelmas Term rolls on – but outlasted the thawing-out process. Tessa basked in it, and, obscurely reminded, washed the dust off her conch shell, pushed aside the copy of Chevchenko and returned the shell to the middle of the mantelpiece. Any reason for the sudden intimacy between them was barely mentioned, only Cathy once saying, 'You too.' Not a question.

'I can't talk about it.'

'Who can? You don't have to.'

Somehow, every few days she spent time with Theodore. He was terrified of being seen around with her alone; of being suspected. So they rode out of the city, or sometimes, when he had the use of Father Max's car, drove. She suggested he should wear a tie; open-necked mufti was getting impracticably draughty in the winter weather. She bought him one, and produced it from her pocket with a flourish as they sat parked in a field gate on Boar's Hill, contemplating Jude the Obscure's famous view. Then – how they laughed over it – she found he couldn't tie it, and had to be shown. Recollections of the hopsack girdle that had belted a gymslip being her own only experience, she couldn't do it facing him; they had to get her in the back seat, leaning over him from behind, tying it as though round her own circumference.

'There! But art Thou he? But oh! how fall'n, how changed!'

'Oh yes,' he said, 'even my Father Provincial wouldn't recognize me; I'm not sure I know myself.'

'Your what?'

'The Father Provincial; the head of the Order in England.'

He was gazing quizzically into the rear-view mirror, and twitching the knot of the tie.

'These things must be very dangerous,' he said. 'One could hang in them very easily if the ends got caught in machinery. Do you know, dearest, I had never realized the sliding nature of the knot?'

'I've never heard of a man dying à la Isadora . . .' she said. 'But to be on the safe side, keep the tie away from your typewriter. I wouldn't like to lose you!'

'Really, truly?' he said, turning away. 'I must be just a complication for you. Ben's demanding friend . . . Tessa, you're not just pretending to care about me?'

'No, I'm not. I do. Shall we go for this walk then?'

And then panic, later, when outside St Winnie's in the dark, they frantically searched the car for Theodore's dog collar, and the little black bib appended to it which made him respectable. He thought Father Max would still be out; he could probably reach the safety of his room without the housekeeper seeing him in suspicious secular clothing; he was calming down when it occurred to him the damn thing might be found, lying in the roadside grass, and give rise to horrible suspicion; he calmed down again when reflection convinced him there was nothing on it to identify its owner.

'But aren't you allowed to take the thing off in your spare time?' she asked him.

'We are supposed to act like priests every living minute of every day,' he said. 'And if you don't they watch you like hawks; especially for any sign of a woman.'

'Father Max would?'

'Well, not Max. But others. There are always others around. It would be their duty to tell the Father Provincial.'

'Yuk, love. Well be careful,' she said, irresistibly reminded of Catherina with her beady little Party Member's eyes.

But she certainly couldn't talk about it, even to radiant and sympathetic Cathy; and when some chance remark over the gas rings made her realize that Cathy thought it was always, instead of sometimes, Ben she went out with, she felt only relief.

She couldn't, of course, spend her whole life thinking about, or seeing, Theodore. Tessa went through the motions of life, read books, wrote essays, drank coffee, resumed going to cell meetings, occasionally had dinner with Ben, but she did all these things dimly, as though in bad weather, as though in all the motions of her mind, only when it dwelt on Theodore did she have light enough to see properly what she was doing.

Or as though the term resembled a visit to the theatre. It opened with dressing up, with excitement, with crowds of people flocking round her. A hum of voices, and constant glancing round to see who else was in the magic brilliance of the auditorium, their senses, like hers, bombarded with variety and colour;

then the lights went down, the curtain rose, and nothing could be seen or heard but the sole occupant of a single spotlight on a darkened stage. The whole of her capacity to give heart or attention to anything was beamed narrowly on Theodore. And what was playing, then, in monologue, on the stage? Theodore's life story, a tragedy? At the time she thought so: a drama, anyway, in which the good man suffers for his goodness. A tale to bring forth pity in a tender heart. Another person might have thought it comedy of course, of a kind; but Tessa, excruciatingly aware of sadness, was blind to folly, as to the colour of the light.

Theodore's account of himself began with the death of his mother, just after his seventh birthday. He had been a late child, born when every hope had been lost of him, like John to St Elizabeth. He could remember very little about her illness, though he thought she had borne it stoically, but he had always known that she had hoped he would become a priest.

On her death his father became morose and restless and his work took him increasingly often abroad. A relay team of tight-lipped, childless, devout aunts tended to Theodore in a storm of shock and disapproval at every act of the boy, at his noise, at the grime on his hands, at his desire to climb trees, or run, or sing in the bath, or splash, or read comics. God, he understood, hated all these actions and disapproved of them as wicked unkindness and disrespect of the selfless aunties who certainly would not have had anything to do with Theodore had it not been God's will that they should. They had been 'called' however, to look after him, and in the purgatory he inflicted on them they pre-paid their entry tickets to heaven.

'But Theodore, what did you do that was abnormally wicked for a little boy? You only sound like my brother!'

'Do I? I always believed I was abnormally wicked!'
'Poor you. Poor little boy!' she said.
The only bright part of Theodore's life was school. He soaked up Latin and maths, and religious instruction. He was always top of the class. The day came when the headmaster asked him to write an essay for the Ravenna Fathers competition.
'What's that, Theodore? Should I know?'
'Well, the Ravenna Fathers are always on the look-out for very clever boys. They are a rather peculiar order really. They started as a group of western theologians brought together to advise the Pope at the Council of Florence – the one that re-united the western and the eastern Church. After the Council they went to Ravenna and ran a house devoted to doing theology, and keeping an eye on the Greek Churches. They do all sorts of things now: running orphanages and universities, and even some parishes, but the whole thing is still run from Ravenna. You write an essay for them, and if it's good enough they will take you under their wing, pay for your education, and train you as a possible recruit.'
When they saw his essay, they had at once adopted Theodore. They arranged a scholarship so that he could be sent away to a seminary school.
'When was this? How old were you?'
'Twelve.'
'Too young to leave home.'
'Surely not. I was glad to go; that I do remember.'
It was a hothouse for academic high flyers, but he had still come top of the class. The place had severe rules. There were hardly any holidays; the great festivals of Christmas and Easter were celebrated at school and when they were over people went home for a few days. Only in the summer was a long holiday given. Once he got into the seminary proper Theodore, however, never went home again. His dread of it somehow showed through to the attendant priests; impassively observant, they knew a lot. Father Michael

asked him what he would be doing in the holiday; coaxed out of him a description of his aunts and his absent father, and asked briskly if, in that case, Theodore wouldn't rather come to the retreat house in Scotland. Not, this time, to pray; to learn sailing.

Father Michael was energetic and cheerful, and a good companion. Theodore was well looked after. Discreetly and systematically the teaching priests saw to it that Theodore had somewhere to go in the summers. An Irish Father took him to Dublin when he was fourteen, for example, where he encountered family life. The atmosphere of affection – and the reverence for priests – enchanted Theodore, who went back to school and wrote an excellent essay on the sacrament of marriage as an agent of God's purpose in the world. He also wrote two or three letters to the priest's jolly younger sister, until she suddenly and mysteriously stopped replying. And sisters were not the only peril against which the seminary guarded him. Rules prohibited the forming of friendships with boys older or younger than oneself.

The summer he was eighteen, with his Higher School Certificate behind him, the Father Provincial of the Ravenna Fathers borrowed him and took him to Rome as his secretary. Theodore could write fluent Latin, and learned Italian in three weeks. He was lonely in Rome, with only a prelate for company. The contrast between the overwhelming worldly glory of the Church and the squalor of the Father Provincial's business disturbed him. The Father Provincial was trying hard to get a dispensation to permit a woman parishioner to return to the communion rail while still using contraception. She had five children; the doctors said she would die if she became pregnant again. The Holy Office said she must abstain. The Father Provincial was angry.

'Aren't they worried about her immortal soul, denied the consolations of the Faith, and the sacraments?' he said, throwing down the official reply.

'*Couldn't* she abstain?' asked Theodore.

The Father Provincial looked at him thoughtfully. 'She is a good woman,' he said.

At Victoria, when they parted – for the Father Provincial had business in London which did not require Latin letter writing, and Theodore had nowhere to lay his head except the seminary – the Father Provincial said suddenly, 'I shall send you for a degree abroad. Not Rome, I think. Germany.'

And Theodore had duly done brilliantly at a German university. He had made a name for himself with a monograph on St Thomas's theory of the just war while he was still an undergraduate, which had begun his reputation as a theorist against nuclear weapons. He had made friends of fellow students, met with only kindness, finished with a highly distinguished degree and gone on to be ordained. People had been ready to take him home, or rock-climbing, or hiking in the Tyrol when the long vacations loomed. On one such hike, which unusually contained lay members, he had met Ben, then an undergraduate.

Then a year working in a parish; then the Father Provincial had sent him to Oxford.

'And Theodore, how did you know you wanted to be a priest?'

'I always wanted to be top of the class. To serve God better than the next man.'

'But . . . Just wanting to do well at school doesn't seem the same as deciding to be a priest . . .'

'I chose it freely, Tessa. I can't wriggle out of it that way. We were always told we could opt out of it at any stage. Nobody put any pressure on me at all.'

'But after all that,' she said, 'they wouldn't need to.'

Another time she asked him, 'And you didn't have any doubts?'

'I had doubts. I do, to some extent, blame those who

advised me to ignore them. And yet I am sure they were sincere.'

'You had doubts and you were told to ignore them?'

'I don't want to talk about my doubts to you, Tessa. I am damned under enough titles of account already without risking the damnation attendant upon sowing doubts in the mind of the innocent.'

'Thank you! But I only want to understand you.'

'Then I had doubts, about which we will not talk. And doubt is difficult for me; I have never been able to understand why faith is a virtue. In every other field of thought rigorous proof, and rejection of the unproven, is better. I was told that everyone feels like that just before ordination. That the devil always takes away people's faith, conceals it from their view, to try to trick them into failing God's purpose.'

'Sounds plausible enough. One would be bound to be nervous . . .'

'But it isn't true. I have talked to many ordained priests now, and they say it didn't happen to them. Certainly it is far from the usual experience I was told it was. And then I already knew that continence was unusually hard for me; impossible, almost. And the same advisers suggested to me I might have some physical abnormality which made it harder for me than most, and that I should therefore forgive myself my lapses . . . that isn't true, either. The thought frightened me. After I was ordained and home again, I went to a non-Catholic doctor who told me not to worry. I was as normal as sin!'

'I don't always understand you very clearly, Theodore. Why does it matter whether you are normal or not, since you aren't . . .'

'Leading a normal life? Well, if there was such a thing as a disability of some kind which prevented a person being continent, then any incontinence they committed would be forced; involuntary, without sin. But if one is a normal person vowed to continence then any failure is sinful. If I am normal, I am in a state of sin nearly all the time. And many times when I get up in the morning and go to say Mass without first making a confession, I redouble my own damnation.'

'Is this what you meant when you said you were certainly damned?' she asked him, incredulous.

At this point in recollection, just for once, time will illuminate Tessa to herself, as well as casting light on Theodore; for she had not, then, read the *Kinsey Report*, and, presumably, neither had he. It was, of course, a scandalous book, having caused an outburst of incredulity and widely reported suggestions that American males were given to gargantuan boasting. Not at all the kind of thing that Tessa read, in spite of her voracious literacy.

'It's a fairly well-sprung trap, Tessa,' Theodore said. 'If the teaching of the Church is true in minute particulars – in every little rule and discipline – then every time I shirk waking Father Max at crack of dawn, yet again, to have a pathetic confession heard before I say early Mass, I commit a terrible blasphemy. I go unclean before God and mock the sanctity of the Mass. I shall go to hell for that, if there is a hell. But if the teaching of the Church is not true in every small particular, then what sort of terrible thing do I do, sitting in the confessional binding others to disciplines which entail, for them, terrible cost, and of the truth of which I am uncertain?'

'Like what, Theodore?'

'Like the prohibition on contraception. Tessa, I am in a kind of hell already. If there is anything worse than needing to wake someone for absolution, it is hearing the confessions of people for whom the teaching of the Church is heart-breaking . . . I shouldn't talk to you like this. Forgive me. But God knows, I am not joking when I say I shall go to hell, if there is any such place for anyone.'

'If you must go to hell,' she said, 'then I shall go there too.'

'Don't joke about such a thing.'

'It's not a joke. If God could really damn you for faults such as those you speak of, then I will turn my face from Him. He will not be what I can worship. I will go with you; wherever.'

'Well,' he said, smiling, 'Beatrice was in heaven. But it was in only the first circle of hell that Dante put those damned for love, less far down the pit than any other kind of sinner.'

'What was it like, the first circle?'

'A great wind swept the lovers for ever and ever round it, giving them no rest.'

'And does it feel like that to you?'

'Somewhat. But only when I am not with you. When I am with you I am in a safe shelter, and at rest.'

'A sort of windbreak, am I?'

'Where no storms come,' he said, 'and out of the swing of the sea.'

And so bizarrely skewed towards the ancient was the Oxford English course that Tessa, who had not yet encountered Hopkins, did not realize that these lovely words compared her to a nun.

Engrossed all the time in the story Theodore was telling her; longing all the time for the next occasion when they could walk freezing without and burning within through a winter landscape; speculating horrified on every dimension of his situation, Tessa nevertheless could not entirely escape the rest of life. Essays were still demanded, the Hungarian appeal still needed envelopes, friends inexplicably failed to realize that she could not attend to anything not spotlit on the stage, and she discovered a talent for seeming to listen, for saying something, while thinking of Theodore at the same time. Her mind had become a dual carriageway.

Only occasionally something let others edge into the bright circle of light that played on Theodore – as, for example, the day that the cell discussed contraception, which they did only because Tessa, knowing that this was a matter on which Theodore was troubled at the teaching of the Church, hoped that her friends might find some resolution, and that their discussion might help Theodore. It was quite unselfish of her really, to suggest it, for she found the whole topic slightly distasteful. But the moment she suggested it, Hubert volunteered to bring a discussion paper on it to the next meeting. Tessa was surprised; she had not thought of Hubert as one of those who would need to know.

Hubert's paper, however, was highly technical. It was exclusively about the state of the Church's teaching on contraception, and the nature of the necessity for accepting it. And that involved a long exposition of the nature of the authority of the Church. No Pope had actually pronounced ex cathedra on the matter. But the present Pope had preached against it, and even issued an encyclical against it.

'Well, but aren't encyclicals binding?' asked Alison.

Theodore said not. While it would be very arrogant, very dangerous, to ignore an encyclical, only a pronouncement ex cathedra carried the guarantee of infallibility. Theoretically, a Pope not speaking ex cathedra could be mistaken.

Hubert went on to explain that what a Catholic was bound to believe was something called 'The Teaching of the Church', to which Papal utterances were a pretty good guide, but actually the teaching of the whole body of the world's bishops mattered too. Theoretically, if another Council were ever called, and the bishops assembled and disagreed with the Pope, the Pope, unless he resorted to ex cathedra statement, would simply have to accept that the teaching of the Church was the predominant opinion of all the bishops.

'What if the bishops assembled and disagreed with each other?' said Dominic.

Everybody laughed. Councils of the Church struck them, like inquisitions, heretic trials, or selling indulgences, as the sort of thing that had been put far behind.

'Surely there couldn't be another Council?' said Paul. 'When was the last one? Hundreds of years ago?'

'No; eighteen sixty-nine,' said Theodore. 'Just the same, I think a Pope would be very foolhardy to call another. It would attract a huge amount of publicity; and if the bishops did disagree, it would be very hard to keep that secret, as was done in the past.'

'And in that case,' said Hubert, 'the faithful would be free to choose for themselves which party of bishops to follow. About those things on which the teaching of the Church is unclear, or on which there is controversy among bishops, a Catholic is free to decide for himself.'

They weighed the prospect, every one of them finding it fanciful. Had an angel in glory appeared to them and told them that Hubert was prophesying they wouldn't have believed it. You might as well have told them they would live to see the Vatican proscribing the Latin Mass.

'There isn't any doubt at all, however,' said Theodore, 'that the teaching of the Church at present is against any use of contraception, in any circumstances. There are discreet doubts on the matter voiced by a very few theologians; otherwise the teaching is solid.'

'And the interesting question is why?' said Tessa. 'What, after all, is so very wrong about it?'

'I have always thought,' said Theodore, 'that a celibate clergy is rather ill qualified on such matters, compared to pious laity. Perhaps *you* should tell *me* what is wrong with it.'

'Well, we have been taught,' said Dominic, 'that it is wrong because sex is clearly designed for procreation; the contraceiver – is there such a word? – takes the pleasure God attached to the act as an inducement while frustrating the natural purpose of it.'

'What about chewing gum?' asked Tessa.

'What about *what*?'

'Well isn't chewing gum another example of taking

the pleasure attached to a natural function, and frustrating its purpose? So if that's all that's wrong with contraception, one would expect the Church to make quite a song and dance about chewing gum too.'

Her companions stared at her. Alison began to laugh.

'Well, I dare say,' said Hubert, 'when Roman vomitariums were in full flow, the Church did condemn the abuse of appetite.'

Theodore said quietly, 'I cannot recall any instance of such a condemnation.'

'When you come to think of it,' said Alison, 'the Church doesn't bother much with greed. One wouldn't really guess that gluttony is as much a deadly sin as lust.'

'Is it?' asked Dominic.

'One of the famous seven,' said Alison.

'And if the Church did take it seriously,' said Tessa, 'we would hear as much about the wicked modern world whipping up temptations to greed as we do now about sexy advertising and sleazy films.'

'Jesuits would rise in the pulpits,' said Hubert, smiling, 'and fulminate against those juicy posters for New Zealand lamb!'

'And instead of condemning the brothels in Soho and admiring the restaurants . . . !' Laughter was overtaking them.

Suddenly Ben got up, took a packet of spearmint chewing gum from his pocket, and solemnly offered one to Alison. She shook her head. He passed the packet round the circle. Somehow, nobody fancied it. When it returned to him he shook the five sticks on to the table, beside the Bible from which they had just been reading. 'If there isn't any further argument against contraceptives, this is serious,' he said.

Theodore tried again. 'Shall we say that the Church is bearing witness to the duty to raise children,' he said. 'Marriage is for that purpose. Deliberately to be infertile is an abuse.'

'But the jump between believing that one ought to have children, and it would be wrong to get married for sex while intending never to have them, and concluding that it is a mortal sin to use a contraceptive on Tuesday night . . .' said Tessa.

'Concluding that it is wrong to preserve one's wife's health so that she can safely have six children, by spacing them out a bit . . .' said Dominic.

'Is one to conclude that a person who knew themselves infertile for some reason could not without sin get married?' asked Hubert.

'The stuff about the sin of Onan is a bit baffling, too,' said Dominic. 'It clearly applies to condoms; but what about this new pill – the thing they are testing in Puerto Rico? Would it apply to that?'

'It is already clear that the official line will be that it does,' said Theodore, 'and, incidentally, it is far from clear that the thing will be safe. I think I would be sorry to see the Church allowing a method dangerous to health, while continuing to condemn safe ones.'

'We ought to keep up with all this, I suppose,' said Hubert.

'Well, where?' asked Alison. 'Is there a *Contraceivers Gazette*?'

'Oh, I suppose we shall be told enough about it,' said Theodore.

'What always strikes me about the sin of Onan,' said Ben, 'is that Onan was being abominably unkind. He was humiliating someone.'

Tessa bent on him a steady gaze, and a slight frown. This, which he took to be serious agreement, was in fact bafflement. She was not quite sure exactly what the sin of Onan was.

'You mean, perhaps it was that which angered God, rather more than the mess on the floor?' said Hubert.

'The question you will all have to face,' said Theodore, as the great bell of Merton, heard in the distance, brought their discussion time to an end, 'is, doubting, as certain theologians do, whether the teaching of the Church is right, you will nevertheless in your own lives obey it.'

'None of us has doubted our duty to obey, Father,' said Ben.

'And the teaching of the Church is what it is. It cannot change, after all,' said Tessa.

'It changed tack about usury, though, didn't it?' said Hubert cheerfully, pulling on his coat.

Yet they were all, really – even Ben who was several years older, even Theodore who was considerably the oldest – in the grip of the single most pervasive delusion of youth. The young all master the times into which they are born as though they were learning the nature of the world, confusing 'now' with 'always henceforward'. Only when someone has lived through more than one epoch, more than one climate of opinion, only when times have changed does it appear how gimcrack and temporary is the spirit of the age – any age. Only when the light changes does one become aware of the colour of the light. In the fifties, people did not know what it was to be of the fifties. The times into which one is born have as much relationship to the nature of the world as the prevailing hemline has to human anatomy. But none of Tessa's circle realized that, then.

Outside, on the cold cobblestones of the alleyway, Ben stomped and rubbed his hands, and declared haste. He was expected at a rehearsal for a quartet playing at a college carol service. Theodore and Tessa wandered down to Folly Bridge, and stood shivering, looking at the flinty water, the dejected barges along the margin of the meadow, and the rain-washed boaty tat of Salter's yard.

'You said something in the meeting that I'm turning over in my mind,' Theodore told her. 'You are very bright sometimes, Tessa. I don't think any theologian has thought of it.'

'Coo! What was it?'

'That remark about a jump between a general obligation and Tuesday night! I suppose that accepting a duty to be fertile doesn't really necessarily entail a duty to be fertile on every occasion.'

'That's it – that word "occasion" worries me. I mean I don't think married people think of sex – I don't know of course, but I'm sure they don't – as a sequence of disconnected occasions. I think physical feelings for someone are just a part of loving them, and the love is continuous.'

'Occasions being how a celibate clergy thinks of sex, whose only experience of it is disconnected lapses into sin. It's a terminology of acts – talk about the intrinsic nature of the act. It comes, though, from very respectable sources. It's from St Thomas rendering Aristotle.'

'This reminds me: I once confessed to pride, and was asked, "How many times?" But surely neither sins nor virtues are necessarily acts.'

'And acts are not necessarily sinful or virtuous? I wish I knew more about ordinary, non-theological ways of thinking about life! And I'm very cold; come and have a coffee.'

'You're nearly always cold; I shall knit you a woolly. Would you be allowed to wear it?'

'So long as it's black. Yes please.'

'OK. Let's buy the wool now, and then have coffee.'

'The coffee is fairly urgent.'

'But we're passing Alice's sheep shop right now!'

Later, clutching a parcel of subfusc wool wrapped in newspaper and tied up with string – having found first the Tackley, and then the Cadena, and then Fuller's Tea Shop overcrowded, noisy and steamy – they finished in Tessa's room with a shilling in the gas meter, two mugs of tea and three soggy biscuits from the less-than-airtight tin. Tessa sat in the venerable cane chair, and Theodore knelt on the hearth rug at her feet, facing the fire, working his blue fingers in the blast of heat. His hair was finely beaded with the cold drizzle outside. An involuntary gesture took her hand to his head and smoothed the hair gently back from his forehead.

At once he turned, still on his knees, put his arms round her legs and laid his head in her lap. They stayed very still while the room gradually defrosted around them.

'Do you mind this?' he said at last, sighing.

'No,' she said. 'But I can't call a man Theodore while he has his head in my lap. Such an unwieldy name. Don't you have a nickname?'

'I'd like one,' he said. 'Give me one.'

'It doesn't shorten easily,' she said.

'American Theodores are called Teds,' he said, muffled. 'Shall I be Ted?'

'Not Ted,' she said. 'Tod. Tod suits you better.'

He looked up at her, startled. 'The fox?' he said. 'Why? Because I am red-haired?'

'Not that.'

'Because I am hunted then? Do I seem hunted?'

'Perhaps. But not that either. Because you are foxed.'

'Frustrated. Well, I can't deny that.'

'No,' she said laughing, and lightly touching his cheek, the pale, softly mottled and freckled skin. 'Foxed like an old book!'

'Ah,' he said. 'Your Tod I am then.'

She removed her fingers from his cheek, and gently lifted his arms away from her, getting up to turn down the fire. The sense of him lingered on her fingers, surprising, his face so slack and soft compared to the taut cheeks of any young man she had ever embraced so far.

'My dear,' he said, getting up, 'when you reached out and touched me just then, was it not just an occasion, but an aspect of a way you feel about me, continuously?'

'Yes!' she said, smiling. Tod's love talk, delivered

with such passion, was so comically unpractised and stilted. 'Shouldn't I have done it? I'm sorry; I couldn't help myself . . .'

'You are to do with me anything you like,' he said. 'I am wholly at your mercy. Whatever you want is what I want; like that aria in *Don Giovanni* – do you know it? I trust you. I know you will not let anything bad happen.'

Below them in the resonant lower reaches of the building, the siren began the clamour that signalled the departure time for visitors in the comic quasi-nunnery in which she spent her days and nights.

'Dearest Tod,' she said.

He had gone before the dinner bell, which followed two minutes later.

The next morning, in her pigeonhole was a 45rpm gramophone record: Anton Dermota singing bits of *Don Giovanni* . . . And a note that said, 'Don't write; any letters to me may at any time be opened. I will write to you. See you next term. God bless you. Tod.'

She stared at this missive in confusion, then slowly realized. Sure enough the back hall was full of trunks, the corridors full of voices. The other note for her summoned her to her end of term report.

'Miss Brownlaw,' said her tutor, regarding her severely over a clutch of notes, 'has a butterfly mind, floating gracefully from *flaa* to *flaa*, giving its full attention to none. This term a remarkable phenomenon has occurred; at the same time Miss Brownlaw's work has shown a suddenly improved perception as to what, exactly, the Elizabethan and metaphysical poets were writing about and a suddenly disimproved discipline, punctuality and attentiveness . . .' She put down her notes and gazed fiercely at Tessa. 'Whereas in the nature of things my pupils are liable to fall in love from time to time, I feel bound to point out that it is not because of the merits of Oxford as a marriage market that a long-suffering tax-payer pays your tuition fees. At this very moment there languishes in a provincial university a young person who but for you would occupy your place here, and who might very well be willing to make better use of it. Happy Christmas.'

Tessa went back to St Winnie's dejected, and began to pack. She had little heart for the task, and indeed, after a while piling things up in a desultory fashion, she lay down on her bed and wept. Then she got up at tea time, phoned home, went to see Reverend Mother to negotiate another night in her room, and started to pack in earnest. She couldn't find her Jerusalem Bible. The cell used the Jerusalem, as the most up-to-date and scholarly Bible available, all newly translated from original languages, and much more accurate than a version based on the Vulgate. The fact that it was obtainable only in French presented no difficulty, (though *Voilà l'hippopotame* made one wince for *Lo, Leviathan*) but ensured that no copy would be found in bookshop or library in North Finchley. Anyway, it had cost a lot. She thought she must have left it in the Newman Rooms; certainly she couldn't remember having it since the last cell meeting. Well, it wasn't far; nowhere in Oxford was far. She had not lost a Londoner's astonishment at a city that you could walk right round. After supper she set out to retrieve her book.

It was a beautiful clear night, bitterly cold, and lavishly displaying stars. There was no moon, but the Camera and Saint Mary's were floodlit. Somewhere down the Botley Road a peal of bells was ringing haltingly, suggesting rehearsal; the faint sound of carols leaked out of St Mary's as she passed its windows, seasonally lit from within. Past Tom Tower, which loudly confided the hour of eight to her, and into Rose Place she went, wondering if she would need to disturb Father Max for the keys. But the door of the Newman Rooms was unlocked. A single dim, unshaded light bulb lit the dusty floor of the lower room, and the stair. And from the upper room came music.

She stopped, disconcerted, not wanting to disturb whoever it was. Two people; someone playing a cello, someone playing the grand piano. A dark music, very argued music with a pattern that tried to say there was a meaning, and failed to contain a flood of something else. She stood listening at the foot of the stair for some time, fighting the consonance of the sound with her own mood, hoping for a break in which she could decently go up. When none came for some time, she tiptoed up the stairs anyway.

The players were Ben and Theodore. Ben had his back to her; though Theodore at the piano was facing her, the room was nearly dark and his eyes were bent on the music, brightly lit in front of him. Her Bible, with its battered oxblood covers, lay in sight on the end of the bookcase across the room. She hesitated; the music argued God. She walked quietly across the room and took her book. She turned, and seeing that neither of them had seen her, or lifted their rapt attention for a moment, she walked quietly back to the staircase and went without a word, pulling the outer door gently to behind her.

Far above her head the disinterested glory of the winter sky arched as before. She felt like an eavesdropper; like the person who hearing what they should not learns only to their own disadvantage. Though she could not think what she had learned that she did not know before. Well, yes; she saw that it had been naïve of her to think that she had, or would ever have, any need to tell Ben anything about Theodore.

Next morning her grandfather's car was at the door; her trunk was loaded, they swept over Magdalen Bridge, and away up Headington Hill. The play was over; the stage had gone dark, the actor had left, and all the bright company of friends in the audience were scattered. Term was over.

* * *

There was, naturally, a comfortable pleasure in being a child again. Tessa slept for most of her first three days at home, and then woke up and played chess with her grandfather, and helped put up streamers and wrap presents. For all the frantic business around her there was a curious stillness in her mind, a state of suspension.

'Who is it, then? Are you going to tell me?' asked her mother after a day or so.

Tessa shrank inwardly. She could not possibly; she did not consider exactly why. But with a sudden inspiration she began to tell her mother about Ben.

Three days later, pat like the resolution of the old comedy, Ben turned up, wanting to take her to a concert in the Festival Hall. He hardly talked to Tessa, in fact, so eager was he to converse pleasantly with her parents. The evening out began with a sung Mass in Westminster Cathedral, continued with the concert, and finished with a meal at Gennaro's; then it was so late Ben brought her all the way home and slept on the sofa. They sat over breakfast, eyed discreetly by Tessa's mother, talking about last night's music and how it certainly wouldn't have done for Hubert, except perhaps as a penitential offering, but how, for themselves, they had enjoyed it vastly. Ben deplored the fact that the Royal Box, which had cost a fortune by upsetting the symmetry and requiring heroic measures to balance the acoustics, had been, as usual, empty. They laughed a lot. The copy of *The Times* they were reading promised the return of students called up for Suez in time for next term. Ben stayed for lunch.

Just as he was leaving he gave her a letter from Theodore, marked, 'By hand.'

'But how . . . ?' she asked.

'I dashed up north to see him,' said Ben. 'He's in a parish, helping out. He's OK.'

The letter had been written in haste; it said only, 'Listen to the record. It will tell you how I think of you.'

Tessa, who did not have a gramophone, went back to reading Chaucer, *omnia opera*, beside the comfortable crackle and hiss of the sitting-room fire and ignored her mother's conspiratorial smiles.

On a colourless, bleak January day – nothing special about it, not bright, not cold, not wet, not anything for the time of year – Tod phoned at last. Tessa, shivering lightly in the unheated dining room where the phone was, staring at the grey garden, melted at the distant voice.

'Am I disturbing you?' he asked. 'Were you working?'

'No. Yes. How are you?'

'Talk to me. I need your voice. Tell me something like the plastic daffodils on the gondolas in Venice.'

'You've lost me. What do you mean?'

'You wouldn't think it could possibly be real . . .'

'A dream upon the waters . . .'

'Yes. And then you see that the flowers on the prows of the gondolas are plastic. And you wouldn't in a million years imagine *that*! So you know you are awake, and the vision around you is real. Say something ordinary and real, Tess. Imagining you is destroying me.'

'Oh, I know what you mean. I keep imagining you, too. We are sucked away by dreaming each other. I've nearly finished your sweater, though. The cat's just come in. Is that what you mean?'

'What did you have for breakfast?'

'Cornflakes.'

'What are you wearing? What are you reading?'

'Old blue lacy sweater. The *Penguin Book of Italian Verse*. Are you all right, Tod?'

'The same. Not all right. But I shall see you soon; I was wondering if there was any chance at all of you coming up a day early. I have to be at a meeting in the morning; I have to make a short speech. But I've got the use of Max's car till the first day of term, and I was thinking if you came to the meeting too, we could go to Kelmscott afterwards.'

'What's that?'

'William Morris's house. Lovely. Not open, but I have an invitation for any time . . . it's by the river.'

'Bablock Hythe direction?'

'Upstream.'

'I'd love to. I don't see why not. When and where?'

'Outside Blackwell's. Eleven.'

'Fine. Not long now.'

'Call me by my secret name.'

'Tod. Dear Tod. Dear Tod . . .'

On the steps of the Clarendon Building, a speaker stood on a tea-chest – not, as it happened, a soap box – addressing the crowd. It was an orderly crowd by comparison with the Suez demonstration, but it was spreading on to the road, and blocking access to the Proctors' Office and the Sheldonian Theatre. Tessa took up a position leaning against the wall of the New Bodleian, and watched. A young woman with a mass of red hair was addressing the crowd on the subject of the appalling iniquity perpetrated by the University on the occasion – Tessa gathered it was last year sometime – when they had awarded to President Truman an honorary degree.

Whatever, Tessa wondered, had President Truman to do with anything? The crowd listened, shouted occasionally, grew. By the time Theodore replaced the woman speaker and scrambled on to the tea-chest, the road was blocked.

'My friends,' said Theodore, his light but always crisp enunciation carrying across the sea of heads between to Tessa's side of the road, 'some of you here today are root-and-branch pacifists, opposed to the use of force in any circumstances, even self-defence. But I am sure there are more of you who think, as I do, that there are some circumstances in which it might be just and necessary to fight a defensive war, and it is to you especially that I wish to speak this morning. If we might have to fight in self-defence, why should we nevertheless abandon instantly all nuclear weapons? I am sure that all of us, of all shades of opinion, are agreed that the only justification for a war would have to be that it was fought in defence of the good; and yet nuclear weapons are so huge, and their side-effects so sinister and widespread, and the retaliation they would provoke so certain, that it is certain they cannot be used for any such purpose. Using them will destroy the good along with the threatened evil; using them will never be the lesser of two evils . . .'

'Hey!' someone suddenly shouted from beside Tessa. 'Hey you! I was in a Jap prisoner of war camp! Do you hear me? I was in a . . .'

And looking towards the raucous heckler, Tessa saw beyond him, marching round from Holywell, a contingent of policemen.

'. . . from 1945 to the end of time, anyone who uses nuclear weapons will be a war criminal,' Theodore was saying, 'and that includes President Truman, whose honour dishonours this ancient university . . .'

At which point a surge of people moving away in front of the line of bobbies displaced Tessa and swept her out of earshot. The crowd pushed down the Broad towards the taxi rank, where there was more space. She found herself standing beside the heckler, on tiptoe, straining to see back.

'He wouldn't know a war criminal if you stuffed one up his arse,' said the heckler.

But his remark was lost in a roar of laughter from all around. The police had brought a van up Catte Street, and were unloading and setting up a pair of temporary traffic lights, some road-up signs and cordons, and a chaotic struggle ensued while some people attempted to get outside the cordons, and others to sit down within them. Those deviants who tried both – sitting down but outside the cordons – were instantly arrested – several Black Marias were now parked in Hertford Lane. A tentative line of cars began to get through the cleared half of the street. A policeman asked Tessa to 'Move along there, now, miss,' and she automatically did, withdrawing further away though all the time craning her head to keep Theodore in view. He was still speaking, though she could no longer hear a word above the uproar. A rhythmic chant of 'Ban-the-Bomb' accompanied by various yells of disagreement drowned out his now distant voice.

But though she could no longer hear him, she could still see, more or less. The police were doggedly clearing the whole area, including access up the steps of the Clarendon Building for the procession to Convocation which was expected at noon, and for that they needed to remove the speaker on his box. And Theodore must have declined to move on, for Tessa clearly saw him lifted from his perch by two officers, and marched off towards the Black Marias.

There was bedlam in the police station. The entire demonstration seemed to have reconvened there in very confined space; everyone who had not been arrested having dashed down there, like Tessa, in pursuit of someone else who had. A long line of people was waiting for the attention of the duty officers behind the desk and the friends and relations were packed, standing-room only in a waiting area. An old lady was determinedly trying to register the loss of her cat to a beefy and heroically patient station sergeant, whom she could hear only if he shouted at stentorian volume.

Tessa tried to hear through the yells of 'Did you say *tabby, Madam*?' to the process going on beyond. It was perfectly simple. 'Are you a member of the University?' each culprit in turn was asked. Then 'Name and college?' And once that was written down, people were released and left, taking their anxious attendants with them. Gradually the press of people around Tessa diminished, until there was room to sit down on the rows of schoolroom benches.

'Why do they want to know which college?' she asked a young man sitting beside her.

'They're washing their hands of it. They'll just report everyone to the proctors.'

'What will the proctors do?'

'Fine them. More than the beak would, probably.'

'That's not very fair.'

'What's fair? The cops and the proctors have got it all sewn up. The cops will even frog-march you back to the college gates if they find you out after midnight. Didn't you know?' He looked round at Tessa. 'Well, perhaps you wouldn't. We're all just waiting for them to pick on someone with enough money to go after them for wrongful arrest.'

Just then their attention was drawn by a grey-haired somewhat scruffy-looking man who said crisply, 'Yes, I am a member of the University. But I am not *in statu pupillari*. I am a senior member.'

The policeman at the desk withdrew to consult with an officer sitting in a remote recess behind the counter. 'Charge him,' this individual said.

A dreadful thought struck Tessa. Was Theodore a senior member? Surely not; he was doing a further degree of some kind. But then he also did some teaching, she thought . . . she wasn't at all sure what his status was.

And there he was, at the head of the queue. 'Are you a member of the University?' said the constable, boredom in every note of his voice.

'I decline to say,' said Theodore.

Slowly the policeman put down his pencil, placing it carefully parallel with his notebook on the desk. He straightened up and confronted Theodore with a chilly stare.

'Now why would you do that, sir?' he said.

'You have no right to ask me. The laws about obstructing the highway apply alike to everyone in this country whether or not they are members of the University, or of any other private organization.'

'Who says you will be charged with obstructing the highway? In my opinion, sir, it is more likely you will be charged with obstructing one of my colleagues in the execution of his duty.'

'Just the same. The laws about obstructing the police – and, incidentally, the laws of free speech – are the same for members of the University as for anybody else.'

Tessa listened with a sinking heart.

'People have been known to prefer,' said the policeman, 'having their names passed to the proctors, when the alternative is appearing in court and acquiring a criminal record. Not to say, reverend, that a criminal record is unheard of in your profession, but there are some who are averse to getting one, all the same.'

'I have not committed any offence,' said Theodore, 'and I will not answer any questions, or give you any information about myself except my name and address, which I am legally obliged to give you.'

'As you wish, sir. Your name and address then.' He wrote it down, and carried it back to the superintendent. Tessa watched as the address was carried round and shown to every policeman in turn. 'Is this a University establishment?' he was asking. Nobody seemed to know. Someone suggesting telephoning 'That Mongsenior. He'll know.' The constable despatched a woman police officer to make the call, but she came back with the news that Monsignor Howe was away, and not expected back till tomorrow evening.

Obstinately the policeman plodded to the back of the room, took a battered copy of the *University Directory* from the shelf and, drawing up a chair to a corner of an occupied desk, began to search through it.

Theodore, standing waiting impassively, with an increasingly restive group of people behind him, cast a rueful glance at Tessa and followed it with one of his rare and dazzling smiles. She was too dejected to respond.

Soon the fatal words, 'Charge him,' were heard from the distant powers, and Theodore was led away. As he went he turned and said over his shoulder, 'Sorry about Kelmscott.'

Tessa rose and, on shaking legs, got herself up to the desk. 'Please tell me what will happen to him,' she said to the officer who had taken his address.

'We'll hold him in the cells overnight, and bring him up before the magistrates in the morning, miss. Nothing terrible. This isn't Russia, you know. And we do a good breakfast in this station.'

'And in the morning what will happen to him?'

'A fine. I can't say how much, that's up to the court. Now if you don't mind, miss, I've got a lot to do.'

'Sorry,' she said. 'Thanks.' And she began to walk back to St Winnie's. She was feeling weak and shaky, and light in the head. As she passed the bakery in the Cornmarket the smell of bread suddenly ambushed her, and she realized that it was now five o'clock, and she had not eaten a crumb since very early breakfast that morning in London. And how she despised herself when a hot meat pie and four doughnuts gave her strength, and made the disaster seem less fearful than before!

The disaster, however, had not yet run its course. The magistrate was choleric and patriotic. He was also incredibly stupid. Though the only question it fell to him to decide was whether certain individuals had obstructed the police, he seemed to think that his own opinion of the subject of the demonstration was relevant, and delivered himself of a comparison between those who objected to nuclear defence now and those undergraduates who had notoriously provoked World War Two by declining to fight for King and Country. An immaculate barrister appearing in defence of the scruffy senior member reminded him courteously that freedom of speech was one of the matters which the undergraduates in question had been called upon to defend, and a remarkably bad-tempered discussion ensued in which the magistrate announced his intention of making an example of anyone in a senior position who had given a bad example and led the young into trouble. Anybody could guess that all this was going to be bad for Theodore, whose case was being called next and who was conducting his own defence. And so it was.

The impartial majesty of the law, however, is constrained to acknowledge fact. Theodore was acquitted of the charge of obstructing the highway because the steps of the Clarendon Building, from which he had been removed, are the private property of the University and, although adjacent to and open to the carriageway, do not form any part of it. But he was convicted of obstructing the police. The solid sergeant, reading from his notes, mentioned that the accused had been very uncooperative, and Theodore got twenty-five pounds or fourteen days.

Whereupon Theodore announced that he would, in that case, go to prison, as he had no money to pay the fine.

The magistrate heaved a huge audible sigh. 'It gives me no pleasure to send a heretofore respectable person to prison,' he said. 'Would you like to have time to pay?' A last flicker of hope entered Tessa's mind at this.

But no, said Theodore. His religious superior paid his keep; he did not have, and never would have, any money with which he could pay a fine.

'Isn't there anybody you could borrow from?' said the magistrate.

Theodore said he would rather be imprisoned unjustly than acquire a debt he could not pay to discharge an unjust fine.

Whereupon the magistrate said, 'Oh, take him away,

before I lose my temper!' and for the second time in two days Tessa found herself wandering away into Oxford in a state of shock.

To go where, exactly? Where in Oxford, out of term, was she going to find twenty-five pounds? She had her first month of term allowance from her mother in the bank – nine pounds – and a present of five from her grandfather. That still left more than ten to find. Ben, of course. Ben would fall over himself to help. But Ben was in retreat somewhere in London. The name of the place was in his last letter to her, in her writing case back in her room at St Winnie's. She began to run.

The telephone number wasn't hard to find, but the number rang interminably and nobody answered. Increasingly frantic, Tessa tried again and again, and at last was found in the phone lobby, in floods of tears, by Cathy.

'Tess! Whatever is wrong?'

'Cathy! Am I glad to see you! I thought no-one would be here till tomorrow.'

'You look upset. Come along. I'll make you a coffee. No; don't refuse, you need it. You can try that number, whatever it is, in a minute.'

'I'm trying to get hold of Ben.'

'Well, that can wait a few minutes.'

'It isn't just a chat,' she said, meekly following Cathy upstairs, wiping her wet cheeks with the flat of her hands. 'I need money. Cathy – I suppose you couldn't lend me some; just till I can get hold of Ben?'

'I'm sorry, Tess,' said Cathy, filling the kettle. 'I haven't got a bean. I've just been fined the entire term's money.'

'You! Were you there too?'

'I certainly was. I feel very strongly about it.'

'I didn't know . . .'

'You never asked me. Why were *you* there?'

'Waiting for someone.'

'Did they nab you? I didn't see you in the cells.'

'No, I'm afraid I'm Simon Peter, disassociating myself.

Certainly I'll step aside, officer, nothing to do with me . . .'

'You've got more sense than I have, then. I don't know what Daddy will say when I need the money all over again.'

'What? Oh, yes. Have some sympathy,' said Tessa. She looked at her watch, considering the possibility of London, and found to her amazement that it was only half past eleven. Time had congealed, and was dragging a rallentando through her woe.

'Look, thanks for the coffee, Cathy, but I must try to get hold of Ben . . .'

Tessa hauled her bike from the sheds, rode frantically for the station, and just caught the twelve o'clock down.

Once in the train, sitting still and with nothing to do but sit still until she got to London, she wept uncontrollably. How a little hindsight would have consoled her! Had she known how many respectable people would maintain a high moral tone in and out of prison cells; had she foreseen a time when one would apologize at dinner parties for never having been arrested at a demo . . . But then, her only knowledge of prison being derived from Oscar Wilde, it was hard to keep Theodore's fourteen days in due proportion. A woman in the opposite seats stared uneasily, but said nothing. Outside the train window a blurred and floating panorama of the bleak brown winter fields and pale sky slipped past her unfocused, flooded gaze. A row of battered, sodden stooks that had missed harvest home stood like desolate dwarf wigwams. By the time they reached Reading the sky was the same colour as the miles of undulating wet slate roofs, except that the slates gleamed, and the sky was smeared with smoke from the effluent of chimneys.

At Paddington she ran out of Brunel's great glass and iron pavilion, and found a bus going up the

Finchley Road. The retreat house was a huge red-brick pile, like a refugee from North Oxford, and it was guarded by a gnarled man with an Irish accent who sat in a lobby inside a huge cold hall. A frozen pot-plant suffered in a brass bowl at the foot of an elaborate and ugly stair. After what seemed ages the porter brought to Tessa, now dry-eyed, a young man in a soutane and dog collar, who took her into a little parlour off the hall and heard her out.

'Someone we know is in terrible trouble,' she said simply, 'and I think Ben can help. Please let me speak to him, or at least give him a message.'

'Is this person in Dr Marshall's family?' asked the young priest.

'What? I don't understand . . .' Tessa was startled at Ben's title; it was easy to forget he was a don.

'Is Dr Marshall the next of kin?'

'No. It is just a friend. But please – it's very urgent.'

'And the unfortunate person who is in need has no family of their own?'

'Well, no, it's just that he's . . .' She broke off. Something warned her not to say that Theodore was a priest, and probably was being penalized for that.

'You see, when we receive people on retreats here, Miss Brownlaw, we make the rules very clear to them. Only for a disaster to next of kin will we break the all-too-short isolation from the world. If all the world's concerns and troubles can come and go through the place, what is the point of retiring here, and how can anyone collect themselves?'

'I know,' said Tessa, 'I am wholly and entirely certain that Ben would want to be told, he would want to do something . . .'

'And I am equally certain that Dr Marshall wished to have a few days for meditation and prayer set apart from the cares of the world, and did not wish to have them thrust upon him. I must ask you to leave now.'

'But this is ridiculous!' she cried. 'What if someone close to him were dying?'

'In such a case we would indeed consider breaking the retreat,' said the cold voice. 'But you, young woman, do not have any such reason.'

'How can you know what I want?' said Tessa, struggling with tears again. 'How can you know?'

'I am old enough to know that the prospect of death makes people solemn rather than hysterical. In the light of eternity, whatever it is that so excites you can surely wait until lunch time on Friday. Pray for a sense of proportion.' He held the door of the room open for her. She rushed out, right across the hall to the foot of the stairs, and cupping her hands to her mouth, she yelled, 'Ben! Ben!' at the top of her voice.

Someone grabbed her at once from behind, clapping over her mouth a row of strong fingers reeking of nicotine. Thus gagged she was lifted off her feet, carried rapidly across the hall and out of the door. Dumped on the doorstep she heard the door close and latch securely behind her.

So she found herself wandering about Hampstead in a rapidly darkening afternoon. She asked the way to a Catholic church, and knelt in the gloom – all the candles to Our Lady had guttered out, and there were no lights on – and asked God what she should do. No very obvious inspiration came to her. The place was ugly, elaborately decorated, cluttered with piety. At the back of the transept a huge stall sold holy books, pictures, rosaries, dreadful plaster St Josephs, medals and crucifixes. A miasma of stale incense hung around. And Tessa was lost. She suddenly saw it as though from outside, as though she were a heathen mind considering dispassionately whether this could be the Kingdom of God upon earth. Wasn't Christ against selling things in church and in favour of helping those in prison? 'Oh Lord Jesus,' she said inwardly, praying suddenly fluently and easily, 'who takes any notice of You, really? Help me help Theodore, who is after all more Yours than mine!'

Calmer, she emerged and took a bus back to

Paddington, to find she had just missed a train. She stood around at the end of platform eight, waiting wearily for the next one. Someone suddenly swung bags down beside her and putting a hand on each of her shoulders, said from behind her, 'Guess who!'

'Richard?'

'She'd know me anywhere! Progress at last, Angel Face!' he said happily, and then, catching sight of her face, 'Why whatever is the matter, Tess? Are you ill?'

And indeed, Tessa seemed to be swaying on her feet. Richard caught her firmly and held her against his khaki greatcoat. 'Let me get you on the train,' he said. 'You were on your way to Oxford?' She nodded. 'No luggage, at the beginning of term?' he asked. 'Never mind, let me get you sitting down, and then you can explain.' He found an empty carriage and put his own cases on the rack. 'Now you just sit there, tell them not to go without me and I'll get us some coffee,' he said, striding off towards the station buffet.

'What about the cups?' she managed, as she sipped the tasteless hot comforting liquid, and the train snorted and pulled out.

'The train will be coming back,' he said. 'Now girl, what's up?'

She told him. She told him she could not bear to think of Theodore locked up, in squalor . . .

'Well, then, we'll have to get him out,' said Richard. 'Dry your eyes, my dear, I will bail the bugger. As soon as we get there, Tess. Cheer up, I'll pay his fine and go and get him, and we'll all have supper together. How's that?'

'You would really? For someone you don't know?'

'Well, I have actually met the fellow – once. In fact, quite a promising relationship seems to be developing. The first time I nearly clobber him – so sorry, took you for a footpad; and the second time I spring him from a dungeon – hope you don't mind, old man, people do feel strongly about these things, it isn't a month since I was thinking of going to prison myself. I can't wait to see what our third encounter will bring . . . What, no smiles, Angel Face? You've had a bad day, I can see that . . .'

'Oh, Richard,' said Tessa. 'Dear Richard, how was the army?' And leaning against his shoulder she fell abruptly and deeply asleep.

At Oxford in the dark he put Tessa, sombrely awake and almost hopeful, in a taxi. 'By the time you've dropped my bags off in the porter's lodge, and got yourself to St Winnie's,' he said, 'I'll be there with Father Whatsit. Promise.'

Richard was as good as his word in not taking long. Tessa had hardly reached her room, and sat down on the bed, hands folded, heart beating palpably, when he was there. But he came alone.

'I'm sorry, Tessa, I was too late,' he said. 'There was competition for the job. Monsignor Something was there wanting to do it for me. Give me credit for trying, love, but it seems your Theodore's fine was paid by the Father Provincial of his order this afternoon, and he was driven off at once and hasn't been seen since.'

Whether Theodore would be happier in the custody of the Father Provincial than in the custody of the prison service Tessa could not imagine. A Father Provincial, presumably, would dislike his priests getting arrested; but then if Theodore was right about the teaching of the Church the Father Provincial would necessarily agree with Theodore about nuclear weapons. Would he think therefore, that it was a Christian duty to demonstrate against Convocation about honorary degrees? However Theodore was, well or ill, it was certain he was cut off from Tessa; she could not attempt to reach him with consolation, when her letters might be opened. And, of course, she did not even know where he was. And could not, without disastrous self-revelation, attempt to find out.

So dazed and obsessed was she that she was astonished that snow began falling, that people kept arriving back, unpacking, eating, talking, singing in the stairwell outside her room and generally demonstrating that life would go on. Reluctantly – but what else could she do? – Tessa joined in. She plodded across the Park to Hartland House, got her first essay titles and began to work.

When Ben arrived, she rushed to find him in his rooms and tell him the horrible story. He was concerned about Theodore, disconcertingly inclined to see the Father Provincial as a happy ending, and not impressed at all by Tessa's anger at having been turned away from the retreat house.

'Tessa, you do dramatize! Theodore was not in great trouble; the Provincial was already on his way to bail him, as it happens. And, my dear, you are too quick to claim not to be "the world" to me; you have not agreed to marry me. You are, as things were left between us, still thinking about it. When the retreat father asked me if I was engaged to anybody, I naturally said no.'

'They told you that I was there, trying to see you, and you didn't come?'

'No, Tessa. Nothing so dramatic. They wanted to know if you had a claim on me. They asked me if I had a fiancée, and I said no. That is the truth, isn't it? Or is this conversation an acceptance?'

'No, it isn't. I'm still thinking about it. And right now I'm too angry to think.'

'You haven't any reason to be angry, Tessa, believe me.'

'How can we find out where Theodore is?'

'He'll let us know when he can.'

'Isn't there any discreet way of finding out? Ben, aren't you worried about him?'

'I'll ask Father Max when I get a chance,' said Ben.

* * *

So the term which had started so dramatically settled into dullness. The weather was dismally cold. Tessa read Chaucer, and then the Scottish Chaucerians.

> A dooly season to a careful wight
> should correspond, and be equivalent . . .

she read. She wrote essays, sat through lectures, finished Theodore's sweater, and packed it up ready to send, somewhere . . . At the end of the second week there was a letter from him in her pigeonhole.

He was in disgrace. The Father Provincial thought politics and religion did not mix. He had forbidden Theodore to take any further part in campaigning against nuclear weapons, and had ordered him not to return to Oxford. Theodore's studies were suspended; he was to work in a poor industrial parish in the Midlands. He had no idea how long for – as long as the Father Provincial thought fit. There didn't seem to be any way he could phone her; he had tried to get her at St Winnie's, but whoever answered had not been willing to climb three flights of stairs to fetch her to the phone. He begged her to write to him, but carefully; the Italians, he added, said *'Ti voglio Bene'* for 'I love you'.

So she packed up his sweater with a note that finished, 'Wishing you well', and went back to Chaucer.

Ben made a chance to talk to Father Max and brought a gloomy tale to Tessa. The Father Provincial had been grooming Theodore for promotion in the Order; his studies were to qualify him to hold his own on behalf of the Church with any in the land. But the Father Provincial was disgusted with Oxford. It had got his ewe-lamb into trouble, and into bad company – 'Gone to his head,' were the words.

Cooling off for a while in the real world was what the Father Provincial now thought would do Theodore good. 'But Max didn't like it a bit,' Ben reported. 'Max said Theodore was unacquainted with the real world, and unfit for it. "If he doesn't find one kind of martyrdom, he'll find another," Max said. "He's delicate; the Father Provincial won't see that, being of coarser clay." '

'Father Max thinks Theodore is some kind of saint?' said Tessa, wondering.

'No. Some kind of child. I got the strong impression Max doesn't approve of martyrdom; it isn't gentlemanly!'

Days passed. It stopped snowing. Tessa's essay on Troilus and Criseyde got high praise and they moved to Langland. Ben took her out to dinner and made her laugh with accounts of very elderly dons, taken back into college on the deaths of wives and weaving wild eccentricity into the ethos of the common room. Richard seemed careful, watching his step. He no longer teased and flirted in the lecture halls; he took her out once to dinner, and once to watch Torpids rowed, and complained that she seemed to him to be sleepwalking these days. 'Wake up, Angel Face; you have eaten a poisoned apple!' he said, delivering her to her door after a Langland lecture.

She shook her head. 'I'm awake, really,' she said. 'But things seem, well, disorganized. Desultory – that's the word I want.'

'The word I want is yes,' he said.

'Yes to what?'

'Ah, well, a general, all-purpose blank cheque sort of yes was too much to hope for, especially since I didn't get sent to prison,' he said. 'Just, shall we go home next weekend and eat one of Mother's good dinners?'

'Yes, please!' she said.

'Oh,' said Richard. 'Good. Somehow I thought you'd say no.'

'Rot, Richard. I'll look forward to it.'

And she would look forward to it; but with only the palest shadow of the longing and expectation with which she looked forward to Tod's letters, for which she was consumed with longing although they caused her only pain.

'Adored Beatrice,' he wrote,

Forgive me many times over for the disappointment you must have felt when I did not take you to Kelmscott as arranged. My punishment is severe enough in the Father Provincial's eyes – exile from Oxford; he does not know, of course, that exile from you makes it into perfect hell. The work here gives me some comfort; the people are poorer than you can imagine, and live in terrible conditions, but they are brave and cheerful, and they need their religion as luckier folk need food and drink. Most of them work in the engineering shops, or in making various fittings for ships. But the company I am in is terrible. The parish priest is worldly and boring. The curate is nice enough, but very badly taught; he preaches a different heresy every Sunday. The thought that these two have been set to watch me makes me cringe with shame. We live in great comfort and luxury, central heating turned up high, quantities of excellent food, and wine with every meal – well, drink with every meal, because the curate has beer with breakfast. The housekeeper waits on us hand and foot. And all this is paid for out of money contributed by the parishioners in their damp and bare houses. I feel defiled and incriminated by it – I can hardly bring myself to eat. I have turned off the radiator in my room and I wear your sweater instead. Thank you.

I wonder what you did with the day we should have had at Kelmscott? Write and tell me – that can hardly harm even if the awful priest does open and read it. I think of you day and night, and you are always in my prayers. Dearest, do listen to that record some time.

With love, from Tod, your poor fox . . .

Tessa took the record from between two books and plodded down the corridor to Cathy's room.

'Could we play this on your gramophone?' she asked. 'It's important.'

So she sat, back to the fire on Cathy's hearth rug, and Cathy, deep in her book lay on the bed, and the needle scratched and lurched, and then the room filled with a clear tenor voice . . .

> Dalla sua pace,
> La mia dipende,
> Quel che a lei piace,
> Vita mi rende . . .

'I think I need to understand the words,' said Tessa. She found a pencil and notepad on Cathy's desk, returned the needle to the start of the record, and tried to write.

'Here, let me,' said Cathy. 'I know them anyway.'

> Quel che a lei incresce
> Morte mi da,
> Morte, morte mi da!

sang the voice. Cathy wrote the words, translated *incresce*, which baffled Tessa, and then put the record on again. She lit a cigarette, leaned back against the wall and watched Tessa weeping soundlessly, kneeling on the rug.

When the record ended Tessa got up and put it on again. Cathy took her hand and drew her down to sit on the bed. She wept on Cathy's shoulder.

'Sorry,' she said, muffled in Cathy's sweater, as the needle scratched across the centre yet again.

'Lucky you,' Cathy said softly. 'Nobody feels like that about me, now. Nobody. Count yourself lucky. And let's have some sherry before the dinner gong, shall we? I have just a smidgen left . . .'

* * *

'Dearest Tod,' Tessa wrote,

I spent the Kelmscott day frantically keeping track of you, and the next day trying to raise twenty-five pounds. You might like to know that with the help of a good friend I had succeeded by six o'clock; though too late. The term just goes on, as you can predict. We have moved from Chaucer to Langland. My tute partner astonished me the other day by saying she wished that she had been brought up a Catholic. (She is as irreligious as you can imagine.) When I asked why, she said that it was impossible she should still believe such a farrago of nonsense, so it would not inconvenience her, while on the other hand she would easily understand Langland's obscure sacramental vision, as I did, without labouring in difficult footnotes!

You have my approval turning down the heat in your room as long as the sweater keeps you warm, but you really must eat. Should you take things on your conscience which are not of your own doing? Do you not sleep, and work, and eat, under a vow of obedience to the Father Provincial, and if anything in your situation is morally sleazy, is it not then the Father Provincial who is responsible?

Remember me in your prayers, as you are remembered in mine.

Wishing you well,
Tessa

PS I borrowed a gramophone, and played the record. Thank you. I feel just that about you.

Richard's mother duly provided the good dinner on Saturday. His brother Jeremy was at home, with a young wife, very cool and graceful, and a baby that wailed from upstairs and had everyone dancing attendance. Two huge golden retrievers lay across the hearth rug in front of a log fire, and the talk was about oil, and how, after the Suez affair, we were to get it. Richard's brother seemed to know a lot about it; not, Tessa gathered, because he worked in oil directly, but because he worked in the City.

By and by Richard noticed that she was bored; she listened, but could have nothing to say, and Richard's mother was nodding quietly over her needlework, drowsing. 'Let's play croquet!' he said.

'Silly,' said his mother, waking up. 'Quite dark. And the lawn is frozen. Shall I find the mah-jong, if you want a game?'

'No; croquet or nothing. Ice-croquet if need be. It might be a wonderful variant game. Who'll play?'

'I will,' said Tessa, standing up, 'if you show me. I've never played before.'

'We must find survival kit,' said Richard. 'You'll never do in those clothes. Come on!'

They went through the kitchen, into a garden lobby full of coats and boots, and even a gunrack, and chose a tacky gaberdine lined with tartan, which engulfed Tessa to her ankles, and a huge pair of rubber boots, and wrapped her head up in a knitted balaclava and Richard's school scarf.

'Fairest of the fair!' he murmured, looking at her, and leaning forward he kissed her gently on the cheek. Then he put on a number of jackets and overcoats, and opened the back door. 'Light,' he said, picking up a torch.

The garden was pitch dark, beyond the pool of light falling through the windows of the drawing room on to the terrace. They walked to the middle of the lawn. Richard swung the torch round, and Tessa saw the frosted hoops, leaning at crazy angles above the white grass. He lolloped across to a garden shed and brought her a mallet and some balls. 'Stand astride, and swing the mallet between your legs, like this,' he said.

'Like what? I can't see a thing, can I?'

'OK. Look, you take the torch, and shine it on me,

and I'll show you. Like this.' He struck his ball, which rolled away into the blackness. They took a while to find it, waving the torch around.

'You try.'

'Try to what?'

'The idea is to go through all the hoops in turn.'

'Without being able to see!'

'Look, there's your ball, and, hang on . . . here's the hoop. I'll keep the torch on it while you play.'

Tessa swung the mallet at the darkness at her feet. There was a loud click. Moments later her ball rolled demurely into the pool of light round the hoop, and she saw it go smoothly through.

'Wow!' said Richard. And then there was, from somewhere beyond the hoop, another click, and he said, 'Oh hell!'

'What happened?'

'Your ball knocked mine into the flowerbed.'

'Oh, Richard, I'm so sorry . . .'

'Don't be daft; you're allowed to knock my ball away. Vicious, this game. You're a natural.'

'Come on, come on, then; what do we do next?'

'The next hoop. Over there somewhere . . . got it. You hold the torch while I try it, and then I'll hold it for you.'

Her eyes were getting used to the darkness, while her feet froze in the cavernous boots on the ice-bound ground. Above their heads was a great cloudy streamer of stars. The ball rolled towards her, whispering as it broke the frost splints on the blades of grass. Richard loomed out of the darkness and took the torch from her. They whooped and laughed as she hit true again. Then suddenly there were other voices, and another torch. The others had rushed out to join them. 'I've got to try this!' said Jeremy. Lumbering about and laughing they soon lost all the balls in the herbaceous borders. The torchlight wavered on their footprints in the frost. Richard maintained that every ball made a track in the grass, so that you turned the next ball into a tram, forced to follow . . .

'The predestination of the spheres!' she said.

'Right, children,' said Richard's mother at last. 'Indoors at once, and no argument. And mulled claret, before anyone dies of cold.'

It was very painful, thawing fingers and ears and feet before the fire. They all groaned, heaped curses upon Richard, and warned Tessa against having anything to do with him.

Later he drove her back, slowly, on treacherous roads. It seemed likely they would be late; Tessa would be gated. As they went, Tessa watched the white coating on the hedges in the headlights, and Richard said, 'You know, Tessa, I'm always teasing you; I do find your religion a touch preposterous. But I wouldn't be difficult about it; I'd better not promise not to tease you, but I'd never more than tease; you could keep it, love, with me . . .'

'But you do know,' she said, 'it is far more difficult than that. For example, anyone marrying a Catholic has to promise to have the children all brought up in the Church.'

'I wouldn't mind,' he said. 'I think children make up their own minds in the long run.'

'One does not make up one's own mind about being a Catholic.'

'Do Catholics,' he said, very softly, suddenly sounding dangerous, 'make up their own minds about anything?'

'Richard, please remember that I didn't want to go out with you in the first place, and you mocked me for it, and told me you only wanted to have dinner with me, and you were engaged to Cynthia, and all that rot. Please remember that I warned you.'

'Yes,' he said gloomily. 'So you did.'

'My Darling,' Tessa read,

I got your dear letter yesterday. It landed on my plate unopened, which is just as well. Do be careful what you write; merely sounding like a close and special friend would be enough to make trouble, and as for that remark about the Father Provincial!

In fact, I rather wish you were right about the Father Provincial, but I don't think you can be. If you were right then presumably all the clergy in the Church could simply lay their sins on bishops like King Harry's soldiers laying theirs upon the King in *Henry the Fifth*. There has to be something wrong about that; it would make it a dubious act to promise obedience to a bishop, instead of a virtuous one, for it is easy to prove that bishops must all be wicked. Do you doubt that? Let me prove it for you. Everyone knows Acton's famous principle that power corrupts, and absolute power corrupts absolutely. When a man is invited to become a bishop he is offered a great deal of power. He could always refuse the offer. But if he accepts it, then either he knows Acton's law, but thinks it does not apply to him, in which case he is wickedly proud – the sin of Lucifer, no less – or he knows Acton's law and does not care if he is corrupted, in which case also he is steeped in sin. I suppose there is a third possibility, that he is too stupid to know and understand Acton's law . . . Pray for me, Tessa, since I have to hope that the man to whom I vowed obedience is stupid, in case he is something worse. I do not lay my sins on him; I eat as little as I can, and keep the fire turned off, and work as hard as I can for the poor of this dreadful place. In the pulpit, and worse – far worse – in the confessional, I too have power over them. I am afraid. Power corrupts, and spiritual power corrupts spiritually. I feel cold all the time.

Nymph, in thine orisons, be all my sins remembered.

Your poor frozen
Tod

Dear Father Theodore,

I have been wondering what news of Oxford would interest you. The term seems very dull. Father Max has found a stand-in chaplain for the group, a Franciscan called Brother Damian, who is making a lot of changes. Firstly he tried to get Alison and me to leave, and start up a women's group; he doesn't like sanctity co-ed; but all the men stuck up for us rather fiercely. Dominic even said he would leave if we did. So that idea hasn't been mentioned again. Then he doesn't like our traditional kind of meeting; he thinks discussion of moral issues isn't much use; all you need is to know the teaching of the Church, and you don't discuss that; you just ask him to tell you what it is. So for the moment we are transformed into a Bible studies group. There's quite a bit of grumbling, and you are sorely missed. We would all and any of us gladly organize a petition to have you back.

However, curiously enough, since I think the Bible studies were supposed to be non-controversial, he is shaking us all rigid!

For example, he says that the shepherds, the birth of Christ in a stable, the coming of the kings, and so on, are not to be taken as having actually happened. It's just that there were a whole lot of prophecies in the Old Testament about things associated with the coming of the Messiah, and the evangelists, knowing that Christ was the Messiah, put all this stuff in to show that the prophecies had been fulfilled in Christ. But all that they meant to say was that Christ was the Messiah, and that's all we should take as having the authority of the Holy Ghost.

'You mean they cooked the evidence,' said Dominic, and Brother Damian got a bit hot under the collar. Alison pointed out that if in any modern context one caught somebody telling lies in order to prove something one would never believe a word they said again. Brother Damian thinks that the Holy

Ghost would realize that in a modern context there would be nothing to gain and everything to lose by such methods . . . I asked about miracles, and he said, well, the Messiah was known to be going to perform miracles, and so if you preached Christ as the Messiah, you would need him to have performed some . . . We are very confused. Did Christ, do you think, actually say for example the words to Peter on which the claims of the Church are based? Or are those put in because they suited some point the evangelist wished to make? We need you . . .

Wishing you well,

T

Dearest, Dearest Tessa,

I'm sorry; you must let Brother Damian expound his own theology. I have enough responsibility already, without sharing someone else's. But sound opinion would always maintain that the authority for the Bible is derived from the Church, and not the other way about. There is no sign of spring here. I do not think the Father Provincial is going to let me back to Oxford. Read, as if from me, the Cavalcanti in your book of Italian verse; the one that starts, *'Perche io non spero tournar giammi'* . . .

And pray for me, my dearest. I am in great distress of spirit. I have just discovered that a large number of the parishioners are working on a navigation device for launching nuclear weapons. They have so little in this world, and must by this be losing their hope of the next. The parish priest has forbidden me to preach on this subject; but I am sure you would tell me otherwise, even though my caution has silenced the love in your letters, and left me without comfort. Pray for me. I cannot see which way to turn.

Your hunted

Tod

Tessa put this letter in her pocket and took it to the

lecture on Middle English Phonemes. When the lecture was over she rode across to Ben's rooms and waited for his tutorial to end. Before his pupils left the next group came clattering up the stairs, and she had to beg their pardon as she slipped in to see Ben first.

'I've got a very worrying letter from Theodore,' she said. 'When can we talk?'

'So have I, Tess. He almost sounds as if saying goodbye . . .'

'I think he doesn't know what may happen. I think he is thinking of preaching a sermon the parish priest has forbidden.'

'Against the naval weapons factory? Yes; I think he might.'

'And what would happen to him?'

'I don't know. There has to be a limit to what a Father Provincial can do; this isn't medieval Spain. But it wouldn't better his chances of being allowed to complete his degree, I think.'

'Ben, I don't even know what his degree is in.'

'It's a doctoral thesis in mathematics. About the nature of mathematical proof. He has the kind of mathematical brain that only comes along once or twice in a generation. Criminal to waste it.'

'But he has a conscience too. What do you think he should do?'

'Well, I wish to God he would keep out of trouble, and work quietly in Oxford. But he isn't made like that.'

'Can we help him? He sounds so desperate.'

'I've been wondering. I haven't any tutorials tomorrow and I've just one thing I must do this afternoon. I think I'll take the train up tonight and go and talk to him. Caution isn't one of the deadly sins, after all. Do you think he will listen to me?'

'Ben, of course he will! What a good idea; you are kind. I wish I thought I could get an exeat to come too . . .'

'Better not. Clerics are suspicious of women. And,

Tessa, dear . . .' He glanced towards the door, outside which shufflings were now audible. 'I've been meaning to find the right moment to thank you for getting so concerned for him.'

'To thank me?'

'Well, after all, you were doing it for me, weren't you? Because I asked you to. And it has helped; I'm sure it has. I'll come and see you immediately I get back.'

Outside on the staircase Ben's next group of pupils had adopted attitudes of exaggerated patience, and they grinned when she emerged and fled down the spiral steps. She wandered out into the Botanical Gardens, where no visions came to her now, and crossed the High into Magdalen, and through the water-walks, taking a long and lovely way home, trying in the grey open February air to cool her heart and steady herself. She tried, passing the patches of snowdrops on the brown mulchy banks of the lower river, to remember the great vowel shift from the morning's lecture. At the top end of Mesopotamia she walked into the Parks, and found herself, in the end, leaning on the parapet of the Rainbow Bridge, praying for Theodore. Asking God fiercely if martyrdom was, in the divine plan, absolutely necessary.

She made herself late for her tutorial. And then needed books from the college library. So it wasn't till after supper that she returned to her room. And there sitting on her window seat was a Pye Black Box gramophone, with a note propped on it. 'Theodore's letter to me asked me to buy you this. Can't wait, or I'll miss that train. Ben.'

She plugged it in, stroked its lovely varnished lid with her fingertips, and put on *'Dalla sua Pace'*. Again and again. Till Cathy burst into the room saying, 'For God's sake let me lend you some more records!'

Next morning she woke early. A faint rose-tinted glow shone on a small patch of wall over her mantelpiece. It lit the shell in a brief restoration of its one-time pearly glory, abolishing the dust of its present state like the last trumpet. Tessa got up, but by the time she had dressed the dawn had moved on, the light no longer came level and could get into her room no more. A faint frost lay on the outside world under a faintly iridescent sky. A delicate sort of day in which the cold seemed to be the medium of the light.

In the cool Nissen-hut chapel the light bathed the white vestments and Father Max's white hair with a golden tinge as of old varnish. The smoke of incense burned yesterday hung coiling in the rays of light, and the little red sanctuary lamp was dimmed into near invisibility by the brazen strike of the sunlight on the brass bowl in which it was suspended. To left and right of the altar the expressionless tranquil faces of the statues of Mary and Joseph looked at the tiny congregation. The Chaplaincy housekeeper, as always, muttered under a heavy black lace veil. Tessa had forgotten her mantilla, and stood in defiance of St Paul. It was the Feast of the flight into Egypt.

'I will go in to the altar of God; to God who giveth joy to my youth . . .

'. . . How distant will my journey be, how long would I remain there, out in the wilderness . . . !

'I confess to almighty God, to the blessed Mary, ever virgin, to blessed Michael, the Archangel, to Blessed John the Baptist, to the holy Apostles Peter and Paul, to all the saints, and to you, Father . . . Lord, have mercy, Christ have mercy, Lord have mercy . . . Remember Lord, Thy servants N. and N.' (Here the celebrant makes silent mention of those for whom he wishes to pray, and Tessa thinks of Theodore, right through until the dismissal, the *'Ite Missa Est'*.)

Later, unable to settle to work in her own room, she took her books to Ben's room, and sat there. She lit his gas fire, and set ready his percolator of coffee. His indecipherable books and his cello leaning in the corner comforted her. The stone mullions of his gothic windows made a diagram of the decorated style in shadow plan on the carpet that swung round her feet as the day wore on. The rich gloss on the cello reminded her of the varnish on her marvellous gramophone. The college porter delivered a clutch of notes and displayed a wooden indifference to the sight of a young woman, ensconced and waiting. He did, however, offer an opinion that gas fires were bad for cellos, and she turned the heat down. Various clocks and bells punctuated time. At five, as it began to get dark, she timed the hour from the first bell to the last in earshot, and found it took twenty minutes.

Ben came back at nine, looking tired. 'It's very bad news, I'm afraid, Tessa,' he said. 'He's in hospital. He did preach his sermon, and some of his parishioners didn't like it. He's been beaten up.'

As far as Ben had been able to find out Theodore had three broken ribs, a broken nose, a broken collar bone, and some internal bruising and bleeding. He looked pretty dreadful, and was only half-conscious. And, no, he didn't see how Tessa could possibly see him; as it was already the horrible parish priest had favoured Ben with the opinion that when young priests started to get silly and troublesome there was always a woman behind it. Tessa in the pit of misery began to cry, and was soon crying in Ben's arms.

She woke long after midnight, every college curfew long overrun, to find herself covered with an eiderdown in Ben's fireside chair.

'Are you hungry, love?' Ben asked.

'Yes. How disgusting of me. But I think I missed lunch . . .'

'No wonder you're a bit woozy. There's a late-night chippy in Walton Street; could you face cod and six?'

'Yes. I'm out too late . . .'

'The best thing now is to sit it out and hope nobody finds your room empty.'

'Your scout will find me in the morning.'

'Not for a guinea. Don't fret. You just draw the cork

from this bottle, and put it near the fire. Won't be long.'

In the small hours of the morning, leaving Ben on his camping mat in front of the fire, Tessa curled up in his narrow bed, the door ajar because the bedroom was so cold. Fish and chips washed down with good claret had strengthened her a little, and she slipped back into sleep.

The scout's cooperation included a splendid breakfast. Over which she and Ben made plans. So that by the time Tessa slipped back into St Winifred's, to discover that only Cathy had noticed her absence, and Cathy had had more sense than to raise the alarm, she had some scheme to cling to. As soon as term ended, Ben would drive them both across to visit Theodore. And Ben was fairly certain that letters to the hospital would not be intercepted; so she could write as she thought fit.

Dearest, Dearest Tod,

How brave you are. Whatever anyone else says, I believe that you are right to follow your own conscience when you preach . . .

Dear Miss Brownlaw,

Father T. has asked me to drop you a line to let you know he is not in too much pain, and we all hope to have him well again before too long. He can't write himself, because of being unable to sit up at the moment, but he says I am to tell you that his brain is not in plaster, and he can think as well as ever, and indeed, has a good deal of time for thinking. I might add that he is a very good patient, and no trouble at all to nurse, not like some.

Yours sincerely, Mrs Peters (nurse).

Dearest Beatrice,

This wobbly writing is the best I can do. I love you. They don't seem quite sure what is wrong with me, but it is making me a funny colour, like a swarthy Mediterranean type. And I hope you like the look of retired boxers, because my nose is flattened, and I can't ask them to fix it as vanity in a priest is unthinkable. They keep laughing and telling me it's just as well my looks will never matter . . . it's peaceful here. I half dread getting better, for when I do all my problems will reappear. The hope of seeing you is the only thing that getting better is worth while for.

Yours always and everywhere, Tod

Dearest Tod,

You can trust me to see Othello's visage in his mind. Your mind I'm sure is unharmed. I think of you every moment of every day . . . and wish you well . . .

Dearest Tessa,

I suppose I should be glad you think my mind is in good shape. My best friend hasn't noticed; perhaps I am not mad. But it feels to me as though the last few years have crushed and battered my mind and spirit considerably more than the poor cross drunken workers bashed my body . . .

Dearest Tod,

Not long now. The term is nearly over, and we shall carry out our plan to kidnap you from hospital for an hour; and I shall see you, Dearest. It seems so long . . . But now it's only a week . . .

There is, though, no certainty in this contingent world. When the end of the term came Theodore had been taken suddenly worse, had undergone an operation on his liver, and was lying inaccessible, mortally ill, perhaps dying.

* * *

That Easter Tessa dreamed about bricks. She woke repeatedly in her pale yellow-washed room at home with the view to the willow tree in the suburban garden, remembering, or imagining – is there any difference in dreams? – a tin trunk full of bricks. The tin trunk was painted blue inside, and outside, battered though it was, was covered in golden scumble. Magenta lines picked out the edges, and the latch. Inside there were two kinds of brick: little smooth ones in bright colours, cylinders and arches and domes, and big coarse rough-cut plain ones which, Tessa found she knew, Cornish Grandad had made himself, and which were not quite regular enough to build together easily. The word 'off-cuts' drifted in her waking mind, and brought with it one morning a clear memory of the fragrant smell of the boatbuilding shed, the floor covered in sawdust and delicate curled shavings, and Grandad picking up from the detritus on the floor chunks of wood of a pale pink mackerel colour, and grained like the flesh of fish. A plane swept back and forth on a work bench somewhere, like the swish of wave on sand. A happiness suffused the dream like the weather of an exotic country; then a black figure stepped suddenly across the light and stood in the workshop door, and Tessa woke abruptly to the prospect of a day to be lived through full of fear for Theodore.

Usually, though, the dream was simpler. Tessa was on a plaited rug, in front of a blazing fire. Someone said, 'What can she do?' and then the trunk of bricks was pulled across the floor towards her. The voice said, 'Anything she likes,' and Tessa began taking bricks out of the box and building with them. The dream began with a vivid sense of joy; she could choose, choose any brick, build anything. But as it went on, and an elaborate tower rose upon the swirling pattern of the rug, there crept into it a fear of scarcity, of running out of bricks . . .

The dream blurred into her waking mind in curious

ways, so that she woke once full of astonishment, knowing that the bricks in her hands were part of the fabric of a boat that had shipwrecked long ago – just a saw cut had divided the section of wood that had gone to the storm-scoured ocean floor from the section that she held in her hand, and was about to build with. Then waking a little further she realized that the bricks were long lost too; gone like the boat in the past. And then she was teased by a faint and fading thought that the bricks themselves didn't matter, that what mattered she still possessed – though, fully awake now, she couldn't imagine what that was.

More and more the dream leaked into her waking moods. She tried to sit quietly reading in her room, to visit her grandparents, to help her mother with the housework, but could not rid herself of the sense of panic in the back of her mind . . . the sense that the days were in some way the last, the last chance for something . . . Some drama was going forward which she did not in the least understand, though it engulfed her. As it had been in the war, she remembered, trying to work out what the fighting was about, what we were trying to stop. She had asked, 'Mother, what will happen if Hitler wins the war?' Her mother had only said, 'He won't,' leaving her as baffled as before.

She got up early in the mornings and went to Mass said at seven in a nearby convent, and prayed for an end to the unease, or at least for an understanding of it. How could she pray for Theodore if she was guilty of an obscure offence? The prayers of the innocent are holy in the sight of God, but she didn't feel innocent any more although she could not name a sin she had committed, and not confessed. After some time it occurred to her that she had not got herself honestly sorted out towards Ben; she did not know clearly what she thought was between them, and perhaps that was what was disturbing her peace for she did believe very sincerely that misleading or tempting young men was sinful. And perhaps what she had been so careful not to do to Richard, she was doing to Ben. That at least could be sorted out. She could get on a train and go to see Ben, any time.

Oxford was quiet, out of term. They walked round familiar places, crossing and recrossing trails of memory of walking with Theodore. They gazed at deer in Magdalen Park, who returned their stares with reciprocal vacant curiosity. Then they crossed the bridge to the water-walks, and to Mesopotamia.

The willows were in fine green leaf, and the violets gave a blue shimmer to the leafy ground, while the river could manage only grey. At last at the top end of the walks, just before they turned back, she found courage to ask him what his intentions were.

He stopped, and turned on her his handsome and unruffled gaze. His expression was always calm, whatever might be happening, and so it was now. 'You know that,' he said.

'I would like you to tell me again.'

'I have asked you to marry me. You have not replied. Until you do, I am bound simply to wait for your answer, for I would not withdraw the offer. I still hope you will accept it.'

'But, Ben, do you love me?'

'You know I do.'

'You have never said so. How should I know?'

'I didn't think you were the sort of girl who would want wooing and flattery, and declarations. Who would want to hear her own praises. I think of you as a serious and devout person who would not expect . . . who would understand love as I understand it. I think you are like that, Tessa.'

'Well, maybe I am. But I think I had better be sure I do understand what you mean by love. Otherwise I don't know what answer I can give you.'

'I am no good at talking,' he said. 'Words don't come freely to me as they do to you. I will write something

for you; a meditation. I will try to get it on paper.'
'Thank you. I'll look forward to that.'
They went back to Ben's room and made tea. Tessa toasted crumpets on a toasting fork like one belonging to a stained-glass devil, and Ben went to his cello, and began to play to her, something that sang quietly, like someone humming in the dark.
'What's that?' she asked.
'It's how you make me feel,' he said, and wouldn't tell her what it was.
Later he saw her off at the station. She leaned out of the carriage window and watched his tall dark-headed form striding away from her down the platform, and called after him, 'Write soon!'

Ben's letter came by the afternoon post, which also brought one from Theodore. She took them into the garden, to the damp seat under the willow tree, and looked at them for some time, wondering which to open first. The multiplicity of fine yellow leaves streaked the sky above her like a shower of stars falling by daylight. A bird sang. The green damp wood laid a chill on her through her coat. She opened Ben's letter:

> I have loved you a long time, since the first few cell meetings at which you spoke. The first time Theodore told me of his feelings towards you I realized that I shared them. So this is no new or quixotic frame of mind.
>
> Has this love, then, grown up? Has childish enthusiasm given place to adult maturity? What is the proper balance between emotion and reason, and shall we find it together?
>
> Marriage is a double commitment, not to each other, but to God. To recap its temptations and advantages:
>
> Its temptations are to double introspection and selfishness; to materialism; to loss of chastity.

Its advantages are virtue through living for someone else, companionship (do we take enough advantage of this?) and an unparalleled opportunity for doing good in the world, offering a warm welcome and moral support, and food, and a roof to others adrift or in trouble or loneliness. God's work for married people is far more than just having children, although it is that too.

Dear Tessa, I think we are well placed to avoid the temptations and enjoy the blessings of a good marriage. I have never met anyone else who seemed to me better able to be my helpmate in this. The danger of materialism, for example, need not trouble us; we shall have all we need, and need not think about it. The danger of double selfishness we shall avoid also, through not having time for it. For the first project God has put in our path is already urgent – looking after Theodore. Though doubtless it is only the first of many.

The last few months have not been easy for me, while you have taken time to think. I hope you have thought, and will think about this letter and pray about it and let me soon have an answer.

Yours ever,
Ben

She left Theodore's letter unopened, and went for a long walk round the comfortable streets, their ornamental cherries and ranks of tulips and suburban birds and wistfully predatory well-fed cats all coexisting and proclaiming domestic delight. She dropped in to the church, and prayed in the gaudy Lady chapel for a quarter of an hour. 'Holy Mary, Mother of God . . .' our example on earth . . . but we cannot be like her; if she is our example, then every woman is flawed. Either mother or virgin; all incomplete . . . but marrying Ben would come near.

And so she had decided before she opened Theodore's letter.

* * *

Whatever seems most natural at the time seems later the most incomprehensible. Time will bring Tessa plenty of retrospective amazement at the young woman sitting under the willow tree and deciding to marry, an opened and an unopened letter on her lap. Deciding to marry Ben without for a moment considering other possibilities – the possibility, for example, of not marrying at all. She had not been in the least alarmed by Ben, and that fact in itself did not alert her. Richard did alarm her; some inner self was always backing away from Richard, however coaxing and reassuring he tried to be. And when she was with Theodore alarm bells rang clear and unmistakable in what warning they gave, and she well knew why, or perhaps, why not . . .

But she was not afraid of Ben; in his company she felt an untroubled profound calm. And so she made up her mind, and opened Theodore's letter in the same moment.

Poor Theodore: afraid of getting better, because they would put him in the priests' prison to recover, where the company would be priests drying out, or serving time for fooling with the choir boys . . . Poor Theodore, longing for his books and time and strength to write and think, and staggering under some other burden which afflicted him all the time he was not with her and which he couldn't put into writing . . .

That night he rang her from the portable telephone in the ward, and she told him that she loved him dearly and not to worry, a rescue plan was nearly complete. Couldn't he imagine what it was? He would have to wait and see . . .

'Dalla tua pace . . .' she said.

'Ti voglio bene,' he said, 'and shall do, in whatever circle . . .'

'It's all right, love. It's *Purgatorio*, not *Inferno* . . .'

Whereupon with little regard for theology or poetry, the pips cut them off.

* * *

On the first day of Trinity, then, Tessa, leaving her bags packed, and barely giving her grandfather, who had driven her up from home, time to get clear of the gates, went to see Ben. She found him surrounded by undergraduates, quaintly gowned, and writing down a revision programme for the desperate final term.

'I'll come back later . . .' she said, to the circle of faces looking at her standing at the door.

'No; wait . . . did you come to tell me something?' asked Ben.

'Just, yes,' she said. 'We'll talk later . . .'

'Don't move, anybody. Just hang on a moment, Tessa, I'll be right back,' he said, and stepping past her he descended the staircase at a run.

The undergraduates all looked at each other, and at her with ill-concealed smirks. Tessa moved to the window and saw Ben disappearing across the quad, his gown billowing and ballooning behind him, running towards the back gate into the High. The young men in the room with her began to talk in low voices, mostly about whether one of them could possibly row in Eights as well as taking Finals.

Tessa picked up a book of Ben's about walking in the Lakes, and idled her mind along the lines.

Ben came up the stairs again two at a time; he hadn't been more than five minutes. 'Have you changed your mind?' he said, to Tessa.

'Of course not!' she said, 'Ben whatever . . .'

'Then . . .' he said, and taking a little box from his pocket he showed her a gold ring with a single diamond on it, and slipped it on her ring finger. 'They'll change it if it doesn't fit,' he said, and everyone in the room laughed.

'We'll come back another time,' one of the students said, and they all got up.

'Ludlow, you have very little chance of a decent class as it is, and if you leave this room without a proper study programme I'll give you poor odds on getting even a Third,' said Ben. So they all sat down again, and it was Tessa who left, smiling at Ben's uncharacteristically precipitate gesture and looking with astonishment at the glinting stone on her finger.

'I seem to be engaged to Ben,' she said to Cathy, meeting her in the back hall of St Winnie's and extending her hand to show the ring.

'I thought you already were,' said Cathy.

That night Tessa dreamed, of course. She dreamed that she had just taken the last brick from the box, and put it on top of the tower. Now there was no more hasty balancing, adding bricks here and there, buttressing or reinforcing to be done; only the tower already made. No more freedom to choose, only consequences.

Consequences came, of course, thick and fast. For one thing, undergraduates were not allowed to get married, or even, without special reasons, to live out of college. Tessa needed permission to do both. The principal poured her a dark brown sherry, invited her to sit, congratulated her, and cursorily admired the ring.

'I don't entirely understand the need for haste,' she said, sitting down herself and looking hard and severely at Tessa. 'The sensible thing, it seems to me, would be for you to be engaged for a year – it's not such a terribly long time, you know – sit your Finals, and then get married.'

'No,' said Tessa. 'It can't wait. We have to get married at once.'

'The excitement of a wedding, and then the duties of running a house are bound to conflict with your own studies, Tessa. And I am responsible, in a general sort of way, for the success of those studies. Would you like to tell me why it can't wait, my dear?'

Tessa blushed. The very thought of telling the principal about Theodore made her flinch. 'Urgent personal reasons,' she said. 'I shall work just as hard as ever. Ben can have a college house somewhere quite close to the centre, and I shall still be able to get to lectures . . .'

'I see you are RC,' said the principal, looking at Tessa's file. 'Would you know what I mean when I say that I wish you people would sin more deeply while you are about it?'

'No,' said Tessa. 'I don't think I would.'

'Ah,' said the principal. 'Forgive me if I ask you, Tessa, if you are really very sure you want to marry Dr Marshall?'

'Oh yes, quite, thank you. Otherwise I wouldn't be bothering you.'

'My dear, you are a clever girl. You may not seem among the brightest here, but then Oxford is very exceptional. In the world outside you are among the few brightest. Clever women in general I think – you must take my word for this, I have seen more of life than you have as yet – are not often very happy married to men who do not respect them intellectually, and who do not acknowledge their equal intellectual needs.'

'But Ben does respect me intellectually . . . !'

'Well, it's not much of a start, is it, getting you into difficulties which threaten your degree?'

'But Ben hasn't got me into difficulties . . . I mean, it isn't Ben's doing; it's more that Ben's trying to get me out of them, really . . .'

Tessa noticed that the principal's expression had become rather strange; she looked pursed and baffled at the same time. The interview was obviously going badly, and so much depended on it.

'If you make me choose,' she said, 'I shall have to abandon my degree. But please . . .'

'It isn't a question of my making you do things,' said the principal. Her expression had lost the prune look, while being more baffled than ever. 'But, for heaven's sake, child, have you looked at a calendar? It seems to me that difficulties apparent to you already will come to a head around Christmas; and thereafter will burden you heavily right through your final two terms. Wouldn't you do better to ask for leave of absence for a year and resume your degree much later? I expect we could arrange that . . .'

'It's far too urgent for that,' Tessa said. 'And it matters long before Christmas; three or four weeks at most!'

The principal now bestowed on her a long and astonished stare, and then said helplessly, 'You will have to leave me to think about this. I need time, and I had better talk to your tutors. I will let you know what view the college takes.'

'As soon as you can, please,' Tessa said.

Proposals must have been in the air. Arriving back from the shops, Tessa was unloading supplies into her bedside cupboard – Cornish wafers and honey, and the butter that in two or three days, unrefrigerated, would have a sulphurous yellow tinge and a rancid taste, and two kinds of chocolate biscuit, the paraphernalia with which undergraduates console themselves for lack of home cooking – when a knock on her door interrupted her. She opened it to find Stefan standing outside.

'Stefan, come in! How are you?' She really was delighted to see him, and smiled deeply at him.

'Not good,' he said, coming in and sitting on her bed. 'I have trouble.'

And indeed, he did look a bit of a wreck, she noticed, rashly opening the nicest packet of biscuits and loading a plate to offer them. His hairline had always been on the high side and he had never been thin, but now he looked fat and balding. His skin was a poor colour, and his face was puffy; whatever had they been doing to him in the Warneford? Whatever it was had not damaged his appetite for biscuits, anyway. 'But at least you're out of hospital,' she said. 'How nice to see you.'

'You are glad to see me?'

'Of course I am. Have some coffee.'

'You are kind girl. You will help me.'

'If I can. What's the matter?'

'I need wife,' said Stefan. 'I must find wife.'

She froze, with the kettle in her hand poised over the mug.

'Is not easy,' Stefan went on. 'People laugh.'

Tessa at least did not feel like laughing. 'Dear Stefan,' she said, trying not to let the preternatural caution that filled her actually poison her tone of voice. 'I am so sorry, but you are too late. I am already engaged. Look.' And she held out her icily glinting finger to him.

'Very bad luck,' Stefan said. 'But you will explain to him . . .'

'What!' she cried. 'Stefan I'm telling you *no* – do you understand? No, I can't marry you!'

'But what can I do?' he said, shaking his head from side to side and clenching his hands together, the picture of distress. 'My mother say find wife, and the doctor say yes, good idea, great help, and I ask, and girls laugh and laugh. You too, Tessa. I thought you would help me. You came to visit me,' he added, reproachfully.

'I didn't laugh, Stefan,' she said.

'Others did.'

'What others? Who did you ask?'

'Oh, some. Quite a few. The girl in the Cadena – she laughed a lot.'

'Stefan *when* did they let you out of hospital?' she said. He looked guilty at once.

'If I find wife I can have house. I would not have to go back,' he said.

A slight sound made Tessa shift her gaze, which had

been riveted on Stefan. Hubert was standing in the door, his hand on the door knob, overhearing. She made a gesture of helplessness towards him. He seemed to catch on very quickly; had he perhaps overheard the whole conversation? He came in and sat in the sagging chair opposite Stefan, reached forward for a biscuit, and said, 'Don't you want to go back, old chap?'

'Is horrible there,' said Stefan. 'Like prison.'

'Have you been there long?' asked Hubert gently.

'Years I think. Maybe months,' said Stefan. Tessa, catching Hubert's eye, nodded, and poured a third mug of coffee.

'And even now,' said Hubert, smiling at Stefan, 'they don't let you out. You have to give them the slip . . .'

Stefan looked at Hubert with eyes full of suspicion, and silently ate another biscuit. Then, 'The others can go out and have tea,' he said resentfully. 'The others go to see wives. They stay out for hours, all weekend sometimes.'

'But perhaps,' said Hubert, 'you wouldn't actually need a wife for that. Perhaps a friend would do. Perhaps if there were a friend who would have you to stay, and take you to tea in Fuller's . . . would you like that?'

'Good idea,' said Stefan, brightening visibly. 'Better tea than here with these girls. They never have cake, only biscuits.'

'Well, let's try it now,' said Hubert, getting up and extending a hand to Stefan. 'And then I could take you back and talk to them, and make sure they will let me come and see you again when the others visit their wives. OK?' Hubert was looking at Stefan, whom Tessa found so repulsive, with an expression of great tenderness.

'I did have friend,' Stefan said, lumbering to his feet. 'Matchek. But he is gone.'

Hubert cocked an eyebrow in Tessa's direction. 'He's forestry,' she said. 'Doing a term on a plantation in Scotland, I think.'

'Perhaps another friend would be better than a wife,' said Hubert, taking Stefan's arm. 'Less trouble for you.'

'That Cadena girl,' said Stefan, turning to Tessa from the corridor, 'she could have been Poelish princess! Thank you for the tea, but I am going now to Fuller's!' And he bowed to her, a slight and noble inclination of the head.

Tessa was left with three mugs of lukewarm coffee, unsure whether first to thank God for Hubert, or to pray for him.

There would be no avoiding consequences with Richard, that she did know. But she had not expected them as swiftly as they came. Richard saw her ring in the Examination Schools, where they were listening to Lord David on Victorian novelists. She had taken the precaution of sitting well away from him in the cathedral gloom which Victorian architects approved of for scholarship, but she had not reckoned on his having telescope eyes. After the lecture she slipped away quickly and biked back to St Winnie's, only to have him follow and burst in upon her before she had even got her coat off and say imperiously, 'Who is it?'

'Ben Marshall,' she said, appalled by the look he was giving her. 'Nobody you know.'

'How can you?' he said. 'You mean you have got over the turbulent cleric and fallen in love with somebody else, all in a single vacation, and not given me a thought? What kind of fool are you playing?'

She returned his gaze steadily, but could think of no reply. She was angry to see him so angry, and without any right . . .

'Worse and worse!' he cried. 'You *haven't* got over the bloody priest! What are you doing, Tessa? What the hell are you playing at? The Ben character must be pretty obtuse if he doesn't know what I know about you!'

'He knows,' she said, turning away.

'And doesn't he know you can't love two people at once?'

'That isn't true, Richard. At least, it may sometimes be true, I think. It depends.'

'It's what is universally thought, Tessa. Can you justify rejecting it?'

'You obviously can't love two people at once if circumstances force you to choose between them. If to serve one you must do what will betray the other . . . but if you don't have a choice, then you can, I think. Why shouldn't you? Don't people in love still love their brothers and sisters and care for their friends?'

'That's different. Entirely. You must, you *do* know that!'

'I don't know anything of the kind. I truly believe what I am telling you. And I am not in a position where I must choose between those I love. Marrying Ben is the thing to do if I love Ben, and marrying Ben is the thing to do if I love Theodore.'

'No, Tessa. You are making a catastrophe. You should marry me.'

'Should I? Should I really, Richard? And could I marry you and take care of Theodore?'

'You bloody couldn't! Marry me, and if that creepy cleric comes within a mile of you trying sanctimonious seductions, I'll knock his ribs through his spine and his teeth into his cranium, so help me God!'

'You see? You should just hear yourself, Richard! Go away, please. Get out!'

He said, 'Tessa . . . please . . .' Then he abruptly left her.

He had left her shaken. She raged at him in her head, and couldn't steady her hand or eye to reading, though an essay was urgent. She felt deadly cold, though the uncertain sunlight of late spring shone through her window. Shortly she crept under her coverlet, and lay there thinking till her internal fury wore her into sleep.

* * *

Sometimes things work out well. The principal gave permission, provided Tessa lived within five miles of the city centre and continued to be bound *in statu pupillari*. Ben's college were unable to find a house at such short notice, but assigned them a little crooked flat in the upper stories of a house in St Giles. And, since Father Knox was to give the Romanes lecture, Oxford was filling up with eminent Catholics, clerical and lay, and Theodore's Father Provincial relented and – granting that he was far too weak to work, and would be for some while – sent him back to Oxford to look for a respectable lodging in which to convalesce, and to study only if it didn't tire him.

Father Max had a full house – a full palace rather – of eminences. You might not get to heaven in purple socks, but purple cummerbunds were to be glimpsed up and down St Aldate's! So, joyfully, Tessa and Ben, having inspected the bare little rooms and assigned Theodore an attic with a charming view into the top of plane trees, descended on Elliston and Cavell's. Ben's lavish diamond had left him temporarily, he assured her, short of funds, but they managed a single bed, and a bedspread in jolly colours to cheer it up a bit, and an off-cut of carpet to do something about a bit of the floor. Tessa begged her mother for the child's desk from home, which came in pieces and could easily be moved.

Preparing for Theodore, in short, was better fun than anything since Tessa abandoned her doll's house, and was no preparation for the shock of seeing him. They were to meet him from the train. Ben thought they had better make quite sure of a taxi, so he got into one and waited while she scanned the crowds coming through the barrier. Theodore came towards her, seeing her long before she recognized him. His face had sunk into all the cavities of his skull; the skin gleamed on the edges of every bone, and his once-sharp nose was broad and blunted. His black sweater hung loose on him like a gown, and when she hugged him it was like holding the bony, palpating body of a bird . . . he looked at her with yellow eyes, and smiled radiantly, the smile of a very old man.

They felt a little shamefaced, showing him his tiny attic. But, 'This is really for me?' he said. 'I have never had a room made ready especially for me!'

'We'll get planks and bricks and make a bookcase,' said Ben, 'when we have a minute.'

But a minute seemed hard to come by. The week was chaotic, with one crisis running into the next. Tessa managed to find a room for her mother in the Blue Boar, but Oxford was jam-packed with people coming to hear Father Knox, and she had terrible trouble finding hotels with any room for her other relatives. The theatrical nature of weddings was comically accentuated by everyone's sudden desire to come; Tessa had not commanded such an ability to assemble the family in one place on one occasion since she had the part of Judas in the school play.

She rushed to distant hotels in Headington, or miles and miles out along the Botley Road trying to book rooms for people. Ben fixed up sherry in the Senior Common Room, and a buffet lunch. His relatives seemed all to be in Brazil; his father was a roving consultant engineer of some kind. They kept telephoning at prearranged times, trying all to speak to Tessa at immense expense. She dashed between booking rooms and the phone in the college office.

'Thank God someone tied him down at last!' said the cheerful voice of a stranger down the line. A long-suffering secretary sat with suspended fingers poised over the keyboard, waiting for the call to end before she hammered out another line. 'We always knew he'd take a lot of catching – there's been enough girls tried and failed . . .'

'I'm very lucky,' said Tessa.

'What's the big rush?' the voice said. 'We could all

be there if you'd hold off a month or two. This shotgun stuff from Ben, of all people, amazes us.'

'I'll look forward to meeting you when you get home,' she said.

An hour later, setting off across the Parks towards college, she met Richard, transparently in ambush for her, leaning against a tree in fresh young leaf like a latter-day Hilliard.

'Can I talk to you?' he said. 'Have you forgiven me for losing my temper?'

'I suppose so. You hadn't any right to talk like that.'

'No right, but every reason. I had just learned my hope of happiness was in ruins.'

'But you always knew . . .'

'Yes, but I had been hoping. Your warnings were so silly I thought you would grow out of them.'

'Don't start again, Richard. Let's just be friends.'

'I couldn't stand being just friends for long. Tessa, don't, please don't marry someone who isn't jealous.'

'And what's so great about jealousy suddenly? One of the deadly sins, and universally known to be destructive of love? Just because you aren't capable of Ben's magnanimity.'

'My mother says – and, yes, it is her business if it's why I have to be unhappy – that the young have no conception of how long life is. Won't you get tired of magnanimity in the long run, and want something a bit more like lust?'

'First jealousy, then lust. Which of the other deadly sins should a partnership be steeped in to please you? Why not anger and sloth and gluttony as well?'

'Come away with me; run away with me now, and we will commit all seven over and over in every possible order, like change-ringing on resounding bells!' And, indeed, from somewhere behind them in the golden maze of the city a clamour of bells came faintly on the wavering wind.

'Richard . . .' she said, exasperated, but smiling in spite of herself.

'I know, I know,' he said. They had come to a fork in the path. 'You would think it wicked, you know, Tessa my dearest, to be as reckless of anyone else's happiness as you are of your own.'

And without a backward glance he set off on the other path from hers.

He had made her late for a tutorial, and she too hastened onwards.

And on top of all the other comings and goings there was Theodore to look after. He needed desperately to eat, but he couldn't manage more than a few mouthfuls without nausea. He needed rest: that was easy, he could lie as long as he liked in the attic room. He couldn't quite manage the walk to the Cornmarket and back to proper shops – even the trip to the little shop in Walton Street exhausted him – so Tessa fetched in food, and cooked it for him when she could. The first time he said the morning Mass which was compulsory for him, the altar wine laid him out and he was brought back, retching, in a taxi. When he couldn't be persuaded to ask for a dispensation from the obligation to say Mass, in case the Father Provincial thought a man as ill as that should be ordered into a holy nursing home, Ben took to getting up early and serving as Theodore's altar boy, so that he could pour the wine for ablutions with the lightest possible hand. Tessa cycled between the two-man Masses and greasy breakfasts at St Winnie's. There seemed to be not a moment's rest anywhere in the day. Pride would not let her confirm the principal's predictions about the distracting effect of all this on her work; she missed not a single lecture and delivered her week's essay on time. Suddenly, two days before the wedding, bricks and planks were delivered in St Giles – Ben had remembered to order them – and dumped in the hall of the house, getting in the way of the tenants of flats on the other floors. Theodore, who had been frantically trying not to be a nuisance, simply couldn't carry bricks up three flights of stairs, Ben had continuous tutorials from one till six, and Tessa abandoned three philology lectures and went to the flat to make Theodore's bookcase.

She carried the bricks up a few at a time in a battered shopping bag. The planks were more trouble, as they swung round behind her and banged the walls on the turns of the stairs. Theodore, wincing at his inability to help, made tea. They began to stack the bricks against the sides of the chimney-breast alcove, and lay the planks.

'It has been good knowing you were nearby,' she said. 'But I've hardly seen you. How have you been?'

'Fine since I got here,' he said. 'Being away was terrible beyond anything.'

'You were dreadfully ill. I can hardly bear to think how ill. Look at you now, poor thing . . .'

'I was ugly already. I must be repulsive now.'

'Oh, rubbish. You weren't, you were rather handsome. And now you could do with putting on a few pounds . . . What do you weigh, anyway?'

'Six stone ten. I used to be nine stone.'

'God. Well, we'll fatten you up.'

'And then my only disfigurement will be a broken nose?'

She contemplated it. Reaching out, she lightly touched the widened bridge of his freckled nose. The impression of toughness which a broken nose confers looked so implausible on his sensitive, ravaged face that the finished effect was that of a little boy acting a tough guy.

'Actually it's rather charming,' she said. 'And Theodore, what is this? You didn't really think I loved you for your looks?'

'Nevertheless there might be limits.'

'Tod dear, you aren't and never have been ugly.'

'Don't you think people's faces gradually get etched

with an image of their minds? And my mind is such a pit of vipers!'

'Everyone has dark thoughts sometimes. And most people's faces stay nice.'

The room was darkening, and rain began to strike the panes of the little window. They laid the last plank in position and tried the steadiness of the structure. Theodore turned away and leant against the window, looking out. His narrow form obliterated most of the light. Behind him the green of the tree wavered and melted in cascades of water running down the glass.

'I suppose most people have nice thoughts as well as nasty ones. I suppose most people have images of love to resort to. Most people haven't got my kind of life to contend with, most people haven't got my filthy mind. I haven't any clean images to protect myself with. When I am with you I can think of your body as just the home of Tessa's soul; as something pure, and living . . . when I am away from you I can't think of you without desire, and desire brings filthy images in its train. I have to struggle so hard not to wrong you in my mind; not to constantly defile you, by association with things . . .'

'My dear, of course you haven't wronged me. You have my permission to think of me in any way you like!'

'Oh, but I don't like it! I loathe it, though I can't help it. The textbooks of moral theology we had to learn from demonstrated every possible sin, every possible perversion, with diagrams, diagrams of the female body to illustrate . . . and I have sat and listened in the confessional to all the petty dirt, all the nastiness you can imagine, much more than you imagine. People come and tell the priest when it goes wrong, when anything foul or nasty has taken place; to set against it I have nothing. Nobody tells the priest if loving brought them joy . . . and the only image in my mind of a woman's body is a diagram to illustrate its misuse . . .'

Behind him, in the dim of the rainlit room shadowed

almost to darkness by his shape against the light, Tessa was silently taking off her clothes.

Then she lay down on the bed and waited for him to turn round. He looked at her for a long time. Neither of them spoke. Then at last he approached the foot of the bed and touched her, gently laying the back of his hand against her naked instep.

'I shall go out for a little while,' he said. 'And any danger to either of us goes with me.'

'Don't get tired!' she called after him. 'Don't go far!'

He came back soon, having so little energy. She was dressed and making more tea. They seemed both to be in some kind of trance, a state almost of weightlessness and unable to take their eyes from each other, so that it was difficult to pour tea or put books on the shelves, and they moved slowly as if dreaming rather than living the time. Nothing was said; and eventually Tessa had to force words out of herself, that seemed to come from the wrong level of meaning altogether.

'Tod dear, will you be able for ever to bear being a priest?'

'Maybe not. Why do you ask?'

'Because if there was a chance, however tiny, however far ahead, that you would want it, I would call all this off even now, and wait for you.'

'Ex-priests can never marry,' he said.

'If you asked me to, I would live with you in sin.'

'That wouldn't be like you at all, my dear,' he said. 'And people always have nervous qualms just before they marry.'

And it was time for her to go and meet her mother's train.

'I always thought, somehow, we'd do this properly, from home, not in a hugger-mugger,' her mother said.

'Oxford isn't Gretna Green,' said Tessa crisply. 'I didn't think you'd mind, somehow . . .'

'No dear. I don't mind. Some of my friends have real

trouble . . . really gruesome son-in-laws – sons-in-law, I mean – and I really do like Ben. In fact, he's almost comically suitable . . . but are you sure, my darling? Are you really sure?' Tessa was relieved when her mother without waiting for an answer went on, 'Where's your dress?'

'Oh,' she said. 'I hadn't really thought. I'll dig something out.'

'Saints give me patience!' wailed her mother. 'For the rest of your life, child, you and everyone else will remember what you wore on your wedding day. You absolutely cannot get married in a pinafore frock and Clark's sandals, do you hear?'

'It's supposed to be a very quiet wedding . . .'

'Quiet my foot! What's the best dress shop in Oxford? The very best?'

'Chanelle, I suppose. It's horribly expensive . . .'

'Right. You meet me at the door of Chanelle's at nine o'clock tomorrow morning, or I'll have your guts for garters, do you understand?'

Tessa agreed at once, because it gave Theodore more time to get up and camp in the Bodleian for the morning. She had been wondering – for her mother was bound to want to see over the flat – whether she could conceal Theodore, or, alternatively, what her mother would think on discovering that the flat was being lived in by an unscheduled man.

Very early in the morning, then, of her wedding day, Tessa got up, grabbed a bath while everyone was sleeping – the last she would need to compete for at St Winnie's – and put on temporarily ancient clothes. She biked to St Giles – how quiet, and how strange with no-one stirring! – and let herself into the flat. The moment she entered the door she heard Theodore weeping. Alone in the place, he was lying face down in a desperately tangled mess of sheets and pillows, with his ravaged frame shaken by sobs. She went up to him, taking the attic stair two steps at a time, and said, 'Hush, love, hush . . .'

He did, eventually, manage to stop.

'I'll get you some coffee,' she said, and went down to the little kitchen.

By and by he came down in his dressing-gown. 'I didn't know you would see me like this,' he said. 'I'm sorry. Why did you come?'

'To see how you were. How you are.'

'Better for seeing you.'

'The plastic daffodils effect; or how to drive out the nasty thoughts . . .'

He managed a smile.

'And I want to ask you what you want as a present for marrying us. Ben has got you something; what do you want as a present from me?'

'Would you kiss me?' he said. 'Properly. Just once?'

'That's not a real present,' she said, 'but yes. Come here.'

Theodore grabbed her, and kissed her so roughly, forcing her head back, jabbing his tongue between her teeth, that she fought free of him, her indignation dying instantly, as she realized how little he knew.

'Not like that, love,' she said. 'Stay quite still and let me show you. Like this.' And taking him again in her arms she kissed him softly and gently, opening her mouth to him after some time, and drinking from his.

She went to him without the smallest sense of danger, and without any thought for how little she herself might know. And she stepped, of course, over the brink. For when one has never kissed a man one loves and desires one is absolutely ignorant of something, which, from that moment forward, is absolutely known.

So now she knew. But it was then seven-thirty in the morning of a day on which she was to get married at three, and indeed, was due to meet her mother to buy a dress at nine. She knew what she ought to do; or rather what she ought not, but the knowledge had come very late, and as for changing course, Tessa had not the courage that would take.

So Tessa got married in a white dress, with a simple veil in a Chaplaincy that was packed to the doors. Was that – could that be – Richard, standing by the door? Certainly there was Hubert, and Matchek, and Cathy and Alison . . . and rows and rows of friends and family. Theodore in white vestments stood facing them from behind the altar rail, his illness giving him an unearthly pallor. Father Max hovered nearby, watching and ready to stand in if necessary, and in unfamiliar nomenclature, *I Theresa Mary . . . thee Benedict Joseph* . . . Theodore led them through the rash magnificence of the marriage vows.

'With this ring, I thee wed,' said Ben to her, 'with my body I thee worship.' But did he? she wondered, did he realize what it sounded as if it meant?

'. . . gold and silver I thee give, and with all my worldly goods I thee endow . . .'

Later, kneeling within the sanctuary during a Mass – the only time in her life that a woman may do so – Tessa anxiously watched Theodore. She was, naturally, afraid that drinking the consecrated wine would lay him out. She didn't seem well able to concentrate as she ought; surely she should have listened carefully to the sermon in her wedding Mass; what had Theodore said? Something about asking God for strength to allow those who took on burdens to carry them faithfully . . . she thought she had seen Father Max pull a wry and disapproving face at it . . . all her life, Tessa thought, she had been trying to be good, and trying to be normal, to behave as she was expected to behave. And it seemed to get harder by the hour. What would her friends and family out there think if they could see that all that was in her heart at the moment was frantic worry about the celebrant's jaundice? Not only his jaundice, of course. Far worse than his folding up under the metabolic impact of the altar wine would be his folding in any way for other reasons . . . God, give him strength . . .

Apparently God did. For Theodore was now reading without faltering the long prayer in blessing of a bride and groom. She knelt at his feet, with Ben beside her, the delicate pattern in the brocade of his vestment just before her eyes.

If a blessing may be read as a prophylactic against what is most feared, then clearly what the Church most feared on this occasion was some failing of Tessa's, for it was largely on her behalf that the intervention of the Almighty was being sought:

'. . . *look graciously upon this Thy handmaiden, now to be joined in wedlock, who begs the safeguard of Thy protection. Upon her let the yoke be one of love and peace . . . let Holy matrons ever be her pattern . . . may she be, like Rachel, dear to her husband, like Rebecca prudent, like Sara faithful and long-lived. Let no action of hers give the Father of Lies dominion over her, but let her ever remain steadfast in the faith, true to her marriage bed, shunning forbidden embraces, of grave demeanour, held in honour for her modesty, well schooled in heavenly lore. May her life be one of proven innocence, and may she come to rest among the blessed . . . May they see their children and their children's children to the third and the fourth generation . . .*'

Theodore read it to the end in an unwavering voice.

Bride and groom are supposed, of course, to be eager to get away from the reception, and so they were. To please her mother Tessa changed, in Ben's room, into the powder-blue suit they had bought from Chanelle; then they departed, waving, got into Ben's car, and drove discreetly round the block, not to be seen to be going at once back to the flat.

Theodore got there just after them. 'I thought you'd gone!' he said, collapsing into a chair.

'I've got an essay to do,' said Tessa, 'and I needed to pick up the things for that. And we were hoping to see you.'

'You can't possibly do an essay on your honeymoon! What is it on?'

'The character of Satan in *Paradise Lost*.'

'I'm an expert on that,' said Theodore. 'Let me write it for you. Couldn't I?'

'All right,' she said, laughing. 'Yes please. I've asked Cathy to come in and make sure you're all right, make sure you're eating,' she added.

'I don't need anyone,' he said. 'Only you. Be happy.'

'We'll be back soon,' said Ben, 'and this is a present for you.' He put down on the table a duplicate door key to the flat.

'I thought I was to borrow Tessa's,' said Theodore, puzzled, picking it up.

'You can't borrow hers for ever; you'll need your own,' said Ben, leading Tessa through the door, and pulling it to behind him.

'A stool with three legs,' said Ben, 'never wobbles.' He was standing with Tessa watching a pair of barges negotiate Godstow Lock. A blazing autumn heat-wave engulfed Port Meadow and gilded the stone of the Nunnery; and they were a little clammy, having stripped and swum above the bridge an hour back, and having brought no towels to dry on. Tessa had just asked him, 'Ought we to be so happy?'

She meditated this answer. 'I suppose it's my convent upbringing again, but I can't help thinking that the wages of unconventionality is misery! Isn't it?'

'Blessed are the conventional, for they shall escape censure?' he said. 'I don't remember that one. And anyway, Tess, *you* are unconventional. I always thought you would need something exceptional; you would find me very dull going by myself, but Theodore . . .'

'Theodore?'

'Could be our special calling.'

'Certainly he's special. So vividly unhappy; then so happy; so alive, he makes us see what our capacity for feeling might be *for* . . .'

'Thinking and laughing, and glooming . . . Yes, I know what you mean. I feel muffled, by comparison.'

'But . . .'

'But what? We are happy because we are doing good. We should quickly become miserable if we didn't have clear consciences. It seems to me quite likely that you need to be intelligent about what God's will is; you can't find out what to do by mindlessly applying rules. But I don't know of any rules we have broken other than those of convention. I don't see what's the problem.'

'There isn't a problem; that's the problem . . .' she said, laughing. 'Can we go home yet? I'm getting cold.'

He looked at his watch. For Theodore had with cheerful impudence that morning announced that if it was his home too, then he needed privacy sometimes, and indeed that afternoon he needed sole possession of the flat until four o'clock. Humouring him they had taken themselves off for lunch at the Trout, and a walk.

'We can now,' said Ben. And they started back across the meadow, making for the Aristotle Bridge.

An Elliston and Cavell van drove away from the door as they reached it, and they let themselves into the flat to find Theodore standing in a living room which now contained a little upright piano. 'I never gave you a real wedding present,' he said, 'and this is it.'

Ben protested a bit. But Theodore said, 'You told me this was my home. And surely I can buy things for my home . . . that's what home means. And not even hypothetical children can grow up in a house without a piano!'

So while Tessa pottered making supper, Tod and

Ben played Mozart. Over supper they talked happily about music for piano and cello, and after supper Tod produced a battered volume of Gilbert and Sullivan, and they sang while he improvised accompaniments.

'This is your song,' he told Tessa. 'Learn this . . .' And he played through for her 'Poor Wandering One.'

At bedtime she made cocoa, loaded with sugar to get calories into Theodore, and a few moments after he went to bed she mounted the stair, entered his room, smoothed and tucked in his sheets and, stroking back the hair from his forehead, kissed him good night. Then she went down to sleep in her proper place, beside Ben. A day in a three-legged life.

A good life. It let Tessa be with Theodore, and Ben be with her. She worked harder than before, partly because of the awe-inspiring example the other two set her, and partly out of stiff-necked determination to show the principal that undergraduate marriage and throwing scholarship to the four winds were not the same. Also she was still hoping to get as much praise for anything of her own as Theodore's essay on Satan had won her. Even so there was time, while Ben – overworked as all young dons are – taught twenty-eight hours a week, for Tod to walk with her, and to try to teach her better Italian. They bought *Werther* translated into Italian, and deciphered that fantastic tale together in outbursts of rueful mirth. In the evenings they went to college concerts – Ben sometimes even playing in them – or walked out to pubs in the villages around, talking all the way. Tessa's undergraduate friends – most of them, not Richard – came in and out, demanding coffee. She seemed to see as much of Cathy as ever; Cathy even brought her books to work beside the gas fire in the sitting room of the flat, for warmth and company.

Every morning began with Mass – in which Theodore gave decreasing cause for concern, though Ben remained the most reliable server to be trusted to pour wine with a light hand. Since they were both going, Tessa got up likewise early and went too. On golden and on misty mornings they walked on the dew-polished cobblestones, making their way through the city's intricate streets as though traversing the convolutions of a shell. By the time they came back for breakfast others were about, and the magical, untouched-beach aura of Oxford, shining like a shore at the ebb of night, had gone.

Sometimes Cathy joined their morning pieties; in spite of which, and although it did not surprise Tessa at all, Theodore was horrified when she announced that after finals she would become a nun.

Tod and Tessa talked about it, alone as usual, sitting in the little kitchen of the flat while Tessa cut and trimmed carrots for their supper vegetable.

'But why, love? Why does it distress you?' asked Tessa.

'I'm afraid she has been influenced by me.'

'Why should she have been?'

He shook his head. 'I conceal my sins, and my dreadful failures. Without thought for the possibility that my apparent and false example may mislead others . . . you are the only one who knows . . .'

'I don't see why you think that Cathy's vocation has anything to do with you, Tod. In fact, something she once said makes me think it is more likely some love affair . . . Could you be becoming a touch big-headed? Is too much love making you vain?'

'Too much love?' he said, looking at her reproachfully. 'Do I have that?'

'You have all the love possible,' she said, 'and the limits on the possible are of your own making.' She was thinking of words exchanged just before she married Ben, but he did not take up her allusion.

'Yes,' he said. 'I suppose we have now done all the things together which are euphemisms for the act. We have lain together, slept together, "made love" . . . I used to be taught, you know, that all such acts would lead immediately to fornication; that what would be wrong, for example, with lying down and fondly embracing a woman would not be that there was any grave sin if it stopped there, but that it could not possibly stop there; as though human desire was a ravening dog once let off the leash . . . and yet nothing like that seems to happen to us; when we embrace I feel, after a moment's struggle, only a trance-like calm; a consolation of the flesh . . .'

'Your instruction was about lust,' she said. 'But love really does hunger and thirst for the good of the other person. So if you are truly, wholly convinced that it would be a disaster for that person to lose chastity, love leads you away from the brink . . . and the more you love someone the less likely you would be to commit sins with them.'

'I have always trusted you,' he said. 'I have known you would not let anything bad happen.'

'Whatever form loving you must take,' she said, 'my love will take it. And right now, it takes the form of getting a good meal ready. So move over, do, and let me have the table to roll out pastry.'

For, of course, it was perfectly true that running a household had devolved upon Tessa. Now that the liverish nausea had left Tod he ate enormously, and gained weight slowly. And besides shopping, there was washing and ironing to do, and the flat to keep clean. Tessa flew around with a duster, singing, and wielded Gumption to leave everything shining behind her. She didn't mind at all; she loved all tasks which in her mind looked after both of them at once – but as her finals approached, Tod began to worry, and pester her with offers of help. Ben didn't seem to worry about it; certainly he was working very hard himself and, it seemed to him, perhaps it was not absolutely necessary to have a graduate wife. A certain school of thought, of course, had always thought a Fourth amusing, and a good Second rather déclassé; Ben said kindly, 'Just do your best; keep calm,' and 'What's for supper?' in the same breath.

Tod pointed out anxiously that Tessa couldn't work the steady hours of treadmill revision that her friends were working – that Cathy was working, for example. Though she rebuffed his offers of help – a less efficient person it would be hard to imagine than Theodore – she agreed that he would cook lunch on the actual days of her finals.

What would be easiest for him? Sausages. A cinch. She left them on the draining board with a tin of beans beside them and a frying pan on the cooker, ready, and, putting on her strange black and white gear and with a dream-like terror in her heart, she went out to a paper on Old English Dialects.

When she came in, gloomy (for God's sake, what *was* the difference between *wict* and *wiht*? She hadn't known; and she had spent far too much time writing about the Vespasian Psalter Gloss), she found Tod wrestling like Laocoön with the sausages in revolt. He had dumped them in the pan, the whole string together, without cutting them up. As they cooked they had unwound themselves, expanded, and combined into one huge sausage that was climbing out of the pan at both ends and in the middle, while Theodore frantically tried to push it back with a fork in each hand. Gasping with laughter she collapsed on a chair while he cursed and the sausages, uniquely combining scorched and raw, continued to win the contest.

Penitent and abashed at his total failure to provide moral support in the form of palatable food, he took them all out to the Taj for supper, and they settled on a plan of fish and chips for lunch and keema peas for supper till all her nine papers were complete.

She thought she would die of indigestion; but she didn't. She got a good Second.

* * *

The principal was pleased. 'You'd never have got a First, you know, anyway,' she said. 'There is one odd thing. You have got a paper graded alpha gamma. How did you manage that?'

'Writing too much about the Vespasian Psalter, I expect,' said Tessa.

'Ah. Well, it's a very respectable degree, my dear. I congratulate you. Will you go on with your studies? I am told your tutor hoped you might . . .'

'No,' said Tessa. 'I don't think I can.' For Ben, who had refrained from getting her pregnant so far, was fully entitled to do so now.

He took her to Greece for a fortnight. And though she did miss Theodore greatly, and write to him every day, she liked it much more than she had expected.

The day before Cathy was to be received, Tessa took her out to tea in Fuller's. They laughed, talking over their degrees just finished as though they were grannies in full flood of nostalgia for the distant past. When Cathy remarked on that, Tessa said, 'The unidirectional quality of time, you see, makes the amount ago that something happened irrelevant, really. Just that it is "ago" is enough to make it distant; we should reminisce all we like!'

'You've been too much with philosophers,' said Cathy. 'Can I have another slice of walnut cake?'

'Gather ye walnuts while ye may!' said Tessa. 'Cathy; Cathy dear, will you be happy?'

'Will you?' said Cathy.

'But that's different . . .'

'No, it's not. I don't know about happiness. I haven't much experience of it. I think that Our Lord wants me as a nun. I shall try my best. I must admit I don't expect it to bring happiness in this world. But I expect my chances are as good as yours.'

'And I repeat: that what you are doing is of a totally different kind.'

'It's funny really, Tess. Has it struck you? All our lives we have been taught about virtue; and constantly, from all sides we have been told about the blessings of self-sacrifice. I have, anyway. And then suddenly, when I propose to do what has been so strongly urged on us all the time, alarm cries go up all round and nearly everyone I know tries to stop me. Now why do you think that is?'

'Who has been trying to stop you?'

'Well, firstly, my mother and father. That's not surprising, really. You can't expect them to rejoice at the thought of never seeing their daughter again, and getting no grandchildren. But the Reverend Mother from my school wrote trying to warn me off, and the priests here are heavily against it.'

'Theodore has warned you off . . .'

'Well, no, not really. Theodore was terribly sad, but he didn't try to change my mind. But Father Max gave me a dreadful going over. He was ferocious. He shook me, he nearly stopped me. And then I thought, but . . . hang on; what is all this suddenly about happiness? It sounds exactly like what they were all calling temptation until this minute.'

'Theodore once said to the group – Cathy, why weren't you a member of the group?'

'All that feels too public to me, Tessa. Just not quiet enough to be holy. What did Theodore say?'

'That all the Church's teaching about loving thy neighbour as thyself assumed that we loved ourselves and would tenderly care for our own welfare. That we did have such a duty, but it was never preached because everyone did it anyway and didn't need telling . . . something like that. They thought they could trust us to look after our own happiness.'

'But could they? Just look at us. Was it reasonable to trust us?'

'We aren't children,' said Tessa.

'When did we stop being, do you think?' Cathy asked.

'When do you have to go tomorrow?'

'Before you get up, I should think. There, don't look so stricken, Tessa. You can write after six weeks.'

Cathy did indeed mean she would be gone early, but not earlier than her friends were stirring, as it happened. For, driving back from morning Mass in the open-topped, clapped-out sports car Theodore had acquired while they were in Greece, they found themselves at the traffic lights at Carfax, directly behind a taxi – the only other vehicle on the road at that unearthly hour – and in the taxi, they realized, was Cathy. Waving and hooting they pursued her up the Cornmarket and St Giles. Theodore drove them past their own door and continued to follow the taxi up the Woodstock Road. Somewhere in Park Town he overtook it and roared ahead, while Ben and Tessa leaned out of the windows waving, and on reaching the roundabout on the by-pass, he simply drove round and round and round it until the taxi caught up with them, and then fell in sedately behind it for a few hundred yards before overtaking it again and repeating the head-spinning manoeuvre.

Until, alongside the endless wall of Blenheim, the taxi overtook them and stopped beside the road. Cathy got out and waited for them. They got out and went towards her. 'All right, then,' she said, smiling. 'Pray with me, now, and for me always.'

They stood in the wet grass under the moaning trees of the park, encountering wind, and bowed their heads.

'Holy Mary, Mother of God, pray for me now and at the hour of my death, Amen . . .'

'No more now,' she said. They stood and watched the taxi out of sight. Then they went, dishevelled and sober, to have breakfast in the Bear.

It was a long hot summer. Theodore worked demoniacally, afraid all the time that the Father Provincial would enquire after his health. His health was improving – Tessa's care and cooking, newly learned from *Tante Marie's French Cooking*, had produced a new, lean Theodore with hollow cheeks and restored energy, giving off an impression of inner fire and glowing with love and intellectual exercise. Something dramatic, Tessa gathered, wholly beyond her humble powers of comprehension but thrilling if you knew any mathematics, was emerging from his thesis. But if the Father Provincial knew how much better he was, he thought, he might be recalled and dumped in a parish somewhere. There was even a plot in hand to put him to bed and paint him yellow again with cake-colouring should any strange cleric – a possible runner for the Father Provincial – put in an appearance. Tessa laughed, and tried out the cake-colouring on Tod's right temple – it took two days to wash off – but she privately thought all the time that the Father Provincial's spy was none other than Father Max, who called now and then, and smiled, and drank a little whisky with them, and sometimes listened to Ben playing Bach.

Once Father Max found her trying to teach herself to type, a Pitman's card covering her hands, which struggled blindly on the keyboard. 'Do you need to do that?' he asked, amused.

'It would be useful. For example I could type Father Theodore's thesis for him.'

He shook his head. 'Dorothea, my dear, will not suit you. If you have time to spare why not help me with the travelling choir?'

Helping in the choir was certainly a pleasant sort of good work. It involved rushing out on Sundays to distant rural parishes, with tiny congregations which could never hear a sung Mass out of their own resources, singing plainsong in scout halls with meadowsweet growing half-way up the windows, or in the living rooms of private houses. Hubert sang in the choir, and some other old friends. Not everyone had departed.

Even so, they were quiet in their little flat. They played music, and read novels, eagerly consuming and discussing *The Sandcastle*, and *The Blue and Brown Books*, which, they decided, though not a novel, was more like poetry than anything else.

One hot afternoon when the leaves outside the window seemed to sweat in the heat and the dust stuck to their jaded planes, Tessa announced a picnic. She bore down protests about how much work the others had to do. 'But I don't have enough to do,' she said, 'and for weeks you've had your brutal way with me, now it's my turn. Anyway fresh air and exercise will do you both good, and the basket is packed with food and wine . . . it's come-away time for all nymphs and shepherds . . .'

They went to Thrupp and, starting with a beer in the Jolly Boatmen, they walked down the towpath, deep in summer growth. The mud-brown water of the canal baked beside them, and twice they saw a water-rat drawing a rapid ripple from bank to bank. Pale blue butterflies, like cut-out scraps of sky, flickered out of the stems they brushed in passing. The sun cooked them steadily through the fabric of their shirts. At the locks Theodore explained in enormous detail how the things were worked, and Tessa sat on a balance beam pretending to give enough attention to understand. They reached the junction with the cut through to the Thames, and turned along it.

The canal and the path slipped under the by-pass bridge, and just short of the bridge a narrow-boat was tied up, with a grimy man in belt and braces standing in the hatch. He nodded as they approached and asked Tessa, who was in the lead on the narrow path, 'What does that say?'

She looked up where he pointed, to a huge sign saying 'By-pass widening starts 1959'. But as she laughed, Theodore kicked her ankle from behind and read the notice aloud.

'Nothing to do with me, then,' the man said, and as

they looked back from beyond the stop-lock they saw him unhurriedly untying his boat.

The cut they were following opened quite shortly into the Thames. They found themselves in a meadow thick with buttercups, lightly shaded by a spaced-out plantation of aspens. Godstow Lock, the keeper's house, the lock cut, were all on the other bank, and beyond them the opposite meadow stretched to the blue wooded whaleback shape of Wytham Woods. At the river brink they sank into the moist, warm grass, and unpacked food and books.

Theodore stretched out, face down, holding the tepid wine-bottle in the water. This water, just as brown as the canal, was dancing, a lively current patterning the surface with scoops and striations, and the afternoon sun burning over Godstow lit constellations of floating stars, blazing and drowning on the rocking surface.

They ate, and sprawled in the fidgeting shade of the tree whose leaves moved constantly, and sounding like water supplied a sound-track to the bright silent river.

Theodore was reading a joke magazine, cyclostyled on cheap paper, and called *Why?* Soon he was laughing, and as Tessa looked up interrogatively from her novel he said, 'Here you are Tessa, here's an exam for you.'

'Why not for Ben too? I don't like exams.'

'Ben knows it all already. Here you go: Existence is, a) a predicate; b) the wherewith whereby the somewhat exists; c) drinking absinthe in black jeans.

'Nobody is a) not the name of nobody; b) not the name of anybody; c) nobody's name . . .'

'Hang on; hang on, what *is* this?'

'A general knowledge quiz; a qualifying competition for the consorts of philosophers. You aren't doing well at all so far. What about Class membership is a) a logical relation; b) a property of non-proletarians; c) a number which decreases as the term progresses . . .' His voice began to waver with laughter. 'Type means

a) a token of the type "type"; b) what Russell's theory was a theory of; c) a French word for a fellow existentialist . . .'

Tessa giggled. 'Go on. More.'

'Well, you can't do the multiple choice. Try some essay questions. For example: "Nothing is more instructive than philosophy". (Spinoza.) Is this a reason for reading nothing? Or, Who won the ontological argument?'

'Oh, that's easy!' Tessa said. 'God did. Definitely.'

'Hmm,' said Theodore. 'What about: How many more things are there in heaven and earth than are dreamt of in your philosophy? (Give a rough estimate.)'

'But however many things are there in this wretched exam paper?'

'You don't have to do them all. It says candidates are recommended to answer at least none of these questions. And the answers are all on page 13.'

He tossed her the magazine – which had, she found, twelve pages.

'It's hot,' said Tessa. 'I'm hot. I wish I had brought a swimming costume.'

'Oh, yes,' said Theodore, sitting up. 'Wouldn't it have been good.'

'Why not, then?'

'We haven't got . . .'

'But who is here to see? There's only us.' And indeed, since the narrow-boat skipper had brought his boat chugging past them and swung round to enter the lock just after they arrived, they had not seen another soul moving.

Theodore, on his feet, turned his back to them and pulled his shirt up over his head and off. She saw the bones of his back under the dappled shadows on his pale skin. He was still too thin . . . He dropped his trousers, and stood briefly absurd in his underpants before stripping them off too to reveal himself beautiful, slender, narrow, and neatly made. He stepped to the bank and went in diving, the huge splash freckling her face with flecks of water, making her blink.

She lay beside Ben, watching. Theodore swam in a shifting mercurial whirl of silver, where the broken water round him caught up the brilliant sun. He dived, midstream, his pale body surfacing and arching under, water-sleeked like a fish. As he neared the further bank, from the shadowy underhang of the rank weeds and grasses there, a kingfisher suddenly broke cover, and in a pulsing spark of colour burned across the surface and alighted on one of the painted posts that held a chain across the weir, a warning not to turn downstream from the canal junction. Tessa watched entranced, and suddenly finding her sticky skin and beaded upper lip intolerable. 'Shall we?' she asked Ben.

'You if you like,' he said, looking up from his book. 'It's far too cold for me.'

She stood and, turning her back on Tod's bobbing head, shed her clothes – though of course she had to face him to go in – and, not brave enough to dive, she slipped in over the compliant bending flowers of the brink, thinking Ben ridiculous, in the heat, to say it was too cold, until the icy water gripped her naked body and scorched her skin all over, and she realized he meant the river not the day. She stood, trembling, shoulder deep, while her nipples flinched and stood up hard and painful from areolas wrinkled tight like prunes, and she felt the coolness seeping into her body below, warming only slowly as it entered her shuddering flesh. She gasped breath into her constricted chest, girdled with muscles in spasm, and struck out swimming as hard as she could against the current, heading upstream.

Tod caught her quickly. He came swimming below the surface and rolling over on his back brushed against her, underneath her in the pull of the river's direction. His half erect member stroked her belly as he swam under her, and her weightless, floating breasts were drawn across his ribs and came to rest cradled against his thighs as she caught him by the waist and held on. Everywhere they touched she felt his blood-warmth consoling her skin, while the molten cold flowed on and burned between them, fire and ice, touching him and not touching him, and marbled together the incandescent glowing of the flesh and the death-cold strength and scour of the changelessly flowing river.

He moved in her arms, gently thrusting her away while he rolled over, and raised his head for breath; she had been holding him submerged. Then he was kissing her. They were floating, extended together full length, face to face, and as his tongue parted her lips she drank river and, upturned, saw the sky and branches together scudding overhead. A stripe of shadow crossed her vision; then they heard Ben calling sharply to them from the shore and, breaking out of their rapt entwinement, they found they had drifted under the chains and past the sign saying Danger.

The current ran faster and fiercer there; it was a hard swim back.

And though the water had become tolerable, had lost its mortal bite while she swam upstream – the kingfisher flew again as she came – the moment she struggled out she did feel cold, and they had brought no towels. Tod ran into the open field and rolled around to dry off among the buttercups, but Tessa, slightly shy, put her clothes on her wet self and only watched him. He came back covered all over with gold, shining with yellow pollen and with petals and grass sticking to his skin. He came back golden, fiercely smiling at her, goose-pimpled, and sat down between her and Ben with his teeth chattering, and Ben said, pretending not to look up from his book, 'I knew it would be too cold.' Theodore picked up the bottle and swigged the rest of the wine. And by and by, dressed and decent, they ambled back to Thrupp and the car.

* * *

And now, at last, Tessa wondered if she had sinned. Had she, meaning no harm – she was quite sure she had meant no harm – crossed the obscure border between chaste and unchaste love? She found it hard to tell. She could derive no map of the emotions from her dealings with Ben which gave her any guidance at all; it seemed a different country, and much less perilous. Theodore had said that they had done everything which was a euphemism for the forbidden act; he had never seemed, tender though his conscience was, disturbed by anything they had actually done. Love itself, she knew, was not only permitted, but a commandment. Tessa examined her conscience. It seemed to her that since the day of the swim, her joy in Theodore had become more immediate, more like a physical sensation. She thought she was no more likely than before to overstep the mark and actually gratify the lusts of the flesh as she had always understood them, but it had begun to occur to her that the lusts of the flesh might include even smiling, even knowing that someone was sitting reading in the next room . . . She knew, after all, enough Anglo-Saxon to know that 'lusts' were joys. And she was full of joy.

Her dreams were full of flowing, falling water. Bright salmon leapt in them, casting a shower of diamonds, casting a shower of golden petals. Brilliant kingfisher-blue mackerel with silver bellies thrust thickly through the waves of the wide sea, or leapt in the well of the boat casting droplets of blood. The blood covered her with brown freckles, freckled Theodore's smiling face. She drew a naked fish up on the end of a line, and it came up Theodore. She walked at the river brink and saw the Green Man dancing under the trees, dancing with the May-Day Morris men, and then the dancers all departed and the boughs of the Green Man's dress parted and out came Theodore, golden with buttercups, holding a silver chalice in his hands . . . She walked in a dewy morning, out on the meadow above Magdalen Bridge, and saw a fox alone in the field, dancing and gambolling, leaping high in the air for joy, and then – since she really had walked there, alone and very early – did not know if she had dreamed, or seen the fox.

She could walk for hours, and not know where she had been walking. And heaven shone out in every common English sight, in gardens, in flowering grasses, in cloudy skies. But when she prayed, and thought of the real heaven, she still saw that meadow, across which she had once thought to walk talking theology with her friends, only now it contained Theodore, naked, and the glorification of the body looked like a coating of pollen . . .

What you did, of course, if you did not know for certain if you had sinned or not, was confess it just in case. All her life confronted with a puzzling possible transgression, Tessa had added it to her confessions. After all, God would know if the confession was unnecessary and no harm would be done . . . Tessa thought about it. She usually confessed to Father Max; and he would know her voice. He would know immediately exactly who she was talking about. The secrecy of the confessional was absolute, but that had not stopped Theodore carrying about the knowledge of things said to him like a burden. She really couldn't face confessing to Father Max. In fact, when she thought some more it didn't seem possible to confess to anyone in Oxford. There were quite a few priests in Oxford, but not infinitely many . . . and how was she to know which of them knew enough to guess at Tod's identity? Not in Oxford.

But she was going to London that week to do some shopping and have lunch with her mother.

The cathedral was vast and gloomy. The centuries-long process of covering its walls and multiple domes with vulgar pictures in mosaic had barely begun; marble and brick in unreflective shapes of great beauty surrounded her. The place had a Marabar Caves effect on the voice of a priest saying Benediction somewhere. There was a barrack of confessionals, like a row of telephone boxes in a railway station, and several kneeling queues in the nearby benches. Tessa knelt, prayed, waited her turn.

'Bless me Father, for I have sinned . . . I don't think it is in any way connected with pride, Father. I don't see how it can be. And it isn't because of trying less hard to be a good Catholic. But I have kissed and caressed someone . . . I don't think this was sinful, but I would like to confess it just in case. In this matter I most need God's help and blessing. So just in case . . .'

'But why do you suspect these actions, child? You are married?'

'Yes, Father.'

'And it was not your husband on whom these endearments were conferred?'

'No, Father.'

'And you think, if he knew about it, he would object?'

'No, Father. I don't think that.'

'Then what is troubling you, child? Is there some other reason why you are afraid you have done wrong?'

'I don't really think I *have* done wrong, Father. But the other man is a priest.'

'I see. And are you alone when you exchange these embraces?'

'Sometimes. Usually.'

'And at these times has either of you disarranged your dress?'

'What do you mean, Father? No, I don't think so . . .'

'And on these occasions are you lying down or standing up? Have you ever touched or seen his private parts?'

'I don't think you should ask me this, Father. I won't answer you!'

She heard an audible sigh from the shadowy shape through the grid.

'Describe a single occasion to me when something that troubles you took place.'

'No, Father. I have told you enough.'

'You are full of self-will, my child. Remember you kneel before God, putting your immortal soul in his hands.'

'God knows what happened, Father. I don't have to describe it to *Him*.'

'I cannot in this case absolve you, child. At least, I can give you only a conditional absolution. You must promise me you will never again be alone with this man.'

And at last Tessa saw where she had arrived. Her refusal to describe any more had been born in fact from concern for her confessor, whose agitated tone of voice made her suspect his motives for enquiry . . .

And now she had before her a choice between God and Theodore.

'I can't promise that,' she said.

'Why not?'

'It is not me you ask to make sacrifices. It is the other person's safety and welfare at stake.'

'How can that be? It is not for you to take responsibility for the sins of a spoiled priest; you are to see to your own salvation. Think carefully. Unless you can promise me you will never again allow yourself to be alone with that man, I cannot absolve you.'

Kneeling in the dark Tessa thought. To keep the promise she was asked for would mean turning Theodore out of what they had called his home. The moment term began again, and Ben started teaching, they would be alone together most of the time. It would mean never again going in to him, tucking in the sheet and kissing him good night . . . never even walking with him, and all conversation about him and his difficulties would cease since they never talked like that with Ben present, though doubtless Theodore talked also to Ben . . . It would mean deserting Theodore, leaving him to fall again into the misery and lusts that had afflicted him before, leaving him, she thought, to encompass his damnation, or unhinge his marvellous mind, or both . . . She had no choice at all.

She did make a last try. 'It cannot be God's will I should desert someone who needs me,' she said.

'God's will for you is what I say it is,' he said. 'It is to me He has given the keys of Peter. Give me your promise, and let your sins be forgiven.'

'If God damns us for loving one another, then we must choose to be damned.'

'You have no choice to make. You must simply obey, and give your promise.'

'No,' she said. 'No I will not. I will leave the Church; now, this minute. And every time you pray, Father, until you die, until the judgement day, remember me, for one of us is lost!'

She walked away down the centre aisle, and out of the great doors, not touching herself with holy water, and not looking back at the High Altar, and emerged on the steps opposite Burns and Oates and out into Victoria Street like someone leaving for ever the entire known world.

Chapter Three

LAPSING : DISMISSALS

And in the unknown time ahead Tessa would inevitably change, and her actions on that morning would come to seem to her impenetrable. Whatever had she been thinking of? Granted that she had supposed that loving Theodore was a sin at all, how could she have thought that it was a venial one? How could she possibly have imagined that she could confess to touching a priest and be forgiven? Or have thought that the reactions of the anonymous power behind the grille would have anything whatever to do with the teaching of Christ?

But if her own mind would be a mystery to her, how much greater would be her amazement at reflecting that in the few years since her severance from her faith, the mighty and immortal Church had changed far more than she. For it would come to pass that the bishops had indeed assembled and disagreed with one another. And people remained Catholics who picked and chose what to believe, what to obey. So the Church would be mirrored with crystal clarity in her apostacy, that was blurred and invisible in the continued faith of her husband and her friends. As the dignity and antiquity of the liturgy would be clearer in her memory than in the continuing service of God which had so garbled everything . . . And that powerful longing to return to the rituals of one's youth, that so often has people back in the benches once they have not much to lose, and little prospect of sin in front of them, would for her be impossible. The altars of her youth would have been turned back to front; the blessings vulgarized.

'*Dominus vobiscum . . . et cum spiritu tuo . . .*' would become, more or less, 'God bless . . . and the same to you, Jack.'

And she would little by little gain unexpected ground in common with her Polish friends; like them being exiled from a country which in the meantime has changed irremediably, and beyond recognition.

Three days after the day Tessa left the Church it was Sunday, and when she would not go to Mass she had to explain herself to Ben.

'Don't be silly, love,' he said. 'All you have to do is find a more intelligent priest, and try again.'

'Blessed are the brainy, who understand the teaching of the Church?' she said. 'No, I don't think so.'

'Why not? Look, Tessa, we're very protected in Oxford, you know. The Church is full of priests who know less theology than we do, whose judgement is very narrow and poor. And the intelligent laity everywhere have your problem. It's not unusual. What they do is sit politely through the sermons, and go and find a Jesuit or a very bright Benedictine to confess to. You just avoid confessing to Father Tom Dick and Harry.'

'But, Ben, to them He has given the keys of the kingdom of heaven!'

'What do you mean?'

'They have the power to bind and loose.'

'The Church has that power. The Church isn't some prurient clot in Westminster Cathedral.'

'I think you don't understand. Maybe you are right, maybe I could find a priest who would absolve me. What about other people who don't know that? Who believe in sermons? Who meekly do what they are told? Weren't we supposed to be in one true Church together?'

'You are right that I don't understand you.'

'There's a kind of cleverness I can't stomach, Ben. My uncle missing Mass the day it wasn't said in the village . . . no, a better example, those people who think the Church has got its own teaching wrong about contraception, and who use it, and go and kneel at the Communion rail beside the Mrs Murphies dying of a fourteenth pregnancy, and who say "*Unam Sanctam Catholicam*" alongside her and feel no shame.'

'All you have to do is keep the rules. The rules do not prevent you from finding a sympathetic priest. What you are doing is deliberately making the rules more strict than they need be, and then saying you can't keep them at all on that account.'

'But the trouble is much deeper than that. I knew I was not going to obey that man. I was, and I am, quite sure that he is wrong. And I am not sure he is wrong because I could find a Jesuit confessor who would say so; I am sure because I judge it so – and so you see, I am a Protestant really. I will act on my own conscience and when it comes to the crunch I judge for myself, and find the Church wanting. I am not really a Catholic, for all the attempts there have been to make me one.'

'You have such a strange idea of what being a Catholic is. It doesn't mean not following your conscience.'

'For you perhaps not.'

'Not for anyone. It isn't for us to say what being a Catholic is. We just are Catholics. You can't stop. You can be a good one, a bad one, a lapsed one . . .'

'Poor Ben; you would never have married me if you hadn't thought I was a rock solid Papist!'

'No,' he said. 'I must go now. I shall be late for Mass.'

'Pray for me,' she said, sitting on the bed, for they had been talking in their own room behind a closed door. He turned in the doorway.

'I will with all my strength,' he said. 'But Tessa, you know, don't you – you do remember? "*Extra Ecclesia Nulla Salus Est.*"'

Outside the church, though, was where she walked

that Sunday while Theodore and Ben attended the sung High Mass.

She walked in the familiar golden streets, while all around her a clamour of heretical bells summoned believers of another kind, and into the Botanical Gardens, where once God had shaken the veils of reality and almost appeared to her palpable.

Could she really so have mistaken virtue? Could loving Theodore really be wrong? She sat down on a stone bench in a patch of sunlight falling through leaf-shadow, and considered. If God exists, she thought, I could more easily by far explain myself to Him . . . and then she stopped, appalled. For the first time in her life she had entertained a thought beginning 'if God exists . . .' thinking truly in a conditional mode. Every time you said this theological catch phrase, you called up, grammatically at least, the other option, *if he does not* . . . and now this ghostly possibility was suddenly made flesh.

If God does not exist, what then?

She saw at once that various consequences allegedly falling on unbelievers were false, were nothing but the Church's straw men. The idea that if God does not exist there would be no foul act, however frightful, that one would not gaily commit, having no fear of hell . . . She herself, for example, was not going to commit frightful acts, had never been going to, and had all the time been restrained not by fear of God but by a proper self-respect. There was, now she came to think of it, something almost sleazy about the hypothetical person who was restrained from foulness of conduct only by fear of retribution, or hope of rewards, rather than from intrinsic revulsion from what was foul.

The other day she had supposed vaguely that she could leave the Church and still believe in God, but more thought made that seem difficult. The Church had in effect ejected her for loyally loving Theodore. Would God underwrite that? If not that, would He underwrite the Church at all? Would He fry you in hell for challenging the Church's authority? Well, if He would, He would not be what we should most love and desire to serve. And if He didn't underwrite the Church's authority, He had in a way abolished Himself. For, apart from the teaching of the Church, what evidence of God did we have?

Tessa looked up, with a lightening heart, with an amazing lift of the spirit, at a possibly empty sky. At flowers and scented bushes, and riotously branching and leafy trees, which perhaps just were, having no reason, self-sown – self sown! – and it seemed to her suddenly likely that the world was empty of morality, and that she stood in no more danger of being hideously punished for loving Theodore than the lovely willow trees along the river edge of the garden for leaning to the water, or the rank weeds of the bank for growing towards the light.

The road from Damascus, however, was not to be taken without challenge. The challenge she expected, from Theodore, did not come. She had her answers ready, having decided not to lay on his troubled heart any responsibility for her defection; never to let him know that it was to keep her door open to him that she had left the Church . . . But he seemed not to notice, and he never asked. But one morning she opened the door to find Father Max.

She made him coffee, and he sat down on the battered sofa and said, 'It is usually those to whom the Faith means a great deal who lose it, Tessa. Did you know that?'

'Is that why you warned me not to come to Mass so often?'

'Did I? That was clever of me. Tessa, I have been a priest for thirty years, and I still have no idea whether God prefers those who take their consciences lightly, take faith for granted, forgive themselves readily, or those who take it all deeply to heart . . . Can you tell me why you have lapsed? Or does Ben exaggerate?'

'I can't tell you why. It's very personal.'

'Somehow I thought it would be. I can believe no harm of you, my dear. If I find you among the others at the Communion rail, I will give you the Sacrament of our Blessed Lord without hesitation.'

'I think you will never find me there.'

'Never is a long time.'

'My grandfather used to say that!'

'Did he? Well, I am almost old enough to be your grandfather. I know that it is moderation, coolness, common sense, that is steady and faithful to Our Holy Mother the Church, not enthusiasm and excess. At least, not among those who remain in the world. In the cloister it may be different.'

'Father, what did you come for? Are you hoping to persuade me to return?'

'I would be immeasurably glad if I could, Tessa. But no. Our Blessed Lord clearly preferred the repentant sinner to the man of common virtue. It may be He prefers those who have too much faith to keep the Faith. I am among the worldly ones, but I do not know that I am right. I have come to ask you to promise me that you will pray for me. Will you do that?'

'I can promise for now. I don't know for how long I will believe enough . . .'

'You could always pray, believing or not. You could pray on Pascal's bet, I think.'

'What's that?'

'The view that we should act as though God did exist; because if He does not we stand to lose only a few superficial pleasures in this life, whereas if He does we might lose eternity.'

'I don't think I understand that.'

'Ask Father Theodore to explain it to you,' said Max, getting up. 'And don't forget me, Tessa. My flock are my only family. I need your prayers.'

* * *

Tod came in so quickly upon Father Max's departure that they met on the stairs, and the coffee was still hot for him.

'What did Max want?' he asked.

'Nothing much. Coffee, chiefly.'

'Oh?' he said, coming and putting his arms round her and leaning his cheek against the nape of her neck as she filled his cup and added his dash of cream. 'Only I sometimes wonder if Max is keeping an eye on me. Did he ask you anything about me?'

'No he didn't. You want to watch out, you know, Tod. I realize that ordination makes you ineffably sacred, but does it also make you paranoid? It was my spiritual state Max was on about, not yours.'

Tod laughed. 'How could a nice girl like you have a spiritual problem?' he said. 'You're sure he didn't even enquire lightly if I am working hard?'

'I'm quite sure. Your name was not so much as mentioned.'

'Phew! Relief, relief. In fact, darling Tess, under whose tender care I flourish like the best bay tree, my thesis is almost finished. And that raises the spectre . . .'

'Of the Father Provincial wanting you back. Oh.'

'I have been thinking it over. I can't go back. I have decided to ask to be laicized.'

She put down the coffee at once, and took him in her arms. 'What does it mean?' she asked.

'Release from priestly duties. No more duty to say the breviary, to say Mass, to work in a parish. One is allowed to go quietly away and live the life of a devout layman. I've been finding out as much about it as I can. I've been such an embarrassment to him, I think he'll let me go.'

'But . . . I didn't know such a thing was possible. You just ask and he lets you go?'

'Goodness no! It means appeals to Rome . . . an awful fuss. Compulsory retreats for me; it may be very nasty. But as far as I can find out I would be likely to get it if the Father Provincial backs the request and not otherwise. I shall have to tell him how I was advised to suppress doubts . . .'

'But when he understands it will be easy?'

'Well, one thing will make it much easier. I shan't need to seek release from a vow of celibacy. You are the person I love; and so I shan't ever want to marry.'

'Hold on, Tod. Wait a bit. That doesn't sound right to me. I think you should try to get free, entirely.'

'I think release from the vow of celibacy is never given. They are afraid there would be such a flood.'

'But you must try to get it. If they won't give it, they won't; but you will always know you did your best to be honourably quit of it.'

'Ah, Beatrice,' he said, softly, 'who cares for my honour . . . you know so much more about the lay life than I do, that I ought to take your advice, I think. Only we both know there will never be anything like this . . . never be any one but you. So, since it will make it much harder for me, why?'

'It's somehow cleaner,' she said. 'Have you told Ben?'

'I will tell him. But I wanted to tell you first.'

That night she found Tod crying when she went to give him good night.

His distress appalled her. 'Tod, is any of this my fault?' she asked him. 'The worst thing imaginable for me would be if I thought you would have found the priesthood easier if you had never met me, never loved me.'

'No,' he said. 'Nothing would have been better, and a lot of things would have been worse. However painful this is, Tess, it keeps things sorted out for me.'

'What do you mean?'

'I know that my doubts are real, and honest. I have no hope of marrying the woman I love, and nothing to gain in respect of love from leaving the priesthood. And still I know that I must go, on pure grounds of belief. Without you I could never be sure that my unhappiness was not the true source of my doubts; that I was not unconsciously persuading myself the Church was wrong in order to feel free to disobey her . . .'

'And that's what you call sorted out?'

'When I seek my release they will look around for the woman in the case. They always jump to that conclusion. And I shall be able to say with complete truthfulness that there is no-one I wish to marry.'

'So it wouldn't help you now any more than it did at first if we gave each other up?'

'It's just the opposite I'm afraid of. I can't see this through without you . . . you won't stop loving me?'

'I couldn't ever do that. I would have to unself myself first.'

'Not even if I fail God, fail the Church, disgrace myself utterly?'

'No. Not at all. I didn't love you because I thought you a good priest, silly!'

'I'm not sure I understand love. If it wasn't for that, I can't imagine why you *did* love me.'

'Why I *do*. You do understand; if I did something wrong, and horrible, you wouldn't stop loving me, would you?'

'That's different.'

'Why?'

'You never would.'

'What I really will never do is stop loving you. Whatever you have to do. Whatever other people think. Never fear it, love.'

'I'll try not,' he said.

Three months after the day Tessa left the Church, she woke one morning to hear the phone ringing insistently downstairs, by the front door of the house. The other flats were all empty until the new term began since the college let them to graduate students who wanted to live out. Ben lay peacefully sleeping beside her, with a sheet of Bach cello music under his cheek;

he had fallen asleep last night while trying to commit it to memory for a concert that would begin rehearsals next week.

Her first thought was of Theodore. She pulled on a dressing-gown and went leaping down the stairs to the ground floor, where the phone, a battered payphone, hung crazily askew on the wall behind the front door.

Theodore; his letters were so miserable. They were putting him through an endless punitive inquisition, keeping him in retreat. They had not, as he thought they might, sent him to Rome, but back to Germany, to the stern oversight of the principal of the college where he had got his glorious degree, and the shocked would-be reformative company of his clerical friends there. She got letters nearly every day, charting terrible interviews with powerful churchmen, charting his humiliation and distress. He was under great pressure from them not to ask for dispensation from vows of celibacy, which would effectively close his way back, and she was spending nearly all her time writing comfort by return of post, though the post muddled, delayed, and delivered complex discussions in the wrong order. He had phoned once or twice, just to drink her voice, and that was usually early, taking her by surprise at breakfast, so that on one occasion, dumb with longing and joy, and commanded to talk she had been reduced to saying, 'They told me you had been to her and mentioned me to him . . .' and he laughed, and said, 'Plastic daffodils!'

This time she looked at her watch as she reached the foot of the stairs – it was even earlier, only six, and somehow the high-pitched ringing at that hour felt doom-laden, as if it could only be disaster . . . Theodore, and something wrong.

So intensely was she expecting Theodore that it took her several seconds to realize that the tear-choked voice on the other end was Cathy.

'Cathy? What's wrong?'

She had trouble understanding what Cathy was

saying; her voice was hoarse from disuse, and she was too distressed to make much sense. Ben had followed her from bed down the stairs, and was standing on the landing listening as she made what she hoped were the right replies.

'Yes; yes of course I'll fetch you . . . yes, I can come right now. I don't know how long it will take, but I'll come as quickly as I can . . . yes, I'll bring some clothes . . . don't worry about money, we will lend you some . . . yes . . . yes, I'll be on the road as soon as I've got some clothes on . . . well, of course we aren't up yet, it's only six o'clock . . . no, I don't mind being woken, no . . . you can tell me all about it when I get there . . .'

'What's up?' asked Ben.

'It's Cathy. She wants to be fetched from her nunnery. Now or sooner. I think I should go.'

'It will have to be you, I think, Tess; I've got a faculty meeting at twelve. Come and grab some coffee, and we'll look at a map.'

It was miles and miles away; Tessa set out by seven, and could not be there before mid-day. She drove steadily, not being used enough to cars and never before, as it happened, having made a long journey alone, so having both to drive and navigate.

She didn't get lost, to her own surprise. The place was locked, and double locked. There was a parlour just inside the door, like the retreat house that had contained Ben the day Theodore got arrested; on a wooden bench in the parlour Cathy sat, weeping. Her hair was crudely chopped off grotesquely close to her head, she had lost weight and her cheeks were sunken. She was wearing a coarse white woollen robe with a rope belt, and roughly made sandals. As soon as Tessa entered she looked up and said, 'I'm sorry! I'm so sorry!'

'Whatever for?' said Tessa softly.

'Bringing you all this way. I didn't know what to do . . . who to ask . . . my parents are in Hong Kong.'

'You did just right. I brought you some things.'

She gave Cathy the bundle of clothes. Cathy got up and moved towards the door. A nun had appeared and was standing firm, her hands enfolded in her wide sleeves.

'I have to change . . .' said Cathy, like a request.

'You can change in here. I will see nobody comes in,' said the nun.

'Can't I go back in, even to change?' Cathy said, bewildered.

'You know you can't,' said the nun. 'Change here.' She stepped back and closed the door, leaving the two young women together.

'I'll help you,' Tessa said. 'Let's get you respectable and out of here!'

Cathy turned her back, and drew her garment off over her head. There was a faint line of round bruises across her shoulders. And, Tessa saw, appalled, she was not wearing a bra: a piece of flannel was wound round her breasts to restrain them. The commonplace peach nylon Marks and Spencer bra with a little cheap lace on the edges that Tessa had brought seemed suddenly like a wicked luxury – and, she raged, like a basic human right. Cathy had lost the knack of catching the hooks behind her back, and Tessa had to help her. She got it done up, and lightly touching the bruises said, 'What have you done?'

'Penance,' said Cathy.

Tessa had brought her a straight skirt and a black sweater. She had chosen them thinking they were austere and plain enough for any purpose; but with Cathy's crew-cut hair they made her look suddenly extreme, like a French film star. 'Gamine' would be the word.

'Do you have any luggage?' she asked.

Cathy smiled suddenly, a smile as suddenly extinguished. 'Not one thing,' she said.

Tessa had been driving south for half an hour, with Cathy sitting silently beside her, when it occurred to her to ask, 'Cathy, where am I taking you? Are you coming home with me?'

'I have an aunt in Salisbury who would take me, I expect. Can we go there?'

'Yes. We must stop and phone to let her know, I imagine. But *we* could have you, too. You can come to us.'

'You haven't got room, really.'

'There's Theodore's room. He's abroad.'

'Oh.'

'Spend at least one night in Oxford, Cathy. We'll go and buy you a change of clothes, and put some money in a bank account for you . . .'

'I'll do whatever you like,' said Cathy. From time to time on the way she wept quietly.

Somewhere around Banbury she said she would much rather go straight to Salisbury.

'I'm so sorry,' said Tessa, squinting at a rain-lashed windscreen, 'but I don't think I can drive any further. We'll have to stop for a rest and a meal, anyway. I've never driven as far as this before, and I'm getting bog-eyed.'

'All right.'

And Cathy said not another word, as they reached, at last, the by-pass and the familiar long home run down the Banbury Road, and sailed into the open spaces of St Giles, and parked under the plane trees outside the narrow crooked house with its pink front door.

She stood in the kitchen while Ben poured Tessa a drink, and shook her head mutely at the offer of gin, at the offer of food, at the offer of a hot-water bottle and immediate bed.

At last Ben said to her sharply, 'Sit down!' and she obeyed. 'Now, say what you want to eat,' he commanded, and thus, talking to her roughly, he got her to consume an omelette, drink some milk and take herself off to bed, and the moment she had gone he grabbed his cello and played himself into serenity with a Bach partita, while Tessa drowsed in an armchair, her head still reeling with miles of rain and road.

'She's in shock,' Ben said. 'We should try to keep

her here a few days. She'll come round.'

At breakfast Cathy said, 'I need some clothes. You'll want these back before I go anywhere.'

'Let's go shopping, then,' said Tessa. 'That'll be fun.'

But shopping with Cathy turned out to be rather hard work. Bras and knickers were all right, but a dress and a skirt and some blouses caused endless trouble. Cathy kept trying to buy clothes that even Tessa thought frumpish. Anything at all fancy struck her as the next thing to going whoring, and in the end they managed only to find another bleak black sweater, a grey skirt, and a white shirt. Tessa bought her a red silk neckscarf as a present, and they found some plain dark shoes. Then, exhausted, they went home to lunch on sandwiches cut from yesterday's bread.

Later, as they sat reading, Tessa glanced up at Cathy, looking like some boy Hamlet, and said, 'Tell me about it if you like.'

'About what?'

'You don't seem thrilled at the wicked world.'

'I'm missing Divine Office.'

'You just go out on to the street. Turn left for Alleywoggers, right for Blackfriars. I recommend Blackfriars, where you can hear them singing office at all the canonical hours.'

Tears spilled over Cathy's eyes. 'Oh, Lord,' said Tessa, 'I didn't mean it unkindly. You have made the right decision. You must have. There are lots of good things to do in the world, and lots of ways to do good. Once you get over the shock.'

'I expect so. Can we go for a walk? I'd like to feed the ducks.'

It was not until they were half-way to Salisbury, three days later, that, on Tessa saying yet again, 'You must have made the right decision,' Cathy said, 'I didn't. They threw me out!'

'But why? Whyever . . .'

'Something I couldn't get off my mind. Something in the outside world, that I ought to have left behind me . . . I can go back if I can get it sorted out.'

'But do you want to go back?'

'More than anything!'

'I'm sorry,' said Tessa ambiguously.

A year after the day Tessa left the Church, Tod came to see her unexpectedly. He found her half asleep in the sunshine on a bench in the back garden, making a raffia lampshade. They were living at that time in a little house in Wolvercote, and Tod, who had become a schoolmaster, required to live on the premises during term, came and went to Wolvercote as he pleased. He had declared himself willing to take a job on the assembly line at Cowley, if only he could come home to Tessa, but he had found more suitable work easily enough.

He came across the lawn to her, and kissed her. But as she looked up, startled, saying, 'Tod, what has happened? What's wrong?' he began, stiltedly, like one who has rehearsed the words well, 'I know you are too generous to stand in the way of my happiness.'

She took a little while to understand what he was saying; that he had met somebody he wished to marry. When she did understand she at first tried to preserve her calm, before him at least, and saying she needed to be alone for an hour, she reached her bedroom, closed the door and lay down on the bed, face down. A terrible, racking weeping engulfed her. After a while she realized, muffling her sobbing by biting the pillow and hearing small sounds in the house, that Tod was outside, perhaps within earshot. Little by little she stilled herself; suppressed the heaving of her lungs and the twitching of her muscles until only a fluttering in her belly remained. She washed her face, though her eyes were inflamed with tears, and went out to confront him.

Years later Tessa found herself sitting in a garden in the summer dusk, talking to a friend who had lived life chained to a wheelchair. The friend remarked that she could not believe there could be a kindly God, not, it turned out, because of her present affliction, but because when she was seven or so, she had accidentally let her pet bird fly free and sat helplessly while it was taken by a cat. Tessa would then reflect that if she too now accused God, it would be because of the moment when Theodore, baffled at her anguish, had said to her, 'But it's not as if we had ever been lovers . . .'

If he truly did not know what intensity of physical passion their mutual chastity had expressed, then the love she had thought of as perfectly reciprocal, mirrored in each of them, could have been nothing of the kind. Well, evidently it could not have been. The thought possessed her as she stood before him, red-eyed, that that bodily union with him which his priesthood had made unthinkable, thinkable now, would be given to somebody else. He came towards her with a face full of tenderness for her distress and put an arm around her, as though nothing had changed; whereupon some superhuman force seized her, every bone in her body began to shake and her teeth rattled so loudly in her mouth they frightened her.

And that state at least, she realized, was perfectly mirrored in his.

Somehow they managed to step back, to separate themselves and the trembling died down to nothing but a weakness, a watery fatigue in the joints. And though naturally she regretted – and would long regret – that she had never possessed him, she would not regret that it had not happened then, when it came nearest, because, after all, there had been an argument underpinning the position she had got herself into, and that argument crucially depended on the idea that she was the only woman Theodore could love and therefore the only person who could help him. And that, it was now apparent, was not true.

Tessa did not behave well. She could not control her grief and begged abjectly, and often in tears, for some small scrap of continuing intimacy with him. And though all four of them subscribed to the fiction that they were to be life-long friends, this mercy, being now really in love, he steadfastly refused her. At last it occurred to her – she remained deeply ashamed at how long it took her to realize it – that he went on seeing her not because he wanted to, but as a means of keeping himself from knowing how wholly he had abandoned her. Then she thought she would cease to seek to see him, and wait for him to make the next invitation. It would be better, after all, if he saw of her exactly as much as he wished and not a moment more. Whereupon all contact between them ceased.

At some point in the terrible destructive scenes which were travelled before that quietus was reached he said to her, 'But if you feel like this why did you make me try so hard to get release from celibacy?'

'As it turns out it doesn't make any difference to you!' she flashed, but to herself she thought, Does he think I could have wished to keep him like a hare with one foot in a trap?

Somewhere along the way, too, he reminded her that she had once said that if he was going to hell she would go there with him. 'God has taken us at our word,' he said, 'and made us into each other's hell.'

From which it was apparent that Theodore could still muster some belief in God; which was more than Tessa could.

Her path was marked out clear, however. For that flickering sensation in her belly that had not been stilled when she briefly mastered her weeping and went out to confront Theodore on the landing, was the first faint palpable movement of Ben's child.

And later, much later, she realized that it was not so much belief in God that had misled her, but belief in love. For just as she had learned so many transient aspects of the world she grew up in and supposed them to be the enduring nature of things, until they changed or vanished; so she had thought that a declaration of love was a revelation of an abiding, inhering quality – an eternal essence of the soul, not merely a report on the present state of the weather. And yet she had been transformed, as the white swans on the backwaters of the Cherwell had been in the moment when the Australian explorer clapped eyes on a black one. In an instant she had become no longer necessary, but accidental. *Love is not love . . .*

Everyone, she came to think, everyone including herself – oh yes, not least herself, however incompetently! – seeks only their own happiness more or less ruthlessly according to temperament. And Theodore had needed to marry; in forsaking her he had no more been specially wicked than he had, ever, been particularly virtuous.

Five years after the day Tessa left the Church she went to see Hubert. Hubert had asked her to. He was living in Bournemouth, with Stefan, who had never been able to manage independently and, she gathered, was now ill. Hubert's note said Stefan often mentioned her, and he thought seeing her might cheer him up. So she left the children with her mother for the day and took an early train.

Hubert did not, as he had promised, meet her at the station. She waited, meditated whether to phone, and then took a taxi. The address was in a large block of flats, with balconies, facing the sea.

Hubert met her at the door, wearing a butcher's apron and yellow gloves. A shockingly nasty smell wafted to her as he opened the door. 'I'm sorry, Tessa, we've had a bit of a disaster,' he said. 'Go into the sitting room for a moment, will you.'

'Let me help,' she said, slipping off her coat.

'It isn't nice.'

'It can't be worse than nappies,' she said. But it could. Stefan was dying of some fearful disease. His digestive tract had been replaced with various arrangements of tubing and plastic bags, and the rupture of one of the bags had caused the present disaster.

'Who will help us?' Stefan asked. 'Is nurse coming?'

'Not yet,' said Hubert. 'But Tessa will help.'

Tessa blenched at the sight of him, and felt deeply for the offence to his modesty that her reckless intrusion brought about.

But Stefan said to her sweetly, 'You always were kind girl.'

Between them they lifted his ponderous form, removed sodden pyjamas, removed the drawsheet, cleaned up the bed. Hubert with delicacy and tenderness cleaned Stefan's body and reattached a bag, while Tessa, watching, sat and threaded a cord through the top of a clean pair of pyjamas.

Hubert showed no sign of any feeling but brotherly concern while they got Stefan clean, comfortable, settled, equipped with a book. Only when she followed him into the bathroom to wash her hands, and saw the fury and meticulous care with which he was scrubbing his cuticles and fingernails, did she know how he felt.

She did her duty first; she sat beside Stefan, and he talked about Matchek, who was married and brought his wife and children sometimes, and about the Princess his mother, who still lived in London, holding a shrinking court. And then curiously, about literature; did she like the recent Iris Murdoch as much as *The Bell*? Stefan thought she was disimproving. He talked well, and as she stood up to leave him, thinking he had become sleepy, he asked her to open a drawer in the bedside cupboard, and she took out a crumpled stack of papers written over in large handwriting. Stefan said they were his poems; would she read them and write to tell him honestly what she thought? He still found English hard, he said, but in poems less so; did that surprise her?

No, she said, it was more interesting than surprising. She leant over him and kissed him lightly goodbye.

Hubert had a stiff whisky waiting for her in the sitting room. A wide balcony gave on to a view of the roofs of the town, and melted into a blurry indigo that was probably the sea in rain. She sat down by the fire, admiring a fine painting over the mantelpiece.

An eighteenth-century Polish artist, Hubert said. He and Stefan had lovingly collected Polish art. 'A lot of it's very good,' he said. 'Unfamous enough to be affordable, too. Of course, we haven't been about to auctions and galleries much recently.'

'Oh, Hubert!' she said. 'And to think you wanted a hair shirt!'

'I deserve this,' he said, sitting down and looking gloomily at his drink. 'I asked for it. Every single thing I am getting. But what did he do? Whatever did he do to deserve it?'

She could think of no answer.

'Poor crazy fellow,' said Hubert. 'He never had a chance really, the way he was brought up. And you never knew a gentler person, or one more innocent of any intent to hurt . . . I don't know what I will do when he has gone . . .'

But Tessa thought she knew, and that this time he would find no obstacles in his path. 'Think of his purgatory all paid in advance,' she said. 'His path to heaven straight, and every small fault purged before he dies.'

'Do you believe that?' Hubert asked her.

But having at last learned the advantages of truth over kindness, Tessa said sadly, 'Not a word.'

Seven years after the day Tessa left the Church, she was baking bread in a kitchen open to the garden, and in which children ran in and out.

'What shall we do today?' her son asked her.

'Go to the shops and the park.'

'The garden smells nice,' her daughter remarked. 'Like washing.'

'I did the washing yesterday.'

'I haven't any money for going shopping,' the youngest said.

'Yes you have,' Tessa told her. 'I have ten shillings from Cathy for you.'

'I don't want ten shillings from Cathy!'

'Isn't there something you'd like to spend it on?'

'Yes . . . well . . . I don't need it! I don't want it!'

'Don't you like Cathy?'

'Oh, *yes*!'

'Well if you like someone you usually let them give you a present.'

'Oh. I thought it was the other way round.'

Tessa smiled, but the children had vanished, running out to the sandpit. Their voices mingled with suburban birdsong reached her as she thumped and kneaded. Momentarily bored she reached out and turned on the radio, and found herself listening to a programme in which guests chose tunes and talked about them a bit. The voice was Theodore's. He chose a folk song that he remembered from childhood. She kneaded dough, and listened. Then he chose some Mozart opera: 'Dalla sua Pace' from *Don Giovanni*. She listened in perfect stillness. This aria, he said, had meant a lot to him at the time when he was a schoolteacher, during which he was meeting and courting his wife.

Tessa wept into the lump of dough, not knowing if it was more terrible if he did remember or if he did not. Her children, who had arrived back from the garden and were sitting round the table making models with stolen bits of dough that were rapidly turning a greasy grey colour, stared at her with mild concern.

She stopped crying and smiled at them. Did it do children any harm, she wondered, to be brought up by a woman who wept constantly, as, when they were babes, she had done? To be put to the breast and dripped on with salt tears? To be played with by a mother with waterfall eyes? Could it do any harm, being, she supposed, below that mysterious, iridescent horizon that marks the dawn of continuous recollection, and which children cross alone at some moment invisible to all around them . . .

'We shall go to the park when the bread is done,' she said.

A few yards from the car park there was a little wooded hill, overlooking a lake. A favourite place, full of hidey-holes and climbing trees. Tessa settled with a rug, a book, and a basket from which apples and chocolate and horrible bright orange drink could be dispensed on demand. Right at the bottom was stale bread with which, before leaving, they would entice and reward a flock of ducks.

Tessa tried reading; but she could not stop thinking of walking long ago in another wood. '*Morte mi da!*' her mind told her. To her fury – she thought she had got over that at least – she was weeping again.

Suddenly the thin delicate arms of her oldest child were twined round her neck. 'Would it help to tell me all about it?' the girl said.

'Would it what, love?' said Tessa, astonished.

'That's what you say to me, when I'm crying,' the child observed.

'Thank you, darling. But no; I'm all right now. Look, see – dry eyes.'

'Has it gone away?'

'Yes. Gone, gone.'

'All better now?'

'Yes. Nothing in the world is wrong.'

'What a waste of all that crying!' the child said, skipping away, with an apple extracted from the basket in her hand.

Fifteen years after the day Tessa left the Church she was clearing a cupboard full of papers. Old playbills;

the proctors' *Rules for the Conduct of Undergradutes* – she opened that and discovered to her amazement that she had been forbidden to keep an aeroplane within ten miles of Oxford without the proctors' permission – an essay on the history of modern English sounds containing a phonetic transcription of 'Let me not to the marriage of true minds . . .' And then a buckram envelope marked 'To be given to Theodore Wytham after my death'. This was in her own hand, and she had added the word 'unopened' with a caret mark. But the quirks of memory had engulfed it; she had no recollection of writing the inscription, and none of the contents. Feeling oddly reckless, guilty of some trespass, she opened the seal.

Out fell letters from Theodore. Hundreds of closely written pages on airmail paper, stuffed into torn envelopes bearing quaintly old-fashioned stamps. She took one at random and opened it. It was from Theodore distraught.

What was he to do? He knew what pain he caused her, but however he tried he could not get it right. If he wrote to her in friendly fashion she complained of being treated like a girl guide; if he wrote to her of his feelings she accused him of deliberately tormenting her. He did not know which way to turn. If only he was as good at loving two people at once as she was . . . !

She scanned this letter in amazement. She had not remembered that he had ever tried to keep faith with her; she had remembered only failure, followed for her by total loss. Well, there had been a time, of course, when she had needed to think badly of him. But now, she thought, tears springing to her eyes, Poor Theodore! – he had spent half his youth torturing himself by attempting the impossible, of various kinds. Just as he had, he once feared, given Cathy a false example, so had she, Tessa, given him. It was not possible to love two people at once; nor had she, whatever she had told herself at the time, done any such thing. Going downstairs she fed the leaves of paper by handfuls to the fire. She had believed you could worship only one God, but more than one man. The truth was opposite.

And however could I have let myself, she wondered, her attention caught by the word 'torment' in Theodore's stumpy uneven hand, blackening and curling in a scorched millefeuille on the fire, become a cause of pain to Theodore, the last man in the world I would have meant any harm to? She considered it a little. Well, I will forgive myself, she concluded, my lapsing from selfless love, since I had lost both heaven and earth. But would he, I wonder, forgive me?

And the thought came swiftly after, Hush, Tessa, he does not think of you now. She thrust the remaining papers swiftly in the fire, and went out.

Eighteen years after the day Tessa left the Church, somebody gave her a prize for Christian art. In one of her more desperate moments, at a time when her children were young, she had turned to a skill which nobody educated by nuns escapes acquiring, but which she had most bitterly resisted learning at the time – plying a needle. She made a quilt, and sold it, and thus inadvertently set herself a new road in life. For this humble skill has made her her own woman: she has long since parted from Ben. Ben, who hated change, remained a devout Catholic; and it is not for nothing mixed marriages have a bad name. These days Tessa works in a large studio built in a converted barn near Ely. If you want Tessa to make you a quilt you must pay an astonishing sum for it, wait, on average, two years and accept whatever colours and motifs she happens to want to work with. Her work hangs in galleries on both sides of the Atlantic, but especially on the far side, and she has travelled and made friends all over the world. The accolade today is for an altar hanging, and she shares it with her dear friend Leon Grunwald who drew the cartoons for her.

They emerged on to the London pavements at about

three o'clock, full of champagne, with Tessa so burdened down by a huge bouquet of flowers she could hardly walk. Clearly it could not be humped back to Ely on the train.

'Is there a hospital near here?' she asked Leon. 'Or a graveyard?'

'St Giles-in-the-Field,' he said. 'A good one. Andrew Marvell is there.'

'The one without world enough, and time?'

'That very he.'

'Right. Let's go and find him!'

They went solemnly into the church and found Marvell's modest tablet in the north aisle. Tessa left the flowers on the pew beneath it, and then, thinking it would puzzle the verger, added a note: 'Andrew M. From an admirer'. Smiling they emerged again into a watery London sunshine. She felt, absurdly, slightly guilty, but only a solitary meths drinker, dancing slowly on the spot with an empty bottle in his raised left hand, had seen them come and go.

Just before they parted at the tube, she said to Leon, 'But really, how strange they should give such a prize to an apostate Catholic and an apostate Jew.'

'We're the only ones who've taken it seriously enough,' he said.

Twenty-one years after the day Tessa left the Church, she found herself travelling to London from Cheltenham on a bright fair Monday morning. Impulsively she turned off the A40, and drove herself into Oxford, to park under the baubled plane trees in St Giles just beyond the little house where she and Ben had had the flat. It was a bright day, and Oxford, cleaned and glorified, basked in pallid sunshine. Changes struck her: changed shops, no gowns, fewer bicycles. The intricate interstices of wall, street and garden enclosed her as she walked, imitating still the gleaming shell awash with dreams. And everybody but herself was either very young or very old; as though the streets abutted immediately on some enormous school, and the bell she could hear somewhere a little way off had just dispersed flocks of the young. She made for Blackwell's, and entered with all the old eagerness and a consciousness of wealth beyond her undergraduate measure. But she found nothing she specially wanted. Nothing that she could not get any day in Heffer's, or even – how the world had changed! – in London. She emerged on to the pavement and blinked at the grotesque new Caesars, realizing her mistake. Oxford had not been a place: it had been a configuration of people, to whom one could never return this side the lawns of paradise.

She thought about them, driving up Headington Hill. Cathy, settled at last, married and raising children; Hubert, a priest at last; and Richard – whatever had become, she wondered, of Richard? She had never heard. But anybody as wholly right-minded as he had been about the deadly sins would surely now be making himself and someone else very happy. She smiled as she put her foot down hard, and swept away eastwards; she herself travelling still.

Twenty-five years after the day Tessa left the Church she found herself in an American city, where Tod held a chair in Creative Mathematics. Having seen her quilts hung in the city art gallery, on impulse she picked up the phone and asked if she could call on him.

He received her in a bare official room, and offered her sherry. They exchanged disconnected enquiries; the small talk of people who vaguely know each other's lives, but have forgotten the plot in all its details. She said she couldn't stay long. And she looked at him with dazed curiosity: a Theodore slightly portly, almost sleek, his glorious blazing colour faded out – grey-sepia hair, bleached freckles – only his eyes familiar. Was this, then, what Theodore was really like? But no, she thought bemused. Once you know how everything changes with the mutability of the light, there is no special reason to accord primacy to the view in common day. Maybe love is blind; and then again maybe only the radiant vision of love is strong enough to penetrate the muddy vesture of decay, and show us, in however fading and brief an illumination, the truth about another human soul.

She had intended to ask him if she was in the end forgiven, but now she saw him this suddenly did not seem what she needed most to know.

'Are you happy?' she asked abruptly.

'Yes,' he said. 'Very.'

She left almost at once, but gladly. The time of her youth, then, had not been a total disaster. Theodore, for whom she had always cared most – how desperately unfair she had been to Ben, though only doing what he asked of her! – Theodore at least was all right.

Twenty-seven years after the day Tessa left the Church, she took an American friend – Caroline from Vermont – to see Ely Cathedral. Caroline had come to dinner, and spent the night, and could stay only an hour or two the next morning, and by bad luck it was bleak, blustery April weather, cold and threatening rain, and an indoor excursion was called for.

They walked happily awestruck round the magnificent spaces of Ely, and found themselves, in a grey rainlight which fell through the vast sombre windows shaded by a heavy showercloud outside, in the Lady Chapel. The sequence of broken glories around the walls, and the bare emptiness of the place struck Tessa. Her shoes tapping on the pavement rang like bells.

'I bet the acoustics are terrific,' she said, and unthinking lifted her voice to try them:

> Salve, Regina! Mater misericordiae . . .
> Vita, dulcedo, et spes nostra, Salve.

A kind of pre-echo in the place did not repeat her sound, but magnified it and lifted it to ring clear above their heads.

Deeply startled, Caroline said, 'I was brought up a Catholic; did you know?'

But Tessa had equally deeply startled herself. The moment she had seen Caroline onto the London train, she looked at a road-map, and began to drive herself northwards, towards the nearest shore. From Ely, a problematic quest. Looking for a road that went anywhere near the southern edge of the Wash, she went up through Wisbech, and to Long Sutton. Her map showed a likely looking minor road going towards Gedney Drove End. At Sutton Bridge she stopped and bought a pie and a bun. A news stand for the local paper blazoned, 'BAIT DIGGER'S BODY FOUND'.

She didn't stop to read about it. At first, beyond the A17 the road she had chosen was surprisingly suburban. Neat houses, close together; gardens with cherry trees. Then the land opened out, and became exactly like the miles and miles of it she had traversed from Ely, wide fen under a vast sky, with farms riding widely spaced like ships at anchor on a bay. In so wise a scope for seeing it is hard to tell if the scene is empty, or full; she could see, as she drove, a rainstorm on her left, she could see its northern and its southern dirty edge, and see the sun falling all round it, and it must have been miles away; while on her right a string of swans rose, flew, and again alighted, flying hard towards her, and not coming near at all. Their pulsing wings throbbed briefly white against a purple cloud, that was all. In any direction she could see, far off, a few farms snuggled in clustered barns and crouched below windbreak trees, the only trees.

At last she realized that the clean line of green on blue ahead of her, where land joined sky, was not a distant horizon, but a steep green bank, quite near. And at an angle of the road, where it turned abruptly south, she took a gravel track to the foot of the bank and parked the car. A notice put walkers at their own risk. Climbing the bank she found herself not yet at the edge of the sea, though she could see it from here. As flat before her as the fen behind, it lay an inky blue in the rich evening light, with a few breakers drawing and erasing lines of white at its nearer edge. There was even a bright little fishing boat, working a short way out. But before the breakers was a stretch of marsh, grey-green grass growing on a plane all crazed with mud-creeks, in a pattern like cracked paint. The creeks gleamed with silken mud and slow water. But it did not look far. She scrambled down the bank, and set out seaward. She kept finding her way blocked by a twisting creek opening at her feet, and it needed care, for some were so narrow that the rough grasses knitted over them from either side. She jumped where she could, retreated, jumped, found another way where the oozing crevasses were too wide. Nothing but grass and the dirty grey bushes of purslane grew where she walked. There was not another soul in sight – even the distant boat had gone now and nothing moved but a flickering of seabirds, black and white, flocking as they flew low over the water.

And she saw that she seemed to make no progress, that the breakers appeared as far away as ever, but she still went stubbornly on, as though to leave the melancholy void in Ely Cathedral ever farther behind. For though she had long realized that every Cathedral is empty, that the Church is empty, that every human shrine is empty, that all of them contain nothing, that they are all of them, even the loveliest, only intricate hollow shells, and we hear in them only the backwash of human sighing, yet she knew that somewhere, however far driven back, beyond the last inland farms, and though silted in occluded waters, and welling sluggishly in foul narrows, there flows at every human limit the infinite water of the One True Sea.

THE END

Knowledge Of Angels
Jill Paton Walsh

SHORTLISTED FOR THE BOOKER PRIZE 1994

'AN IRRESISTIBLE BLEND OF INTELLECT AND PASSION . . . NOVELS OF IDEAS COME NO BETTER THAN THIS SENSUAL EXAMPLE'
Mail on Sunday

It is, perhaps, the fifteenth century and the ordered tranquillity of a Mediterranean island is about to be shattered by the appearance of two outsiders: one, a castaway, plucked from the sea by fishermen, whose beliefs represent a challenge to the established order; the other, a child abandoned by her mother and suckled by wolves, who knows nothing of the precarious relationship between church and state but whose innocence will become the subject of a dangerous experiment.

But the arrival of the Inquisition on the island creates a darker, more threatening force which will transform what has been a philosophical game of chess into a matter of life and death . . .

'A COMPELLING MEDIAEVAL FABLE, WRITTEN FROM THE HEART AND MELDED TO A DRIVING NARRATIVE WHICH NEVER ONCE LOSES ITS TREMENDOUS PACE'
Guardian

'THIS REMARKABLE NOVEL RESEMBLES AN ILLUMINATED MANUSCRIPT MAPPED WITH ANGELS AND MOUNTAINS AND SIGNPOSTS, AN ALLEGORY FOR TODAY AND YESTERDAY TOO. A BEAUTIFUL, UNSETTLING MORAL FICTION ABOUT VIRTUE AND INTOLERANCE'
Observer

'THE LUCIDITY OF JILL PATON WALSH'S STYLE AND THE DEXTERITY OF THE NARRATIVE ARE SUCH THAT HER BOOK READS MORE LIKE A GOOD THRILLER THAN A WEIGHTY NOVEL OF IDEAS . . . AN INGENIOUS FABLE'
The Times

'REMARKABLE . . . UTTERLY ABSORBING . . . A RICHLY DETAILED AND FINELY IMAGINED FICTIONAL NARRATIVE'
Sunday Telegraph

0 552 99636 X

BLACK SWAN